WRITTEN STONE LANE

WRITTEN STONE LANE

A. J. Hartley

Illustrated by Janet Pickering

uclanpublishing

Written Stone Lane is a uclanpublishing book

First published in Great Britain in 2019 by
uclanpublishing
University of Central Lancashire
Preston, PR1 2HE, UK

978-1-9129790-7-3

1 3 5 7 9 10 8 6 4 2

A CIP catalogue record for this book is available from the British Library.

Printed and bound in Great Britain by Clays Ltd, Elcograf S.p.A.

To my family. As usual.

PROLOGUE

Preston, Lancashire, England.

Ralph Radcliffe considered his face in the fragmented reflection of the leaded windows, the way the bubbled and uneven glass transformed him into something monstrous with each fractional turn of his head. For a moment he became quite still, looking into his own eyes hoping to see only determined singularity of purpose, and not the ghosting of dread he had fought over the last year to beat back. Instead he saw only weariness and resignation.

His time was over but – with a little luck – the nightmare would end, if not for him, then for his friends, his family, for the village and the land that ranged from the fell down to the River Ribble.

And that is worth something.

He thought it deliberately, forcefully, trying to suppress the doubts which he knew would chase the notion through his head, worrying at it, stealing its force and clarity till it had sapped the strength he needed to do the deed. The door behind him creaked open and a flicker of light and colour in the glass made him turn.

It was his wife, Constance. She entered and stood in the doorway, regarding him steadily. She took in his clothes, his bearing, the sword he had left discarded on the bed, knowing he had no further use for it.

"You mean to go through with it, then?" she said.

"I must," he answered. "For you as much or more than all the rest."

"Then let me come with you. I will stand at your side and let the creature do its worst."

Ralph shook his head.

"That cannot be," he said. "The monster's bargain has been made. Only my blood will satisfy it."

"It will trick us, Ralph! You know it can't be trusted. And it wants revenge for your return."

"Aye, that's so," said Ralph. "But this is all we have to offer it."

"And what of the boy? Surely Thomas should not be sacrificed when we fought so hard to bring him back before?"

"His time, like mine, is spent," said Ralph, implacable. "We have had twelve months longer than was allotted to us. Now we must face death with the calm and resolution we could not muster before."

"He's but a child, husband! How can you look your brother in his face?"

"Robert understands."

"And is willing to sacrifice his son?"

"The child is dead already! So am I."

"You came back!" she retorted, her face pleading, her eyes full of tears, though they had been over the point too many times for her to think he would change his mind.

"Thomas died a year since, wife!" Ralph retorted. "Robert knows that. So do you. We cheated mortality then, Thomas and I, and what did we achieve?"

"We got you back," said Constance, simply. "Was not that enough?"

"For me, my love," he answered, crossing to her and taking her hands tenderly in his. "And I wish with all my heart that that was all that mattered. But you have seen the consequences of our trickery. The horrors we have seen, and now my brother Edward's son, dead before the blossom of his youth had chance to fall. It is a judgment on us for our misdeed, and I pray the Lord we can repay the fault, if not to Edward then to those who might yet lose more. The boggart knows what we did and calls it treachery. So long as Thomas and I live, it will plague us, tear down all we hold dear and carry off all those we love to God knows what torment. Compared to such terrors, death is welcome. I am ashamed that I have fled from it so long."

Constance was pale and silent, but as he spoke the tears had begun to flow freely and now she sat rigid. Ralph slipped his arm around her shoulders and squeezed her to his black doublet, but it was a moment before she softened enough to lay her head against his neck. Time seemed to stop and he felt a stillness in the universe, a harmony and peace he had not thought possible on this of all days.

It was a cold night, but the window above the box seat was open. The darkness beyond the candle light of the room was thick and impenetrable. No owl called or fox barked. The cattle were still and the night itself seemed to be waiting, its eyes covered as if in dread of what was to come.

Somewhere out there it would be watching, waiting for him to step outside and meet it at last.

A year, he thought. A year that began with the joy of a life he thought he had lost forever. But that joy had given way to anxiety, and finally to horror and the certainty that his return had come at too high a price. Worse, it was a price born heaviest by those he loved. So he had agreed to the boggart's bargain: a year of life for him and Thomas in return for their going willingly to death at the demon's hands after which, the creature promised peace for the village.

And did he trust its word?

Not for a second. Even if the spirit meant to be faithful now, Ralph saw the hunger and malice burning within it. His blood and that of Robert's boy, Thomas, would satisfy it for a while, but it would be back soon enough, all deals forgotten, and ravenous for more.

But Ralph had one last card to play. He turned to look out through the open window and down to the old standing stone. Even from here he felt the power of it. Constance felt the shift in his focus and she followed his gaze.

"You think that will bind it?" she said.

"Perhaps," he said, "but once in place, the stone must never move. Never, you hear me? And that falls to you, wife. See that it lies there forever."

Her face hardened with resolve, but she could not suppress a pang of doubt.

"Forever is a long time, husband," she answered.

"Aye," he agreed, getting to his feet and turning to the door and the thing waiting for him out there in the dark. "It is at that."

CHAPTER ONE

Ribbleton, Preston, Lancashire.
September 15th, 1978.
9:23 pm.

Preston nodded again, still smiling, then he took another step forward and extended his hand.

"Hi," he said. "I'm Preston."

"Tracey," said the girl with the chestnut hair and the clever eyes, taking his hand and shaking it once.

The touch of her, the warm reality of her palm against his, was like a bolt of electricity through his body. She seemed to flinch as if feeling it too, though maybe that was just a reaction to the intensity of his grip. He let go quickly.

"You have cold hands," she said.

"It's a cold night," he shot back, quite comfortable, as if he had known her all his life.

"No gloves?" she said. "Shouldn't you 'Be Prepared'? You're a scout," she added with that playfully skeptical smile.

"No," said Preston.

The girl made a face, her eyes moving over his uniform.

"So what's that, a costume?" she said.

"I mean, I was a scout," said Preston. "But I quit. Tonight. Just now in fact."

It wasn't a lie: not really. He made the decision as he spoke, and he would stick to it. He was done with scouts. He was done with a lot of things. Preston Oldcorn had been gone long enough to know that now he was back he would not waste a second of life. Because while Tracey obviously had no recollection of what they had been through together, Preston remembered every detail of it.

Preston Oldcorn had been dead, trapped in an endless moment for what had felt like months, years even, killed by a spectre called the Leech which had turned out to be a boy, bullied to death on a train and bent on revenge. But in his final conflict with the thing which had killed him, Preston had stumbled into the other boy's own time and, in changing the past, had saved them both. The Leech, now simply a boy again, had been able to move on to whatever came after death, and Preston had woken up in the same time and place where he had been killed, only a few hundred yards from this very spot.

Logically he knew he shouldn't be able to remember, that if the ghost which killed him had never existed and Preston had never died, none of what had happened in that awful nine twenty-two limbo should have stayed with him, but it did. Every moment of it. He remembered the ghost dogs and the Roman legionaries, the spectre which had emerged from the painting at the Harris Library, Dolly Bannister and Margaret Banks, his friend Roarer, who was gone now, and all that that happened in the Miley tunnel as he made his fateful way to Cold Bath Street. He could see it all, bright and certain and real as brick and pain and darkness. And he remembered Tracey's part in it all. She had been older for most of it. Not much older than she was now. A year or two, perhaps. But he looked into her face now, a face that was already dear to him, and he could tell that as far as she was concerned they were meeting for the first time, and all their strange history together was, to her, blank. Time had unravelled, and one strand of it was gone from every mind in the world but his.

"You got a phone number?" he said. "I need to go home, but I'd like to call you."

Tracey raised an eyebrow. Over her shoulder, her father was watching them closely.

"Pretty forward for an almost ex-scout," she said.

"Yeah," said Preston, shrugging and smiling, though even he was surprised at what he had said. "Life's short, you know?"

"Ah," said Tracey, dry as toast, "adolescent wisdom."

"So what do you say?"

She considered him frankly, then fired a question back.

"Best song in the charts right now?" she demanded. "And if you say 'You're the one that I want', this conversation ends here."

Preston, who had felt so composed, so ready for this, for life, gaped, wrong footed, and thought back. It all seemed so long ago, listening to music in his room before he had been trapped in that nine twenty-two no-place. He thought about arguing with Roarer over which Elvis was best, Presley or Costello, and then something else came to mind, something caustically exotic, vibrant and odd.

"Hong Kong Garden," he said.

"Siouxsie and the Banshees," said Tracey thoughtfully, approving. "Alright then."

She pulled a notebook from her back pocket and scribbled down a phone number in blue biro, watching him out of the corner of her eye. Behind her, her father frowned and adjusted his stance to look Preston over. They were house-hunting. In the other time line, Preston's grief-stricken parents had moved and sold them the house on Langdale Road so that Tracey had grown up in his room, but not now. Now he was back, alive, and his parents would stay where they were. If Tracey was ever to see his room, Preston would have to show it to her himself.

Feeling Tracey's father watching him, Preston met his eyes and gave him a nod, partly respectful, partly man-to-man matey. He had never done anything like it before in his life. And then he was thanking her and saying it was nice to meet her, taking her hand and shaking it like he was at a job interview. He walked away, but – driven by a rash and boundless joy – the walk became a run when he turned down Stuart Road and made for home. His heart thumped in his chest as he made the corner of Langdale Road and he laughed aloud with delight.

In under a minute he was home, down the side and through the back door into the wash house. The kitchen was quiet but the battery clock on the far wall above the old teak dining table was ticking round as it should and Preston could hear the television in the front room. He was usually home in time to catch the end of the nine o'clock news but judging by the noisy soundtrack, 'Target' – the noisy police show his dad sometimes watched – had already started.

Preston burst in so suddenly that his parents looked up, startled, his mum where she always was, on the end of the couch by the gas fire, his father in the armchair just inside the door, his pipe cradled absently in his left hand.

It was as if he had never been away.

But he had. For so very, very long.

"Alright, love?" said his mum, putting down a white paper bag: a quarter of pear drops from Cuffs. One of her few extravagances. "How was scouts?"

Preston, suddenly incapable of speech, said nothing, but hugged each of them in turn, snatching them into embraces fierce and out of character, as if defying the world to ever force his family apart again. Then his father asked if he'd been drinking and Preston laughed and wept a little so that his mum began to worry, and he just held them hard and told them it was all right. At last, it was all right.

He was home.

* * *

Tracey's parents drove back to Longridge in disappointed silence. The house they had come to inspect wasn't right, as the one before it hadn't been right, which was to say that neither were what they wanted while being all they could afford. So they drove out of Ribbleton, over the motorway and through the leafy seclusion of Grimsargh, up to the Alston Reservoir where they turned onto Lower Lane, past the Corporation Arms to the little narrow and weedy road where the old farm houses stood. Tracey knew the roads all too well, and gazed out of the window into the darkness looking at nothing, thinking vaguely about the odd boy she had met who her mum and dad were pointedly not talking about, though she had caught their surreptitious glances. They didn't think she had time for boys, not with her school work to do, her future riding on those magical *qualifications*, which were what they called her upcoming O-Level exams. She suspected they were right, not that it had ever given her much concern either way. She wasn't interested in boys.

Or girls, she added hastily in her head knowing that if her friend Carol Drinkwater could hear this internal monologue she would have already made several *nudge-nudge-say-no-more* jokes. She had sort of fancied Howard Flynn for a while last year, but had never said anything to him and then one day she had woken up and realised she didn't actually like him anymore. Why the funny-looking boy scout had made any impression on her at all, she couldn't say.

Probably because he didn't have time to get boring, she thought, knowing herself a little too well. Give her a half hour to actually talk to him and she'd probably never want to see him again.

On Written Stone Lane itself the nettles and hawthorn rattled the sides of the aging Austin Allegro and Tracey's father made a familiar tsk of annoyance.

"They want to cut them 'edges back more," he muttered to no one in particular. "Scratching up mi paintwork."

Written Stone Lane was supposed to have once been part of the Roman road to Lancaster but it was now little more than a track between two farms, named after the curious old sandstone slab some eight feet long, two feet wide, and a foot and a half deep, surrounded by ancient hollies. It lay lengthways on a raised bank where the lane curved toward Cottam House Farm on the right, while immediately to the left were the buildings of the other farm – a small cottage of which was where Tracey's family had been living for the last eight months. Tracey's room was the closest to the written stone. It was weedy and overgrown with ivy but the rock was clearly carved in block capitals proclaiming

RAVFFE: RADCLIFFE: LAID: THIS STONE TO LYE: FOR: EVER: A.D. 1655.

Why Mr. Radcliffe – Ralph, was the way Tracey read his first name – had placed the stone, no one knew, but there were garbled stories about what had happened to a local farmer who tried to move it. All nonsense of course. Tracey, like her parents, was a hard headed realist unimpressed and unintimidated by tales of the supernatural. "Used to keep the people down," her father liked to pronounce about ghost stories and the like. "Slaves to church and the so-called nobility." Tracey wasn't sure how campfire stories about graveyard apparitions were supposed to keep the masses downtrodden – another of her father's phrases – but she gave them no credence either. She wondered vaguely if the almost ex-scout did.

Well, there's your test, she thought vaguely. *If he turns out to be a credulous idiot, he's not worth your time.*

She nodded to herself at that. Real life was hard enough without a lot of superstitious rubbish getting in the way.

And besides, she reminded herself, as they parked and got out of the car, *he might not even call.*

She looked away from the dark car window so she wouldn't catch her sly, smiling reflection as she thought it through, because she didn't really believe he wouldn't for a minute. And then, as if for luck, she touched the ancient stone while her father unlocked the cottage door.

* * *

Preston sat up in the lounge talking to his slightly baffled parents, asking about their days, grinning, soaking them in. When their confusion started sliding towards alarm he assured them that all was well and went up to his room. There he lay on his bed with the light off, pulling out rattling cassettes at random, listening to a song or two from each on his headphones, laughing silently with an excess of joy so acute that tears ran down his face until, finally exhausted, he properly slept for the first time in a very long while.

But some eight miles away something that had slept long in the earth, stewing in bitterness and muffled rage woke and, finding its ancient bonds strangely fractured, began to stir.

CHAPTER TWO

Agnes Tattershawl had had about as much as she could stand. It wasn't right, a woman of her age, having to walk home at this time of night. And her with a bad back and all. Was it her fault if she had missed her bus because it actually left on time, for once? Now she had to walk all the way along to Ward Green Lane, barely able to see her hand in front of her face. The chips were getting colder with every step, and would she get any sympathy from Joe, shiftless lump that he was? Not on your nelly.

So here I am, trekking halfway across the Pennines for his tea. There ought to be a law.

All the way up Kestor to Little Lane then down Fell Brow to Dilworth, past the Corporation Arms and on. Still the Stonebridge chippy on Derby Road did a nice cod, chips and mushy peas, and the newspaper package, sharp with vinegar, kept her hands warm.

If she was being honest with herself, which she rarely was, the walk was entirely her own fault since she had flatly refused to let Joe cook, and had insisted on chips, even though Doctor Fleming had told her she needed to cut back on fatty foods. *Obese*, he had said. The nerve of him! Skinny little whippet of a man that he was, and only out of medical school about twenty minutes. Well, it was the last time she'd visit that quack. She'd complain to the NHS and see what they had to say, you see if she didn't. Maybe she ought to start going to that place in Clitheroe, the one with the columns outside that Netty Jackson went to. Netty was no trimmer than Agnes, not really, and she got to eat whatever she liked without having to write a manifesto in her own defence. Made you wonder what the country was coming to when a respectable farmer's wife couldn't order chips when she felt like it.

That's life under a Labour government, she concluded with a sniff and, liking the righteous sound of the words in her head, felt better.

She trudged along Blackburn Road, past the pub and under the shade of the reservoir wall. The traffic was horrendous these days, compared to when she was a girl, that is, but it seemed quiet now. Hadn't quite hit chucking-out time at the Corporation Arms, mercifully, so she wouldn't have to deal with Jed Atkinson three sheets to the wind, and sloshing about all over't shop. With the traffic as it was these days it was amazing that fool hadn't been hit yet. Never did have any sense, even when he was sober, which didn't happen often. Agnes hugged the packet of chips to her bosom and huffed her indignation, albeit wheezily.

It was a cold night, not raining, thank God, but dark and misty so that the fields over the road seemed indistinct as if they weren't really there. You could see the sheep as pale blotches where they had bedded down, but it was still, and except for the occasional car, you could hear nothing but Agnes's footsteps and her laboured breathing. She had half a mind to find somewhere to sit down, maybe eat some of her chips while she got her puff back. 'Course, that would make the rest cold and Joe would have something to say about that, but she could always put t' oven on for a spell. Wouldn't kill him to have to wait a bit longer.

The movement by the gate on her left startled her because whatever had been there had been too dark to see till it moved. Even then Agnes thought her eyes were playing tricks on her. Still, her feet hesitated midstride and she almost stumbled. If the precious fish supper got dropped now there'd be hell to pay. That flash of irritation made her stare defiantly at the shadow over the stone wall, angling her head to try and make out the deeper blackness in the night.

Something *was* there. Something not tree or bush or sheep or trough. Something large and, she would have sworn, something that had not been there a moment before.

It was tall and broad and irregular. A cow at an odd angle, perhaps, though what a cow was doing in this particular field she couldn't say. The herd were back up on the higher field and usually stayed there. A bull perhaps. It looked big enough. But Ken Shakeshaft had never kept bulls before, and that was his land right enough.

17

Something about the shape bothered her, and her steps slowed still further, even though there was a wall between her and it. She stared into the dark, her mouth dry, her breath coming quick and shallow, her heart starting to roil in her chest.

There was something strange in the field. It had moved but it was still now, and though she didn't know why she thought it, she felt sure it was watching her. She knew the area inside out, had walked past this field a hundred times or more, and she didn't have the imaginative room in her head for fear. But something felt different about the place tonight, wrong, and she stopped, wary of getting closer.

It moved again, and this time she was looking right at it as it shifted, and that was worse. It seemed to get taller, and she realised that – big though the creature had seemed – it had actually been bent down. Now it was immense, black, glossy and wild. A horse, she thought, but a horse bigger than any she had ever seen, despite a lifetime in the country. Its long mane and tail seemed to float in the air around it as if each strand of hair was stirred by some pocket of wind that affected the beast alone, and even its flanks seemed to ripple as the bristles flexed and relaxed.

It was black as pitch, black as hell.

She wasn't sure why that last word came into her mind, but as it did, the thing took an improbably large step toward the wall and she saw scarlet pinpricks in the night. She knew what they were, though they couldn't be.

Eyes. Eyes like glowing coals.

Agnes froze where she was, and in that instant the beast leapt

the wall and landed on the pavement only yards in front of her. It didn't move like a horse. It splayed its legs as it absorbed the hoof-sliding shock of its landing, moving like something that looked like a horse but wasn't. Like something pretending.

And it was just *immense*. Too big to be real, to be possible. It's lips fluttered and she saw massive yellow teeth and ropes of thick drool spilling from between them. This was not a horse that would eat grass or hay, she thought, with horrible certainty. This was something else entirely.

Agnes took a hurried and unsteady step backwards. Her ankle turned on the curb and she lost her balance, going down hard. The carefully wrapped newspaper parcel exploded beneath her, spewing chips like the entrails of an animal, its body split by a slashing claw. Agnes flailed and scrabbled at the road surface, feeling her heart racing. The impossible creature with the mad, burning eyes and floating hair, loomed over her now. Its muzzle stooped toward her horror-stricken face, her gargling, wordless mouth, her blank eyes. It made a noise that might have been a whinny, though it sounded more like something squeezed out of hunger and malice, and it had a metallic edge like a blade that cut through her chest.

Agnes gasped, clutched at the left side of her rib cage as if the monstrous thing had dipped its awful head and ripped a bloody mouthful from her body. She smelled it then, the fetid animal odour and something sour beneath it that stank of soil and death, of graveyard earth.

Her heart fought, overloaded, and stopped.

Tracey Blenkinsop rolled over in her sleep and frowned. Her eyelids tightened then fluttered and opened. Her mind slid into wakefulness like a dolphin coming up for air. She lay still on her side, registering the dark and trying to decide what had woken her. Something wasn't right, and for a moment her confusion teetered on the edge of fear. Then she shivered and realised with a flicker of relief that she had somehow kicked all her covers off. It was already a proper Autumn in Lancashire and the room was cold, much colder than it had been when she went to bed, so why – or how – she had come to push all the blankets off the bed she couldn't say.

She reached vaguely down the side to the carpet, but found neither sheet nor covers. Frowning again she patted the floor exploringly, pushing her slippers aside, then reaching wider, sweeping blindly around in the dark.

Still nothing.

Irritated, and feeling the chill of the room making her arms and legs break out into goose pimples, she sat up and fumbled for the bedside light till the little yellowish bulb snapped on. As it did so, she noted two things. First, her bedclothes had not slid sideways onto the floor but had somehow gone off the end of the bed, falling in a neat pile by the door. The second thing was that the door was, in defiance of all custom and practice, open; not cracked at the latch, but swung wide, so that the light from the bedside lamp fell into the landing beyond and made strange shadows.

She leapt to her feet, hugging her nightdress against her in a flurry of annoyance and embarrassment, and pulled the door closed as quickly as she could. Her parents' room was just down the hall, and the idea that they might have seen her sprawled out on her bed in nothing but her night things if they had got up to go to the bathroom, made her face hot. Even so, puzzlement overmastered her mortification. The bedroom door was stiff and noisy, and it never came unlatched by itself. When she was little, her mum and dad had liked to stand in the doorway and watch her sleep, but that hadn't happened for years. If the thought of moving house had got them all nostalgic and they had let themselves in without asking, she would have something to say about it.

She gathered the sheet and blankets up around her and sprawled headlong onto the bed, dragging the covers up around her and kicking her legs till they lay right. Then she turned off the light and buried her face in the pillows as if trying to tunnel through them, her jaw set and her mind full of the things she would say over breakfast about privacy.

Even so, and though she was already sliding back toward sleep, her half-conscious brain registered one more small discrepancy on the air: a scent, not exactly unpleasant, but wrong. It was an outside smell, slightly damp and touched with an edge of sourness like decay or, more precisely, of soil.

Yes, she thought dreamily, closing her eyes. *It smells like newly turned earth.*

CHAPTER THREE

The next day was, for Preston, a series of little glories, moments of forgotten bliss which came back to him one after another as life – true, real life – progressed in all its wondrous ordinariness. First it was sunlight in his bedroom bringing brilliance and colour to a place he had known only in shadow for so very long, then it was bringing in the milk in the cold glass bottles left at that door, their silver foil tops pecked through by blue tits. Next it was breakfast and the sheer sensory joy of Weetabix and toast with Hartley's strawberry jam, flavours so intense and yet so familiar that he was briefly brought, once more, to tears. Real tears at that, the kind that ran wet down his cheeks and tasted faintly of salt. He sat, moist eyes closed, munching contentedly, drinking in the aromas, suddenly sure that there could be no greater sensory ecstasy and that this was what the Greek gods ate in Elysium: not nectar and ambrosia but Weetabix and toast with strawberry jam washed down with a mug of good, strong tea! To say he was happy to be alive did not do the feeling justice, and he moved through the morning on a cloud of joy, delighting in all the things of which he had been deprived until his parents asked him again if he was feeling all right.

It was Saturday, so there was no school, no church, no structure for the day, but that was probably as well. After so long spent in the same day, the same moment, he wasn't sure how well he would adjust to schedules and clocks. For almost as long as he could remember, time had been a near meaningless concept, and he was glad he could wait a bit before he would have to go back to checking his watch so that he caught the bus, or made it to class. He went outside and gazed up at his bedroom window through the branches of the pear tree in the front garden, revelling in the colour of the tree after all the grayness of the nine twenty-two limbo, and inhaling the rich, sweet aroma of the fruit.

On impulse he left the garden and walked briskly down the street and round the corner onto Cromwell Road where he could climb onto the railway bridge and look down the track. In one direction was the Miley tunnel. In the other was Grimsargh where the brakeman had patrolled endlessly. It looked different now, green and lush in spite of the oil and smoke stains, the graffiti on the embankment. It looked alive, which was as it should be. He missed Roarer, but it was good to be back here where the blood sang in his ears and his heart throbbed.

He made a snap decision to visit his grandma and granddad on Woodlands Avenue, delighting in the sound of the sliding door which admitted him to the wash house and kitchen, the familiarity of it all chiming like a bell. It was the same as always: the glossy ceramic mixing bowl – tan on the outside, white on the inside – sat on the counter beside an old green weighing scale rusted at the edges with its conical stack of iron weights, and the white enamel bins of flour and sugar. The cracked frosted window glass over the sink. The stainless steel draining rack with the dish rag that smelled damp and very slightly musty. The hatch by the cool, cellar-like pantry that communicated with the living room. Preston took it all in feeling, in some ways, more clearly *back* than he had at home.

His granddad was watching telly in the living room – the front room being considered too posh for use so that the couch still had a plastic cover on it. His granddad barely glanced round when Preston came in but that was because it was hard for him to twist his waist since the stroke, but when Preston said, "All right, granddad?" he nodded and tapped the newspaper significantly.

"*Magnificent Seven* on tonight," he said approvingly. "Mighty fine picture."

Granddad loved his Westerns: horses, open skies and taciturn men with six shooters. They were about as far from his experience of the world as films could be, and he couldn't get enough of them.

His grandma was sitting in the corner armchair, scowling at a book, angling it as if there was something wrong with her reading glasses. She was wearing a buttoned grey frock with white flowers on it and her steel grey hair was pulled back in a bun. She rose smiling when he came in, filling the room with a familiar benevolence, soft and warm and caring. Even so, she seemed pleasantly taken aback by his hug. Preston was surprised by it too, overwhelmed by how good it was to see her again, how much he had missed her. Caught up in his own emotion he looked for something ordinary to mask it. The book she had set down was a paperback by Mary Stewart called *The Gabriel Hounds*.

"Any good?" asked Preston, stepping back and trying to look merely curious.

"Aye," said his grandmother, "except that I can't seem to focus. I reckon I need to see the optician."

"Blurred vision?"

"More like seeing double," she said lightly. "Gives me a headache. Tell me about school."

Preston's grandmother was a former teacher and always wanted to know about school. It was her way of saying she loved you.

Preston shrugged the question off with generalities because school seemed so long ago and he didn't want to discuss what he did remember only to find that he had told her about it weeks ago. He took in the room with the hearth where he had set up his toy Napoleonic soldiers once when he had been recovering from chicken pox, sleeping upstairs in the little bedroom. He considered the long gray curtains at the window where he had played hide and seek, the well-tended garden beyond where he had kicked a ball over the hedge and had to go and ask the scary neighbour with the old bomb shelter behind the house if he could get it back. And he looked at her, the soft papery skin, the fine lines around her kind and thoughtful eyes, wondering at the way she made him so comfortable, so loved without ever really saying it. He had never heard her angry or upset. She was always a rock, in spite of everything she had to do for granddad. She made everyone feel welcome, supported, which is perhaps why – without really thinking about it – he suddenly said,

"I met a girl."

She blinked and raised an eyebrow in surprised pleasure.

"Oh yes?" she said. "And who's that then?"

"Her name's Tracey."

"Right," said his grandma, beaming. "And she's nice, is she?"

"I think so," he said. "Don't know her that well yet."

"Better work on that then," she said with a playful wink. "Time waits for no man."

He laughed out loud at that because he had expected her to advise caution, moving slow and not getting in over his head, which is what his parents would have done. And with her encouragement established, the confidence shared, she moved on, which was also – he thought – both kind and smart because he didn't want to say more about Tracey yet.

"Fancy a brew?" his grandmother asked.

"Aye," he said. "Granddad? Cup of tea?"

"Just a splash of corporation pop for me," he replied.

In the kitchen while the kettle boiled his grandma asked if he

27

had written anything lately – she had always been a champion of the little stories he produced as school writing assignments – and he said he was thinking about a ghost story in which the ghost was the main character.

"Sounds scary," said his grandma, with that twinkle that was just so her that he had to resist hugging her again.

"Maybe more sad than scary," he said. "Better that way. More like life. In the end, I mean."

She seemed to consider that seriously, her smile puckering, and Preston, not sure why he had made the remark or what he had meant by it shrugged and grinned to make light of the moment. She poured the water onto the tea leaves in the old stainless steel pot with the black knob on the lid, and Preston stared at it, amazed again by how good it was to see something he had forgotten about.

"What about today?" she said. "Going on the North End?"

"They're away," said Preston. "Oldham. Maybe I'll go up town or . . . I don't know. Something good."

And that was the question he wondered about as he walked back home, lifted by the buoyant kindness which surrounded his grandmother always. It was, as the cliché said, the first day of the rest of his life. How would he spend it?

He wanted to listen to music, and watch movies, and see his school friends, he wanted to be near his parents just to remind himself that they were there, or rather that he was, but most of all he wanted to see Tracey. He forced himself to wait till ten o'clock, then watched the kitchen clock add another four and a half minutes before announcing he was going to make a phone call. His mother gave him a curious look.

"Who to?" she asked.

He shrugged.

"Someone I met," he said.

"A girl?" asked his mother, reading his blush and failing to conceal her surprise.

"Yeah," he said, with the same failed nonchalance.

"When did you meet her?"

"Last night," said Preston.

"Last night? Where? At scouts?"

"On the way home."

"In the street?" said his mother, as if such a thing was a violation of public decency.

"We sort of knew each other before," he muttered.

This was why his grandma's approach had been better: accepting, brief, moving past it . . .

"How?"

"Can I just call her, please?" said Preston.

"Of course, love," said his mother relenting. "I just like to know who your friends are."

He grinned knowingly at that but was still too glad to be home to be irritated by it. The phone was on a table in the hall, the least private place in the house. He closed the kitchen door after himself, but still felt exposed. Maybe he would have been better ringing from a call box, but the nearest was by the bus stop near the top of Woodlands Avenue and he had just come from there. This would have to do. And besides, he had nothing to be embarrassed about. He was, he thought, a new man.

Or he meant to be.

He picked up the receiver and pinned it against his shoulder with his chin while he checked the number, then put the tip of his finger into the rotary dial at the number seven and swept it round evenly, listening to the familiar mechanical drone as it rewound, then repeating for each digit. A woman answered on the fifth ring, reciting the number he had dialed in a voice which he guessed was slightly posher than her usual.

Preston said, "Is Tracey there, please?"

"I'll see. Who should I say is calling?"

"Preston. Preston Oldcorn," he said. It felt like a confession, but he gritted his teeth and waited as the phone went quiet for a moment, then strained to hear the distant muffled voices on the other end. He half-expected the same voice to come back on, telling him she was in the bath or washing her hair, which made no sense at all given the time, but then it was Tracey saying, "You're keen."

He grinned at that but managed not to agree.

"Wondered what you were doing," he said, as if they had known each other for years which, in a way, they had, even if she was oblivious to that. "Thought you might fancy . . . I don't know. Coffee or something."

"I don't drink coffee."

"Perfect. Neither do I. Tea?"

"We have tea, thanks," said Tracey.

"Right," said Preston, deflating.

"Why are you calling me, Preston Oldcorn?"

"Well, like I said, I thought we could, you know, get together . . ."

"I mean why me? We just met for like ten seconds."

"It was at least a minute," said Preston, squirming.

"Why me?" she said firmly, defiantly, showing all the spark he found so appealing but was also a little scary.

He didn't know what to say. The truth about how he had haunted her and she had helped him stay sane in the land of the merely dead would absolutely guarantee that she would never speak to him again, and he couldn't do all that hearts and flowers stuff about her eyes and her hair even if he thought she'd be taken in by it, which he didn't.

"Just thought we might get along," he said, knowing how lame and childish that sounded, how inadequate. "I mean, I had a feeling we could be friends, you know, but we might never meet again so . . ."

He tailed off. The phone was making his ear sweat he was pressing it so hard to the side of his head, but he could hear nothing but the soft white noise of the line.

"You still there?" he said at last.

"A walk," she said.

"What?"

"You can come for a walk with me. If you like."

"Right," said Preston again, cheerier this time. "A walk. Yeah. Brilliant."

"Preston?"

"Yes?"

"No, I mean do we take the walk *in Preston*, the town, or out where I am? Near Longridge."

It was a nice enough day, cool and overcast but dry, as good an autumn day as Lancashire afforded, and Preston thought that a stroll in the country with this girl was exactly what he wanted.

"I'll come to you," he said, hardly daring to believe it.

CHAPTER FOUR

Tracey was staring shrewdly at her dad when there was a loud rat-tat from the door knocker.

"Oh, listen to that!" called Tracey. "Someone knocking. As if they want to come in but think they should ask first. Fancy that!"

She had already spent several minutes regaling her parents with her policies on people going into her room without permission, policies she was astonished to see had to also be applied to opening her door in the middle of the night. They had responded with bafflement and proclamations of innocence but she wasn't convinced. It was just about possible that her dad might think that pulling her bed clothes off and leaving her half-freezing was funny, some dim-witted attempt to rediscover the kind of playfulness they had had when she had been smaller. Still, normally he would have laughed and received her stern admonition to treat her like a young woman, rather than a child, with a grudging, hangdog apology. This time she got only denial.

"Honest, Trace!" he protested. "I wouldn't! Swear to God."

Her probing glare had been interrupted by the knocking on the front door. Probably Ken Shakeshaft, the dour farmer who owned the land on which the cottage stood, or his equally taciturn wife.

Taciturn, Tracey thought, liking the rightness of the word even as she went into the hall to answer it, giving her dad a last look which said she wasn't done with him yet.

But it wasn't their farmer landlord at all. Tracey opened the stiff door – dragging it judderingly over the tight and unevenly worn stone threshold – to reveal a tall man in a blue-black uniform, his helmet under his arm.

The policeman seemed to rethink whatever he had been about to say and managed a smile.

"Your mum or dad in, love?"

"Why?" she said. It was just curiosity, but it came out like defiance, and the hulking officer seemed taken aback.

"There was an incident down there on the road during the night and we're gathering witness statements."

"Right," she said. "You'd better come in."

She stepped aside, peering past him through the open door and down the lane, craning to see, but the lane looked quiet and normal. When her father appeared from the kitchen, drying his hands, his face wary at the sight of the policeman in the hall, she moved behind him to close the door but hesitated, listening. The officer announced that his enquiries were routine and there were no suspicious circumstances, but there had been "a fatality" late the previous night out on the road. It sounded like something off the telly. As they moved into the kitchen, closing the door behind them, Tracey hesitated, still listening but torn between curiosities: to hear what had happened, or to see where it had happened? In the end the decision was made by her pangs of guilt at eavesdropping and she slipped out of the front door, pulling it softly behind her.

Out in the cool air, sharp with the tang of muck spreading, Tracey wrinkled her nose, wondering what the smell reminded her of . . .

Newly turned earth . . .

. . . and made to walk down to Lower Road, but was stopped in her tracks where the farm drive met the lane. Tussocks of grass strewed the ground and dark clumps of dirt had spilled down the bank where the written stone had sat. The great stone itself was intact, but had rolled down from the weedy embankment and into the road, coming to rest face down like a corpse. Where it had lain before was a dark gash in the undergrowth, like a wound in the earth.

Tracey stared, unable to believe it. How could a car have hit the stone and not woken her up? Her room was mere yards away. She considered the long, pale rock and the black earth which had spewed up around the place where it had lain, like a bomb crater, or the crown of a very small volcano, then she went back into the house and straight into the kitchen.

The policeman, a young man with a pale, open face but watchful and unblinking blue eyes was sitting at the scrubbed table with her parents. They all looked up, startled by her entrance. Her father took it on himself to break the news, voice serious, somber even, but no-nonsense.

"Seems Agnes Tattershawl died last night," he said. "Just outside."

Tracey gasped. She hadn't especially liked Agnes, who had always reminded her of Ena Sharples from Coronation Street – the one with the hairnet and the permanent scowl – but the idea that their neighbour was dead shook her. The woman had lived just over the road and Tracey had seen her several times a week since they had moved to Longridge.

"Heart attack," said the policeman. "In all likelihood. She wasn't in the best of shape and may have overdone it. She was carrying fish and chips."

"Liked her chips, did Agnes," said Tracey's mum.

"What time did it happen?" asked Tracey without preamble.

Her mother looked instantly uneasy, keen to change the subject or usher her out, but the young policeman glanced at a notebook he had on the table in front of him and said,

"Just after half past nine, we think."

"No chance," said Tracey. "I was awake. I would have heard."

"All the way down there?" said her dad, shaking his head. "No, love."

"It's right outside my window!" Tracey replied.

Her dad made a face.

"Couple 'undred yards, Trace," he said. "And there was nothing to hear. You 'eard him: heart attack."

Tracey gave each of them a baffled look.

"What?" she said. "It's right outside the house!"

"What is?" asked her mother.

"The written stone!"

Her father shook his head again, smiling indulgently this time.

"She weren't there," he explained. "She were down on Lower Road."

"A car accident, right?" said Tracey.

"No, love," said her father. "Old dear just dropped dead on the side of the road. No one hit her."

Tracey shot the policeman a look.

"You said there had been an accident!" she said.

"An *incident*, I said. I didn't say crash," he said, sounding defensive. He rallied, adjusting his uniform as if to restore his dignity. "What made you think there had been a car accident?" Tracey looked at her parents.

"Have you not been out today?" she asked.

"Only to get 't milk," said her dad. "Why?"

"Come look," she said, leading the way.

No one protested. They might have exchanged glances, but they followed, and once outside they stood and stared at the uprooted stone which lay stranded at the foot of the overgrown bank. Only the policeman looked a little abashed.

"Oh that," he said. "Yeah, I were going to ask you about that. Happened last night?"

"Definitely," said Tracey.

"You think someone hit it?" asked Tracey's mum. "A lorry or a tractor?"

"A road accident wouldn't pull it up like that," said Tracey's dad who was always certain. "It were up on't bank. Deliberate, that is. Kids. Vandals. Someone has nicked a tractor and dragged 't stone up for a joke. I wonder if Ken's seen it. I'll stop by on my way in. He'll need to get it out o't road."

"Funny that we didn't hear anything," said Tracey's Mum. "Did you, Trace?"

Tracey shook her head but managed not to point out that she had already told them as much.

"Quiet means deliberate," said Tracey's dad. "An accident we would 'ave heard. Ripping it up like that? That's stealth, that is."

"You want to make a report," said the policeman.

"Aye, all right," said Tracey's dad. "Criminal, that is."

The policeman nodded sagely.

"But no reason to think it was connected to the death of Mrs. Tattershawl," he said. "So if you've nothing further to add on that matter . . ." He closed his notebook, considering the great slab of etched stone which was slewed halfway across the lane, writing side down. "I appreciate your time. You will have to get that out of the road, of course. Don't want any more injuries."

And that was all there was to it as far as Tracey's family were concerned. It was a nuisance, an inconvenience, and probably a further indictment of what was wrong with Britain under Callaghan who was, Tracey's dad said, determined to snatch defeat from the jaws of victory and hand the country to the Tories. Tracey was less sure, and while the policeman took down the details of what had apparently been done to the stone overnight, she clambered up onto the bank and peered into the dark hole where it had lain. She couldn't help but think that it looked as if something had pushed the massive block up and away from below, but since that made no sense she didn't say so.

"You'd better be getting ready for your young man," said her mother, as the policeman wandered down the lane to the parked Vauxhall Victor with the blue light on its roof.

"He's not my young man," said Tracey.

CHAPTER FIVE

Preston didn't know what to wear. On any day when he was supposed to meet a girl this would have been a problem but today it was exacerbated by the fact that he had – in his head – being wearing nothing but his scout uniform for months. Since the dead don't sweat or bleed he had never felt the need to change it. It had become a part of his Merely Dead existence. Now that he was faced with the variety of his wardrobe in this world of daylight and colour, and absolutely needed to make the right choice, he found he was paralysed by all the possibilities. The sheer range of ways he might screw things up was too vast to be considered. He knew Tracey Blenkinsop far better than she knew him. He *remembered* her. If he got the clothes wrong, she would say so, not in a mean way, but with that eye-rolling, deadpan wit which already seemed so familiar to him. He didn't want her to think he was an idiot.

But his wardrobe had been mostly picked out for him by his mum, his 'smart clothes' at least, and they all felt just a little Radio 2, a little *Family Favourites*. The thought made him feel ungrateful but he couldn't help it, considering himself in his wardrobe mirror, the starchy jeans with their slight flare, the shirts with the wannabe hang-glider collars: it was all a little bit yesterday's trendy, just old-fashioned enough to have become respectable and very slightly comic. Even his hair now he came to look at it: too long to be sharp, not long enough to be any kind of statement. He looked like a Beatle, and a "Please, Please Me" era Beatle at that.

Well, he didn't have time to get his hair cut before going to see Tracey, and he didn't know how he wanted it cut anyway. Like the clothes, he couldn't put his finger on what he wanted, and was left with a niggling dissatisfaction that there was no way he was going to look anything like cool. In the end he settled for his oldest, most colour-drained jeans and a collared, orange shirt with an off-centre blue and white stripe which made him look like a substitute for Luton Town. He scowled at himself in the mirror and blew out a long sigh.

He was doomed. And that, he thought with bleak amusement, was coming from someone who'd spent most of recent history dead.

"It's just clothes," he said. "It doesn't matter."

But he didn't actually believe that. In the end Preston switched the shirt for a plain white one and shoved the sleeves up in a way he hoped looked casual, though he suspected Tracey wouldn't be fooled for a moment.

Life, he thought, fiddling with his shirt collar in the mirror, was harder than he remembered. But then this version of life – going to see a girl – was new to him.

When he told his parents where he was going they exchanged the smallest of looks which he pretended not to see, then his dad asked if he wanted a ride.

"No thanks," said Preston. "The bus is fine."

His dad seemed almost relieved. Neither of them wanted the inevitable halting conversation as they sat waiting at traffic lights about who this girl was, how they had met, and how to treat her with 1940s courtesy.

"Got some money?" said his dad.

"What for?"

"In case you go out for an ice cream."

"An ice cream?" said Preston, puzzled. It was turning into a broody, overcast autumn day.

"A hot chocolate then."

"I'll be fine, dad," said Preston, grinning. His dad's anxiety was making Preston feel paradoxically calmer, more mature. "I'll see you later."

"Right," said his dad, adding out of old habit, "be good."

Preston knew the bus route as far as Grimsargh but had to watch closely for his stop as they went on through Alston and into Longridge, getting off just past the Old Oak. Tracey was waiting for him, leaning languidly against a stone wall in a sky-blue parka and a skirt with tights. His nervousness had returned on the bus and he had been half-convinced she wouldn't show at all. His relief and pleasure at seeing her further jeopardised his poor attempt at cool, but he didn't care.

"Hi," he said, knowing he was grinning like an idiot.

"Hi," she said, calm, amused. "This way."

"Where we going?"

"My dad wants to see you," she said. "Don't worry; you won't have to talk to him or anything. In fact, I told them they weren't allowed. But they want to be able to look out of the window and see you. It's a parent thing. You know."

Preston wasn't sure he did but he nodded knowingly and babbled his agreement, privately wondering at the girl's ability to order her parents about.

They walked back past a pub and along a road next to a grassy embankment surrounded by a stone wall which Tracey announced as a reservoir, and then an old stone church with a sign that said "St. Lawrence's," surrounded by a graveyard dotted with trees. In the shadows of one a heavy set old woman in a Nora Batty coat and curlers watched them pass, giving Preston what seemed to be a long, thoughtful look.

"Weird," said Preston, as soon as they had rounded the corner.

"What?"

"That old woman watching us," said Preston.

"Didn't notice her," said Tracey. "How well do you know Longridge?"

Preston shrugged.

"Not well. Come through it to go walking sometimes. Or cycling."

"Scouts?" she asked, with that flicker of amusement again.

"Sometimes," he conceded. "Orienteering. Fell walking," he added, conscious that he was trying to make them sound impressive even though he mostly hated doing it. "Bird watching too," he said. "With mates from school."

That had happened twice. Preston wasn't what you would call social. All of a sudden he found he was looking at himself from the outside, seeing his life and personality the way she might, sure it would seem drab and unadventurous. He wanted to take her hand or put an arm around her, remind her of all they had been through together. Except that as far as she was concerned, none of that had happened and they were meeting properly for the first time. It was maddening. The conversation turned to their respective schools, the subjects they were studying for O-level and then, in a desperate attempt to sound interesting, Preston abruptly changed the subject to music, the one area where he thought she might think him cool.

She gave him a sidelong look and he felt instantly transparent.

"You're weird," she said. "I mean, that's all right. I'm pretty weird myself."

"Yeah?" he said, pleased and hopeful.

"Yeah."

He caught her eye then looked quickly away.

"Pretty nice round here," he said. "Countryside. Fields and all. Trees. Sheep and what not."

By comparison Ribbleton seemed to be all brick and tarmac.

"There are sheep, yes," she said, as if he was a bit simple.

"Not a lot of sheep in Ribbleton," he said dryly. "Except in the butchers."

"Nice. I'm a vegetarian."

"Oh," he said, back tracking wildly. "Sorry."

"Yes, you are responsible for meat."

He gave her another desperate look, unsure of what to say, and she seemed to take pity on him.

"It's fine," she said. "I'm practically the only vegetarian in my school. My parents keep giving me nuts and lettuce like I'm an exotic pet they bought without an instruction manual. *This is green*," she added, apparently mimicking her mother or father, "*maybe she'll eat this*. If it didn't used to walk around, my dad doesn't think it's really food."

Preston laughed, then racked his brain for something quirky he could relate about his own parents. He couldn't think of anything, and given how desperately he had wanted to see them again not so very long ago, the very impulse seemed disloyal, so he just nodded.

"So why do you want to move to Preston?" he said at last.

"I don't. My dad's a baker. The shop he worked at closed last year and he didn't have the money to buy it, so he's been working as a farmhand and odd job man. That's why we live up 'ere. There's a cottage on the farm. But my dad wants a proper job. He's applied to Goss's, the printers."

"Big career change," said Preston.

"He was a mill worker when he first left school so he has some factory floor experience."

"Enough?" asked Preston, realising too late that it was a rather personal question.

She gave him a sharp look, then decided to be frank.

"Probably not," she said. "But when you don't have a lot of choices . . ."

"You'll make do with what there is," Preston agreed.

"Right. What do your parents do?"

"Both teachers," he said, rolling his eyes.

Tracey grinned.

"Which school?"

"My mum's at Blessed Sacrament primary, where I went. My dad's a woodwork teacher at Southworth." He paused before adding the kicker. "Where I go now."

"No!" said Tracey with horrified glee.

"Yeah," said Preston ruefully.

"That must be fun," she said.

"You have no idea."

"Must be a help with your school work."

"Maybe," said Preston. "But everyone else gets to leave school at the end of each day. Me? Never. Anything that happens in class – like if I get yelled at for talking or I do badly on a piece of homework or something – my mum and dad know. Every little thing, every time. So I get in trouble at school and then I come home and get it all over again. And having a parent in the school is worse than being 't teacher's pet. No one trusts the teacher's son. They think you're gonna grass everyone up all the time. Like I'm not really on their side."

He hadn't meant to say so much. It just spilled out of him and he felt immediately embarrassed for revealing so much, followed by another rash of guilt for disloyalty to the parents he had missed so desperately. But it was all true, the way that his parents being teachers somehow put him on both sides of a divide which was, for everyone else, absolute: a fundamental *us and them* separation which amounted to a state of war. And it wasn't just that he felt that his classmates didn't trust him: it was also that his loyalties really were divided. He remembered Pete Maddingly talking about some film where the kids in a school had rebelled against the teachers, got a load of guns and finally shot them all. *If. . .* , it was called, and while Preston hadn't even seen it, the idea of the thing haunted him. While everyone else had discussed the film with a kind of grim glee, celebrating it as a fantasy victory against an obvious enemy, Preston had felt a kind of unspeakable horror, because his *parents* were teachers. The whole thing had left him miserable, because he was neither on one side nor the other, not really, and Pete Maddingly, who had seen it in his face, had taunted him relentlessly for it.

Now Preston just shook his head and waved the subject away, so that for a minute they walked along the rustic road in awkward silence.

"It's OK," said Tracey at last. "Doesn't mean you don't like them."

Preston gave her a quick look, amazed. It was like she

47

had been in his head. It was a disconcerting feeling, but then, recovering, he nodded, managing a smile that was oddly grateful.

"Yeah," he said. "I know. What about you?" he added, redirecting. "You like school?"

"It's OK," said Tracey. "Some of the teachers are pretty nice, some . . ." She made a face which hinted at more than the usual pupil discontent.

"What?" he asked.

She shrugged, embarrassed, but said,

"There's this one bloke. Mr. Goggins. Teaches PE and wears Hai Karate aftershave."

"Drives women wild!" said Preston with a grin. It was the TV advertising slogan. "Be careful how you use it!"

Tracey didn't smile back.

"He's always, like, watching," she said. "Ferrety, you know?"

"Right," said Preston, still grinning, unsure why she seemed so repulsed. "Yeah, we have those too. Always on your case, making sure you're not talking in class and . . ."

"No," she said. "Goggins is different. He's always *watching*."

He gave her a quizzical look. He was missing something.

"The girls, Preston," she said, spelling it out. "He watches the girls. And he thinks. You can tell."

Preston felt himself caught between embarrassment and indignation on her behalf, but mostly he felt stupid, as if he had just figured out a maths problem everyone else had mastered months earlier.

"Oh," he said lamely. "Right."

"This way," said Tracey, turning onto a narrow and overgrown way that looked barely more than a farm track. "Home sweet backwoods desolation. Welcome to the seventeenth century."

"I like it," said Preston, looking about him appreciatively. "More fields and trees. Very . . . rural."

"We have established how much you like the country," Tracey answered with another patented eye roll.

"You're lucky to live here," Preston said, meaning it.

"Because you live on the mean streets of Ribbleton," she said.

This is banter, thought Preston, enjoying the thought. *We are bantering.*

"Well, I just mean," he said, "you take all this for granted, but me . . ."

"Right," she replied. "The other man's grass . . ."

"And trees," Preston inserted.

"And trees," she conceded. "A woman died out here last night."

"Died?"

"Yes," she said, giving him a slightly dazed look, as if she didn't fully understand what she had said. "Lived just over that way."

"That's awful," said Preston. "What happened?"

Tracey shrugged.

"Heart attack, they think. My parents didn't really want me to hear about it so . . . you know."

"Right," said Preston.

"This is us," she added, nodding toward the cottage ahead, where a still smaller track went through a gate to a farm on the left. The junction was marked by a long, square-sided stone which was slewed halfway across the road. Mud and clay mounded around it. Tracey followed his eyes.

"Thought maybe that was connected to Agnes dying at first," she said, "but my dad reckons someone with a truck or a tractor pulled it up."

"Why?"

She shrugged again.

"Because they could?" she said, wonderingly. "I don't know. Why do big kids wrap the swings around the top of the frame so that the little kids can't reach them?"

It was clearly a rhetorical question so Preston just nodded solemnly.

"Sit," she said, nodding at the stone. "I'll get you an ice cream."

"An ice cream?" said Preston, amused that his father had been right after all.

"My dad's idea," she said with another eye roll. "Because he thinks I'm seven. Later he figures we'll play hopscotch. He'll probably get the clackers out."

Preston returned her knowing grin and settled on the long stone, as she went to the front door of the cottage.

So far so good, he thought.

He looked around, suddenly sure he was being watched from the cottage window, and his hands fell absently to the stone he was sitting on.

He snatched his palms away, and looked at them. For a fraction of a second the stone had felt hot to the touch. Red hot. His hands, however, looked perfectly normal, and when he cautiously replaced them on the rock he felt only the course, gritty surface of the sandstone, quite cool and ordinary. He frowned, rubbing his thumbs testingly against his finger ends, but if there had been any strange sensation, it was quite gone now. Probably he had imagined it. It had been so long since he had felt much of anything that his mind was playing tricks on him.

"Ice cream," said Tracey, holding out a little pottery bowl with a milky hunk sliding around in it. Preston looked up in time to catch her mum pulling back from the kitchen window. "Eat up and we'll take that walk."

* * *

Ken Shakeshaft, the farmer and landlord to Tracey's family, scowled at the overturned stone.

"And you 'eard nowt?" he said. It wasn't quite an accusation, more a faintly disbelieving statement of their deafness and stupidity. Tracey's dad bristled.

"Told you, didn't I?" he said.

"All right, Jim, keep your 'air on," said Shakeshaft, waving his indignation away. He was already more concerned with the logistics of putting the matter right. "Well, it can't stop there. Could wrap some chain around it but we'd 'ave to get 't tractor up above that bank. That won't work. We can shove it back up where it was, but not without 'elp. Must weigh a ton."

"Bulldozer? Snow plough?"

"I'm not bloody renting serious gear like that unless some

bugger else is paying," said Shakeshaft decisively.

"Could put it somewhere else," said Jim, looking speculatively around. "Drag it up through 't gate to't dairy. Set it alongside loading dock. Put 'milk kits on it."

The *kits* were what he called the old-fashioned milk churns.

"'appen we could at that," said Shakeshaft, liking the idea. "Make it easier to get 'em on't truck."

"Would save time," Jim agreed, privately thinking that Ken Shakeshaft would jump at anything which improved what he liked to call *efficiency*, so long as it didn't cost him anything.

"Where there's muck, there's brass," Jim Blenkinsop's dad used to say, and it was still true. For all their griping about taxes and regulations, Jim had never met a poor farmer.

"There's fifty foot o' cable in't barn," said Shakeshaft. "You grab that and I'll get 't tractor."

* * *

Agnes Tattershawl had seen no one for hours, not since the boy had looked at her as he walked past the churchyard. At least she thought it was hours. It might have been days.

Nights, more like.

It was dark, had been since that moment with the horse-thing on Lower Road down by the fields that went up the side of Written Stone Lane. That had surely been days ago, but the sun hadn't come up, and there was no sign of Joe back at the house. No sign of anyone, for that matter.

The chips had disappeared, though she found she wasn't hungry. Or tired, come to that. She was glad of it, but there was a stronger and less comfortable feeling too, a sense of wrongness that she couldn't quite nail down. It had taken her a while to notice that her heart didn't seem to be beating at all, and though she had decided not to think about that, she couldn't quite put it from her mind. She tried to tell herself that everything was normal, but the time seemed to pass strangely, like she kept falling asleep and couldn't remember what had happened. And where was everyone? The centre of the little town was always quiet at night, but completely deserted?

And then there was the boy.

Preston Oldcorn.

She didn't know how she knew who he was, and so far as she knew she had never seen him before, but she was quite sure of the name. It had come to her bright and clear and hard as the pavement where she had found herself lying after the moment with the impossible horse. Like it had been left there for her, muttered into her ear as she lay there insensible, but by who – or what – she couldn't imagine. For a second there had been a choice in front of her, like a door, and though she didn't understand why she knew she really wanted to go through that door, needed to. It was what was supposed to happen next. But when she tried the handle, it was locked, and the name came back to her.

Preston Oldcorn.

Then she had seen him walking by the churchyard, talking

54

as if he was with someone, though there was no sign of anyone else there, and she had had a keen sensation that whatever strangeness was happening to her was because of him.

Yes.

The idea hardened in her head, turning cold and angry as she pictured the boy's face. His name whispered through her mind again – Preston Oldcorn – and she was sure now, both of the horror she had tried to deny and of his hand in it. Something terrible had happened to her, and while she didn't know for sure what it was, she knew that it was somehow the fault of that boy.

Well, she thought darkly. *We'll see about that.*

CHAPTER SIX

Preston and Tracey walked and talked half the afternoon. For Preston it all felt muffled and surreal, but touched with the thrill of danger, like he was riding his bike along Blackpool Road and knew that if he strayed even a few inches from the curb he'd be clipped by a passing car. He wanted to rehash everything that had happened in the Miley tunnel, talk about the apparition of Margaret Banks and the Leech itself, the boy whose name he did not know, who had been the heart of everything, but knew he could say none of it. She should have known every detail, should have been able to celebrate and commiserate and thrill to the horror of it all with him, like she was right there when it happened – as she had been – but he knew that he could say nothing without sounding like a lunatic. So he was careful, guarded even, terrified of giving away anything he might know about her that he hadn't just learned in the last few hours.

And in truth, he *had* learned plenty about her today, stuff they had never been able to talk about before about her family, her school and the books she liked and what she watched on telly and the music she listened to: all stuff they had been too busy, too desperate, too terrified to get to in those previous encounters she did not remember. It left Preston bewildered and anxious. He still liked her as much as ever but where his memories of her had been full of darkness and horror, they were now in the open fields of Longridge, enjoying the autumn colours and an idle, meandering chat. They talked about telly, reciting moments from *The Two Ronnies* and *Morcambe and Wise*, from *Reggie Perrin* and – both of their favourites – *Fawlty Towers*, of which there was supposed to be a second series next year. They debated whether *Close Encounters of the Third Kind* was actually better than *Star Wars* – Tracey said it was – and laughed about Phil Jenkinson – a boy in Tracey's class – who hadn't gone to see it because he said he hadn't seen the first two. They made fun of the bloke with the posh accent who couldn't pronounce the local place names in the ads they ran before the films ("Pen*worth*am"!), and argued about the best flavour of Spangles and Opal Fruits. Tracey told him he needed to listen to XTC, and Preston, who had never heard of them, said he would. It felt comfortable, and for all the exhilaration of being with a girl he liked, sharing the weirdly intimate emptiness of country lanes and the stillness of sheep and cow pastures, it also felt ordinary.

Not normal, not for him, but also neither big romantic drama nor the dread of ghosts and monsters in dark tunnels.

Ordinary.

Which is a good thing, right? he asked himself as he stared unseeing through the bus window on the way home. He found the end stub of a packet of Pacers he had forgotten about in his jacket pocket, and he unwrapped the last of the green and white striped mints as they passed the Duke William. It had started to rain, the droplets running down the grimy windows in fat, oily rivulets which made the world outside grey and indistinct.

Yes, he decided, chewing thoughtfully. *It's a good thing.*

It was, after all, life, and there could be nothing better than that.

"Alright?" said his dad as he walked into the kitchen where Radio Blackburn was playing.

"Yep," said Preston. "You?"

His father frowned and turned the radio off.

"Lost two nil," he said, adding – as if this made matters significantly worse – "to Oldham."

Preston gave him a bleak smile.

Yes, he thought again. *Ordinary is good.*

* * *

It had called itself the Leech.

It knew that much, though the why of it was lost in a fog of unremembering, a swirling mist of pastness now alien to what it thought itself to be. It lived only in the present, a kind of boggart, though, like all such things, it was old. Some thought it as old as the Lancashire hills themselves, a spirit of earth and stone, fen, river and pool, an ancient terror to the people who lived there in the darkness of the night. Perhaps it was older than the settlements of humankind itself, though it had grown up to feed on their fear and their rage and their grief. As it did so it became less elemental and more like them, the ordinary people who lived under the shadow of Longridge Fell, forgetting what it had been as it took on the shapes they dreaded. It haunted them, learning to terrorise and, when the chance arose, to kill.

It did not recall what it had been, but it knew what it was, a monster of darkness and malice, a thing that preyed on dread and sucked fear like blood, slurping it out like marrow from cracked bones. Or it would be when it fully woke. Such things were beyond it now, but the longer it stalked the earth, drawing power from the land, the darkness, and the terror of the people who lived there, the mightier it would become.

It hadn't expected to have the strength to kill the woman. She had fallen to it in a confused frenzy of physical pain and mental panic, the weakness of her body combining with the weakness of her mind. The Leech had felt her heart stop and had crowed its awful triumph. It had been using one of the old shapes then, a thing like a horse. Those came first because they were easiest, the beasts and trees that had been there longest: horses and cattle, sheep, fox, hare and badger. Ancient things. Creatures of instinct. The human forms were harder, in the same way that acting within their houses and churches was harder, requiring more strength, more wakefulness. That would come, but for the moment the Leech flitted about the lane, now crow or bat, now stagnant pool, now ancient tangled hedge, waiting.

Watching.

It would remember more too, as time passed and the human world came into focus, it would recall more details of the Radcliffe family the boggart had terrorised and destroyed before it had fallen prey to the twice-killed old man's cunning, before it had been the Leech. Long ago, that had been, after the tumult of the war which set brother against brother and neighbour against neighbour. It didn't remember how Radcliffe had outwitted it, but it did remember the long darkness under the stone where it had been pinned, and an icy fury coursed through it for the family in the old farm house. All those years in the cold ground! The boggart was no horse however terrible. It had been too long among humans for that, and it had learned as much from them as it had about them.

It had learned the steel-hard pleasure of vengeance which no beast understood.

The demon moved from shadow to shadow in the lane, and its red and ancient eyes fell on the low hulking shapes of the old farm buildings. They weren't the original structures of the Radcliffe house. That had been a stone's throw to the west, but it was long gone now. This spot was where it had been imprisoned and so the creature hated it, and the house which sat beside it. And the people who lived there. It didn't have a sense of the adults yet, but the girl . . . The girl whose room it had been able to enter. Just. The girl it could feel.

Revenge.

It knew that word. And with it came two more that required more thought before they cooled and hardened into meaning.

Preston Oldcorn.

Oh yes. It remembered him too.

* * *

The boy in question was an altar boy at eleven o clock mass the following day, the parish's last remaining vestige of the Latin liturgy. Preston had always liked the sound of it, the familiarity coupled with that collision of the theatrical and the mysterious, and the parallel translation service books they used meant he knew where they were in the service. This morning, however, as he went through the pre-mass rituals of dressing in cassock and cotta, then lighting the altar candles including what they called the Big Six which flanked the brass tabernacle, he couldn't help but wonder at the strangeness of it all. He had, after all, seen death, and it had taken none of the forms offered up by the church's prayers and teachings. It left him feeling oddly displaced, different, in spite of the comforting predictability of the mass. Perhaps even because of it.

It was a four-man team today. George Hardwick, the sixty-something senior server who put aitches in front of words that didn't have them and dropped them from those that did, was the cross bearer and was doubling as the reader. There were two Southworth first years who were the acolytes – they carried the tall brass candle sticks immediately behind the cross – and Preston who was thurifer, the best job by far. It was his task to light the old thurible's little charcoal disks before the service began, his task to keep it alight and smoking throughout the mass by swinging it gently on its chains, and his task to bless the congregration with the incense – bow, three to the left, three to the centre, three to the right, then another bow. There was a knack to working the chains so that you could pull the upper case up and expose the coals for a sprinkle of the aromatic incense grains, and Preston had always taken pride in having it down pat. It made him feel special.

But the best part of being thurifer was that after the consecration, and the last use of the incense timed to the chiming of the bells as the priest elevated first host then chalice, he got to go off into the sacristy and put the little fire out. Over the years he had learned that no one ever noticed how long this took, so he would amuse himself, playing with the candle wax and matches, while the sounds of the service droned in from beyond the heavy wooden doors. Sometimes he would wrap the match heads in the scraps of silver paper peeled from the charcoal packaging, then shove the stick part into a candle and see how long it would burn before the match head exploded with a flare and a pop that blew the silver foil to ribbons. That was cool. And in truth he loved this tiny rule-breaking, the publicness of his exit to do what looked important, holy things, when he was really just playing. He was always back on in time for communion, re-entering via the altar entrance, and no one any the wiser, but he liked to be alone in the sacristy, a dim, curious little space with its aromas of floor wax and cut flowers. It was the business end of the church, he thought: the backstage, where the public magic of vestments and candlelight was made, but it was also where he felt the mystery of it all – God and myth, spirituality and death – most deeply.

He especially liked it today, though he found himself content to look at the ebbing flame in the tar-blackened heart of the thurible as he listened vaguely to the drone of Father Edwards and the dull mumblings of the congregation's responses.

Pax Domini sit semper vobiscum

Et cum spiritu tuo.

The peace of the lord I give you always.

And also with you.

Agnus dei qui tollis pecatta mundi: miserere nobis.

Agnus dei qui tollis pecatta mundi: miserere nobis.

Agnus dei qui tollis pecatta mundi: dona nobis pacem.

Lamb of God who takes away the sins of the world, have mercy on us.

Lamb of God, who takes away the sins of the world . . .

"Preston Oldcorn! What are you doing?"

Preston spun round to find Nora MacIntyre standing in the doorway of the vestry and looking at him as if she had been there for some time. Preston's mouth fell open and his eyes got big, thrown not simply by being caught fooling around like this, but by who had caught him. Father Edwards' housekeeper was severe and aloof and always dealt with the altar boys as if they were insufficiently reverent and careless in ways that made her job harder, both of which were certainly true, but she was also Roarer's sister. She had been present when Preston had watched his parents grieve for his death and when he had gone to meet the Leech in the Miley tunnel. Like Tracey, of course, such things belonged to a timeline she could not remember because for her it had not happened.

Still, her presence unnerved him, and he stared at her stupidly.

"Well?" she demanded again, her voice just low enough to ensure she wasn't heard in the church itself. "I asked what you were doing."

"Nowt, miss," he said reflexively, like an eight-year-old caught straying onto the lawn outside the church which the little kids called God's Grass. "I were just . . . about to go back on."

"On?" she echoed.

"Into church," he said.

"Then you had better do that," she said in those crisp but slightly musical tones that were the last of her Irish accent. Preston wondered why Roarer hadn't had it too. "Before you burn the building down. Go on then. Off with you."

Preston moved quickly, stooping to the thurible and blowing the flame out, before sidling past her, through the vestry and into the bright and echoing hallway with the sink where the flower arranger had left piles of green oasis and leaf cuttings.

He could feel her watching him go and knew his face was red, though he hadn't really been doing anything wrong. Still, he hoped she wouldn't tell the priest.

* * *

Nora MacIntyre shook her head and was about to frame a bleak, private smile at the boy's back when something strange came over her and she caught her breath. She trembled, a shiver which ran through her aging bones as if the temperature had just dropped twenty degrees. It was a curious sensation, the kind of feeling which made people glibly remark that someone had just walked over her grave.

The words froze in her mind and her smile stalled, her eyes lingering on the back of the altar boy as he went through the little wooden door and onto the altar.

Just for a moment.

The feeling passed and she snapped back to reality with a flash of amused annoyance at how easily she was getting distracted these days. She needed to get the priest's vestments laundered and ironed.

Sunday might be a day of rest for everyone else, Nora MacIntyre, she told herself, *but for you it remains the busiest day of the week, and don't you forget it.*

CHAPTER SEVEN

Preston's dad clicked on the radio and the theme music for *Family Favourites* wafted across the room as his mum dealt out the roast beef and Yorkshire pudding. Preston rolled his eyes, but he couldn't help but smile at the same time. A few weeks ago the sound of all those "easy listening" songs from the mellowest Elvis to the Carpenters, Roger Whittaker, Glenn Miller, and Max Bygraves, would have set his teeth on edge, but he couldn't deny that there was something comforting in the familiarity of what he had once dismissed as *offensively inoffensive*. His dad caught the look and shrugged.

"You want Radio 1 on?" he said.

It was a magnanimous gesture, like offering to buy him the leather jacket they had quarreled over, and Preston knew it cost his father something. The international request show with its old-fashioned, middle-of-the-road sensibility had been a staple of Sunday lunch in the Oldcorn household for as long as Preston could remember.

"Nah, you're all right," said Preston.

"See what they play," said his dad, offering a middle ground. "If none of it is any good . . ."

"It's OK," said Preston. "I can listen to the Top 40 later."

The conciliatory tone was new. They weren't a family who rowed a lot, but they had been needling each other of late. "Growing pains," his mum said, though to Preston it felt less like he was growing than that the house was shrinking, tightening around him like a straitjacket. He knew the feeling made him surly, fiercely protective of his privacy, and quick to argue. Since the nine twenty-two nightmare he had, in some ways, felt more comfortable in his own skin, but he was also different than he had been, and his parents seemed wary of him. Offering to change the radio station was a sign of that. His parents had been *Talking*.

It was a strange program, *Family Favourites*, left over from post-war years when soldiers were stationed all over the world and relied on the radio to convey messages of love and togetherness tacked onto some generic song from a former age, "The Anniversary Waltz" or "The White Cliffs of Dover." It was unbelievably corny, but also sad, touching and strange, all those deeply personal memories and hopes for future togetherness filtered through radio-friendly politeness and greeting-card sentimentality. Preston knew the pain of being separated from those you loved, but he couldn't imagine trying to bridge that gap by unpacking his heart in words for some radio presenter to read out to the world.

Preston recognised the plucked harp opening to the Beatles "She's Leaving Home", and rolled his eyes again. *Family Favourites* only seemed to play the early Beatles singles and a handful of the more melodic tunes like "Blackbird", so that it had been years before he had stumbled onto the harder, stranger stuff.

"The thing about this," said Preston's dad, half-turning to the radio, "is that even though it makes fun of the parents for being middle class and closed-minded, it still allows them to grieve, you know?"

Preston looked at him, feeling like some version of this speech had been poised in his father's head, waiting for the moment it could get out.

"How do you mean?" he said.

"Well, it's their fault she's leaving, right?" said his dad, looking at his plate. "They are controlling and pressuring and the girl . . ." he hesitated, then said it again, as if emphasising it would save him from anything more personal and direct, "the *girl* feels trapped by them. But even though the song mocks them, you still feel their sadness, their loss. They were wrong, and they've forced her out, but they didn't mean to and their grief is real. You know?"

He looked up briefly, caught Preston's eye, then looked away again, and Preston didn't know what to say.

"Anyway," said his dad, as his mum returned from the kitchen with a bowl of roast potatoes. "Good song."

* * *

That evening Preston listened to the Top 40 on Radio 1 with his cassette player plugged in to the five-pin socket on the back, the play, record and pause buttons all pressed so that he set the tape rolling the moment something came up that he wanted. 10cc's "Dreadlock Holiday" had taken over the top slot from the Commodore's "Three Times a Lady" which Preston considered a win, and Jilted John was up to number four, which was kind of funny. Boney M's "Rivers of Babylon" was slipping down the charts at last, but so were Siouxsie and the Banshees and the Rezillos, while the *Grease* onslaught continued unabated. If he had to hear "Summer Nights" one more time, Preston thought he would scream. Blondie's "Picture This" was up to number twelve, and the Jam's "David Watts" – featured on *Top of the Pops* last week with Bruce Foxton singing lead in a white suit, and Paul Weller stealing the show on backing vocals – was up to number twenty-five. Preston thought it unlikely either would get any higher, and most of the rest of the top thirty were ballads and disco. He didn't have anything against disco really, but he didn't dance and it all felt very shiny and American, a world away from his life here in Lancashire. Still, he'd be lying if the love songs didn't sound a little richer and more urgent than usual, didn't make him think vaguely, wistfully of Tracey and whether she was listening to the same songs at the exact same moment . . .

The idea embarrassed him a little, which was stupid, but it also made him smile. He thought about calling her but he wasn't sure of what he considered the "rules" of going out with girls, or whether he and Tracey were actually going out. They hadn't kissed or held hands or anything like that. Maybe Tracey wasn't thinking of him in that way at all. Maybe she thought they were just mates. Actually, it might not even be mates. He had to keep reminding himself that as far as she was concerned they had just met.

He turned the radio off and sat frowning at it, suddenly deflated. He hadn't recorded a single song except the 10cc, and even that had been grudging, a sense of obligation as if he was commending the universe for the momentary respite from bloody *Grease*. He rewound it and listened to it again, liking it better this time, the menace of the lyric coming through in spite of the upbeat reggae guitar. The song's idea of being a long way from home and out of his depth settled into him, reminding him dimly of the nine twenty-two no-place where he had spent so much time.

But he was back now. Everything was fine. He was back, and there was a girl who liked him, or seemed to, and all the strangeness and misery he had been through was no more than a bad dream which would eventually blow away in the everyday breezes of home.

* * *

Tracey was in a tight, dark place. A hole, perhaps, though now it seemed more like a box. It closed her in on all sides but the top, and even though she was not moving she thought she could sense the air above her. Her eyes were open but it was too dark to see, though she felt her confinement against her arms and legs. All her weight was on her left hip and shoulder and her knees were drawn up into her belly like a foetus, but when she pushed her feet down they met something hard and unyielding which might have been wood.

A coffin, she thought. *I'm in an open coffin at the bottom of a grave.*

She wasn't sure where the thought came from, and she knew it couldn't be right. In fact, she thought, though it felt like a coffin now it had been something else just moments before, though she wasn't sure what. It had still been dark, still confined, but it had felt different and it hadn't been so tight.

A dream, then, she decided. She was dreaming, or had been. If the world around you changed it meant you were dreaming.

She squeezed her eyes shut, held them like that, then opened them again, and as she did so she shifted and flexed her legs again. There was no sense of the box – coffin now. She straightened her legs, cautiously at first and, when she encountered no resistance, more decisively, pushing them all the way till she was stretched out, her back and neck unarching. She rolled then onto her stomach, feeling the way her face burrowed instinctively into her pillow. Fingers and palms flexed, exploring the darkness, kneading the sheet and mattress beneath her. As the certainty –

her own bed, her own room – returned to her and the nightmare fell away, she smiled at the absurdities the sleeping mind could make you believe, and it was a moment before she realised she was cold.

She stirred again, frowning now, reaching vaguely with one hand for sheet and blankets, but they were gone. Blowing out an exasperated sigh, Tracey sat up and felt around to be sure all the covers were gone, then scooted down to the foot of the bed, not bothering to turn on the bedside lamp. She drew herself into a crouch on the end of the mattress and reached down to where the mound of sheet and blankets were, just as they had been two nights ago. She started sorting them blindly, hunting for the edge so she could drag them up and over herself as she crawled back into a sleeping position.

It was while she was down there, her hair hanging down in her face as she grasped the covers, that the cold air seemed to shift. She became quite still, moving only her eyes. She looked straight ahead. It was too dark to see anything for sure, but she had the impression that the blackness was deeper where the door should be, which would only make sense if it was open.

Again.

She hesitated, touched by a prickling of her skin which was not entirely about cold. She stared at the rectangle of darkness where the door should be, trying to make sense of the deep shadow, and she caught it again, a scent of newly turned earth and something else that was rank and sour beneath it.

Something animal.

She became very still, staring fixedly ahead, and as she did so the darkness seemed to shift, the deep core of the blackness in the doorway moving silently sideways, as if some person had been standing there, watching her, but had now moved off onto the landing.

For a second she stayed exactly where she was, too afraid to move, eyes wide and staring at nothing, and then she was up and slapping wildly at the wall where the light switch should be. She found it on the second try, flicked it, and flooded the room with a light so hard that even in her heart-pumping terror she flinched away from it.

Her bedroom door was indeed open, flung so wide that it was folded back against the wall. The light spilled out onto the landing and she stepped quickly into it, reaching immediately for another light switch though it was already clear that there was nothing and nobody there but her. She took a hurried step to the head of the stairs and looked down, but she knew as only a teenager can precisely how the stairs creaked under foot, and she was unsurprised to see no one descending. For a moment she stood there anyway, drinking in the light and the ordinariness of the sleeping house, feeling her heart slow to something like normal, watching the fractional unsteadiness of her hand which she held up in front of her face until the minute tremors had all but gone.

But the strange scent she had caught was different now. Where it had been all animal musk and wet earth, it had changed to something familiar but unplaceable. Where the previous aroma had been straight out of the fields, this was human and synthetic. It reminded her dimly of school, and not in a good way. She thought of getting self-consciously undressed for PE, as if the smell might be from the changing rooms, but that wasn't it. She sniffed again, trying to home in on it but it was already fading.

A door latch behind her snapped and she spun around to see her dad, bleary-eyed and tousle-haired standing in his pyjamas in the doorway to her parents' room.

"What's going on?" he muttered, vague, still half-asleep. "You alright, Tracey love?"

She hesitated, blinking, and said,

"yeah. Went to the toilet."

"Oh," said her father. "Right. I saw the light and . . . Go back to bed, love."

"Am doing," she said, managing a smile. "Everything's fine."

She wasn't sure why she said that. He was already walking away and closing the door behind him. He didn't need reassuring.

"Night," she said to his back.

She returned to her room, wondering why the face of the creepy PE teacher had come into her mind just as she was about to close the door. She had felt like she was being watched. Maybe that was why. For a second she could almost imagine him, Mr. Goggins, standing still in the shadows of the landing and smiling that secret, leering smile of his . . .

She shuddered and closed the door, pushing it hard till she heard the snap of the latch. Maybe its opening had been something to do with the weather? Shrinking timbers or something had caused the door to swing open? She didn't really think so, but she held onto the possibility like a candle in the dark, if only to shake off the uncomfortableness that the thought of the PE teacher gave her.

As she climbed back into bed and pulled the covers protectively over herself she thought of that image, the candle in the dark, and it stirred another memory of the dream she had just shaken off. Before the confined space had felt like a coffin, it had been something else, something big enough to walk in, though still tight and claustrophobic. The ground had been stony, but there was something else that she had to step over which was straight and regular and cold as steel. She could feel it with the toes of her shoes, a long metal thing like a girder. Or a railway line. She scowled to herself again at the memory, thinking of the space around her as tight, a long tube smelling of damp and ancient soot. The dream resolved, hardened in her mind for a second and its location swum suddenly into her conscious mind and became clear.

It was a tunnel.

CHAPTER EIGHT

Monday morning came, and Preston's delight in being alive and present again shattered against the hard reality of being back in school. He rode in the old Cortina with his dad as usual, dropping his mum off at Blessed Sacrament School, then driving up over the motorway toward Grimsargh and the looming chimneys of the Courtaulds textile factory. There were two hourglass-shaped cooling towers and two massive smoke stacks, sharp as gun barrels raking the sky for enemy aircraft. At three hundred and sixty five feet high – Preston had done a project on them in primary school and knew this to be true – they were the landmarks of the area, the tallest man-made structure between here and Blackpool Tower.

Preston looked to the left where the old railway line ran, the same one which passed within a hundred yards of his home, the same one which ran from the Miley tunnel up to Longridge where Tracey lived. From time to time he would see a goods train there, usually while he was scanning the fields for a hovering kestrel, but the passenger line which had once carried school children on day trips was long since defunct. Preston thought of the spectral boy who had died on that line, the one who had called himself the Leech, and he marvelled that he still did not know the child's real name.

Because his dad had to be early for meetings and such, Preston always arrived at school before the buses. Sometimes he stayed outside where he could watch the pied wagtails and house martins, but today was cold and wet, so he found a place near his form room to read. There was a chair down in an angle of the corridor by the metalwork room, an area which smelled of steel and oil and, during class time, rang with the pounding of hammers and the whine of drills. At this time of day it was silent, a different place entirely, its tools locked away, its forge cold, as if it had forgotten its own purpose. Preston settled into the chair and started rummaging through the battered briefcase he was hoping to replace with a sports bag. His parents might baulk as they had baulked at the leather jacket, but he would stand firm. He dimly understood that their attempts to make him more respectable than they really were had something to do with their hopes for his future, but he was sick of being sneered at by the other kids, and the briefcase wasn't even big enough for his school stuff. He dragged his copy of *Romeo and Juliet* from it now, gazing at its ragged cover like it was some ancient artifact he had dug out of the ground. In the nine twenty-two no-place he had abandoned the idea of ever being in school again and had given his classes no thought in what felt like years. He was suddenly struck by how badly behind he might be now. English and history wasn't so bad, but French would be hard, and maths would be impossible.

"Alright there?"

He looked up, it was Mr. Simpson, the ancient school caretaker whose house was on the corner of the bus park. He must have been seventy, his face deeply lined like a bloodhound's, and his movements were slow, grandfatherly. Preston knew from his dad that the teachers thought he was too old for the job, and that the cleaners did most of the real work, but the old man was a fixture at the school, familiar as the corridors he paced.

"Hello, Mr. Simpson," said Preston.

The caretaker smiled and nodded, then shuffled off on whatever rounds he did to begin the week.

Preston read for fifteen minutes, and some of his panic about his neglected studies subsided. The Shakespeare was quickly becoming familiar again, mostly because – though he wouldn't admit it to his classmates – he enjoyed it. Some of it was ponderous and difficult but he liked the sound of the words when he whispered them to himself, even when he didn't completely grasp what they meant. Feeling better about the day ahead, he tried refreshing his memory of where they were up to in his maths textbook, but got the opposite response. Struck by how little he understood, he kept turning further and further back in the book, re-reading the term's early work, trying to find something that seemed familiar; but even where he could see his own pencilled marks in the margins, it all felt foreign and new, as if he had never seen it before.

By the time Mr. Blake arrived to open the door of the form room Preston was feeling thoroughly despondent again, though this dissipated somewhat as the other kids arrived from their buses. They entered cheerfully, noisily, yammering on about the weekend, about music and football and who was going out with who, till the teacher told them to quieten down on pain of demerits. Preston sat on a stool in the back behind the heavy, dark benches, their file-scored worktops broken regularly by scarred vices bolted in place. It was his usual spot, though it seemed strange to be back there. He stared at where someone had carved STONKER WOZ ERE into the desk. He had seen it a thousand times without giving it a thought, but he now found himself wondering who "Stonker" was, when he had been sitting where Preston was now, and what had happened to him.

"Oldcorn! You in't tuck shop today?"

It was Pete Maddingly, a big, gangly ape of a boy, one of a few Preston did his best – unsuccessfully – to steer clear of. Preston's heart sank.

"Oy! I asked you a question. You deaf or what?" said Maddingly.

Preston focused but couldn't come up with a satisfactory answer. It was true he worked the occasional shift at the school tuck shop, selling Wagon Wheels, Mars Bars, Mojos, Blackjacks and packets of Golden Wonder crisps from the little window overlooking the playing fields, but he had no idea if he was supposed to be there today.

"Can't remember," he said.

"Yeah?" said Maddingly. "Well you'd better. I'll be coming at lunch time."

Preston knew what that meant. The boy would come to the window, hold up his hand as if he was clutching some coins and demand what he wanted like the other customers. But there would be no money in the closed fist. Just a little menace for later if Preston didn't play along.

"I wouldn't bother if I were you," said Preston. "Not unless you've got some cash."

"Oh yeah?" said Maddingly, leaning in close and grimacing. He bared his teeth and rolled his eyes ridiculously, but it was still scary.

Or had been.

Preston had seen scarier things since the last time he had tangled with Pete Maddingly, and in his gut he knew that like a lot of bullies the boy got by mostly on swagger and menace. It was true that he was bigger than Preston, stronger, and less caring of whether or not he got into trouble – which was ninety percent of what gave kids power in school – but he didn't often get into actual fights, and when he did, he didn't always win. He had famously and gloriously been beaten up by Chris Enfield last year, a large but mostly quiet and gentle West Indian boy, who was generally considered the cock of the school, and who had finally given in under Maddingly's supposedly funny taunts about his colour. Preston still treasured the memory of watching Maddingly running down the stairs and out into the playground with Enfield at his heels, plaintively gasping, "Don't Chris! Come on. I were just kidding . . ."

Preston remembered that now as he smiled back at Maddingly's menaces.

"Your face will stick like that one day," he said mildly.

Maddingly winced as if slapped.

"You better watch it, Oldcorn," snarled the bigger boy. "I'll smash your face in."

"Yeah?" said Preston, still smiling, still curiously calm and unconcerned. "You're welcome to try."

It was a crazy thing to say. Preston could no more batter Pete Maddingly than go to the moon, but for the first time in his dealings with the boy he felt absolutely no fear.

"Yeah?" said Maddingly, closer still, close enough that Preston could feel the boy's breath on his face. He smelled of aniseed balls.

Preston considered him with his cartoon expression, and he felt something like contempt for the boy, even pity, so that his own smile vanished and he said with certainty, "Yeah."

Maddingly made a fist, and faked a little head-bobbing lunge designed to make Preston flinch away, but he looked uncertain, and when Preston didn't respond, he turned back to the front of the room.

"Living dangerously?"

It was Dez Hopkins, Preston's only true mate in the class.

Dez wore glasses and had long hair which fit the progressive rock music he listened to. Preston shrugged.

"Maybe," he said. "Just tired of being pushed around."

"Fair enough," said Dez, another occasional victim of Maddingly's bullying, though not so much as Preston. Dez had a temper, and if pushed too far, he'd lose it. Maddingly was thick but he wasn't completely stupid.

"Fair enough," said Dez, though he looked uneasy. If it came to a fight in the school yard, no one would be there to take Preston's side. That wasn't how the code of such things worked. People might try to break it up, especially if it looked one-sided, but they also might just gather around to make sure it was conducted fairly. Early in the term Preston had seen Dave Jenkinson square off with Barry Melling, and the latter had waited patiently for the other to get up every time he got knocked down. It might have been a professional boxing match. Of course, usually a teacher got into the middle of things before it really got going, but there was a lot that could happen in those first few seconds, not least to your pride. Preston eyed the back of Pete Maddingly's head with the kind of trepidation he had somehow managed not to feel while facing him, wondering if his sudden and unusual defiance might have been a very bad idea.

He might have even said something to Maddingly, backed down a little, but Mr. Blake – who was a gaunt and pale-faced Polish immigrant who sometimes confused his Vs and Ws and was therefore known as The Count – got their attention.

"Special assembly today, class!" he shouted without preamble. "You'll go to first period direct from the hall. Line up now. Single file. And silence!"

Normally there would have been grumbling, jeering, but an unannounced assembly was unusual and the kids' curiosity was piqued.

"Sir? What for, sir? Why we 'aving 'ssembly?" shouted Diane Cartwright, a fierce, thin-faced girl who tended to bark.

"You'll find out when you get there," said Mr. Blake with a prim look.

"You don't know, do you sir?" said Billy Jennings with a knowing grin.

Blake flushed pink but managed to sputter,

"Of course I know."

"I think you're belming, sir," said Billy.

Blake went scarlet.

"Ooh sir, you've gone all red," said Billy.

"I want you all to line up now!" shouted Blake, turning redder still. Though, of course, he didn't say 'want,': he said '*vant.*'

Billy, like a dog smelling fear or weakness pounced.

"Vat do you vant sir," he called back in his best *Hammer House of Horror* vampire accent. "You vant to suck our blood?"

Big laugh from the class.

"That's enough!" shouted Blake, losing the slender grip he maintained on his rage almost as quickly as he lost control of the class. "Demerit, Jennings! Von more vord and it will be detention. I vill not varn you again!"

"What for, sir?" Jennings returned, clearly enjoying himself. "It veren't me. It vere Cartwright."

The girl spun to face Billy Jennings, her narrow face a mask of hard, lunging fury. Preston had seen her like that before. It was like having a hatchet thrown at you, and he was glad he wasn't involved.

Billy Jennings danced a couple of steps away but couldn't resist a jab.

"You should be in a cage, Cartwright. He gives me detention, he should put you in a zoo."

Diane Cartwright swung for him and Blake had to intervene grasping her wrist and pulling her back.

"I vill not tolerate such vildness!" he bellowed, completely losing it as usual.

"What's 'vildness,' sir?" asked Jennings innocently.

"Vhat?" sputtered the teacher, genuinely baffled. "I said 'vildness.' I von't tolerate it."

"Oh, *wildness*," said Jennings as if coming to some huge realisation. "I thought you were speaking Transylvanian."

"DETENTION!" roared Mr. Blake.

At which point a cluster of boys started flapping imaginary bat wings and booming out their best Dracula laughs. All order and discipline collapsed into chaos.

Preston couldn't help but grin at Dez. For all the time he had been away, school was picking up exactly where he had left off.

He was feeling good as they walked the corridors round to the hall and filed in, lining up by form, while Jimmy Sargeant did his best Dick Emery impression – "Ooh you are awful . . . but I like you"– and Aftar Patel countered with Tommy Cooper as presented by Mike Yarwood.

Dez was rolling his eyes.

The usual, said his face.

The school had just under 400 pupils, and this was the only indoor space big enough for all of them, a great barn of a room with a parquet floor and a broad stage at the front. It was where they came for school plays or performances by the reliably awful orchestra during prize giving evenings and, since they had no chapel, where special school masses were held. Today it buzzed with interest and confusion, though he caught two of the teachers conferring under their breaths and he thought they looked somber.

Something had happened.

In spite of all the muttering and occasional peals of laughter that were normal when you got this number of kids together, all no more than sixteen, Preston felt a prickle of unease. He scanned the teachers' faces, glancing around where they stood silent and downcast at the end of the rows of students. Miss Wilkins, he was alarmed to see, looked like she had been crying.

"This isn't good," he muttered to himself.

Dez gave him a sharp look, but then there was a crackle of static and the headmaster, Mr. Collins, was on the stage.

"Good morning," he said, in a tone that confirmed Preston's anxiety. "Thank you for coming to this special assembly. I'm afraid I have bad news. We are, as I like to remind you, very much a community here at Southworth, so when we lose one of our number, we all feel the loss of it." He hesitated, as if he hadn't decided what tone to take. He was a big man, unusually tall and commanding, but now he looked a little shrunken and unsure of himself. "You all know Mr. Simpson, our beloved caretaker who has lived and worked on these premised for almost thirty years. I'm sorry to say that he died this past weekend. A special mass will be said in his memory . . ."

But Preston didn't hear the rest.

Mr. Simpson died this past weekend?

That couldn't be right. It wasn't possible. Not even close. Because Preston had seen him – had *spoken* to him – this morning.

CHAPTER NINE

Formal courtesies were spoken about Mr. Simpson, how well respected he was, how efficient, how much he would be missed, but the truth was that few of the students really knew him at all. The caretaker had been a remote figure who mostly appeared when everyone had gone home or showed up to handle some minor emergency which he did with taciturn economy. Most of the kids had never spoken to him, and his death made little impression on them, except to remind them that such a thing as death existed.

Preston was one of the few who had anything like a personal relationship with the caretaker. That was solely because – being reliant on his dad for coming and going most days – he tended to arrive earlier and leave later than his classmates, and his presence in the building thus overlapped with the old man's. They hadn't talked much, barely a word really, beyond the grunts of acknowledgement which were the full extent of Mr. Simpson's conversation. Once or twice the caretaker had talked about the school football team, about which Preston – who was no sportsman – knew almost nothing of, or had asked him what he was reading, but mostly it was just "Alright?" And when Preston said he was and returned the question Mr. Simpson would reply "Aye, not so bad," and head off down the corridor, pushing a mop or dragging a wheeled dustbin.

Like today. Except that when that snatch of almost conversation had happened, the caretaker had already been dead thirty-six hours. According to Preston's dad, Mr. Simpson's daughter – whose existence was news to Preston – had found him on Sunday morning. He had died the previous evening. She had found him in his pyjamas and dressing gown, sitting in an armchair in front of the telly.

"Like he'd nodded off," Preston's dad had said, musingly, as if he was wondering if that was how he'd like to go himself: just drift off, slide away painlessly, moving easily into whatever came next . . .

But Mr. Simpson hadn't moved on. He was still here, pacing the school hallways and corridors. He might not even have fully grasped what had happened to him, not without some equivalent of Roarer to explain to him the nature of the Merely Dead limbo he had strayed into. Preston wondered vaguely what time it was for him. Not nine twenty-two, for sure, but maybe not that different.

But the caretaker had spoken to Preston this morning in

the living present, something Preston, when he had been dead, had only been able to manage partially with massive effort and practice. It didn't make sense.

After the assembly Preston had said he needed to go to the bathroom so that he had an excuse to search those corners of the school where the caretaker was most likely to appear, but there was no sign of him. Preston wasn't really surprised, not because he knew the old man was dead but because it was day time, and the caretaker was hardly ever around when classes were going on. He thought it again: it didn't make sense, and that was even taking into account what he knew from personal experience about death and ghosts.

His confused feelings cast a pall over the rest of the day and kept him awake that night, uncertain and – in truth – fearful of what might await him at school the following day. He wished he could confide in Tracey, but he knew that impulse came from a relationship she no longer remembered, a relationship which – in real terms – had never existed. Without her as she had been, without Roarer, Preston had no one to talk to who wouldn't think he had lost his mind, and that somehow made his apprehension worse. He considered telling his parents he was sick and should stay home, but that was only a stalling tactic. Much as he might want to, he couldn't hide from school forever, from Pete Maddingly, from algebra, nor from the spectre of the caretaker.

And besides, he told himself just before he went to sleep. *There was no need to be afraid of ghosts.*

He should know. He'd been one.

Preston was quieter than usual in the car the next day, and his father noticed.

"Everything alright?" he asked. His voice was nonchalant, but there was something in his eyes that suggested real concern, and Preston had seen the way his mum and dad had looked at each other when she got out of the old Cortina at Blessed Sacrament.

They've been talking about me, Preston thought. *Again. They're worried.*

"Fine," he said. "Struggling with maths a bit, but I'll get it."

He felt his father's sidelong glance, his hesitation as he decided whether or not to push the issue, and when the car went quiet again, Preston wondered what it was in his behaviour which had triggered his parents' concern. Was it about how he had been since he came back, or was this a long-term concern which extended back before the nine twenty-two period when he had been, he now thought, a different person entirely.

"I'm OK," he added, if only to head his father off before he started asking Preston about Tracey. "Really."

His father nodded, and though he didn't seem entirely satisfied, he let the matter drop. Preston breathed a sigh of relief and watched the fields and farms of Longridge Road as they passed under the great chimneys of Courtaulds, familiar as ritual, and he felt better. Maybe the ghost of the caretaker had been no more than a momentary flicker, a kind of after-image which had happened because he had died so recently. Maybe he would now have passed on and Preston would never see him again.

That thought kept him upbeat and determined to spend the minutes before the school buses arrived as he always did. He left his father at the staffroom door and headed down the corridors to the very end of the school building where the woodwork and metalwork rooms were.

Mr. Simpson met him around the first corner.

The ghost looked quite solid, quite real, but he was uncharacteristically still, staring at a wall with a kind of fierce curiosity. Preston stopped where he was and was about to retrace his steps, to get away, when the old man turned slowly to face him. It was true that there was nothing misty about the figure, but he did not look precisely as he had in life. His eyes were sunken but shining, and his face had a strange pallor. Most unusually, he looked angry.

Preston had seen the caretaker when he had had to clean up graffiti and he had a kind of set irritation, but that had been nothing compared to this. Now he looked livid, possessed of a cold fury which blazed within him even though he just stood and stared. Then, very slowly he raised one arm and extended an accusatory finger at Preston. As he did so his jaw dropped open slow and wide as it would go, descending almost to his chest, and from his dead throat came a terrible cry of rage which seemed to fill the corridor, the school, the world.

Preston slammed his hands to his ears and staggered

backwards. Still the scream came, and – without even really deciding to – Preston rounded the corner heading back the way he had come, stumbling blindly and colliding with Mr. Blake who was on his way to form room.

"You all right, Preston?" asked the teacher.

Preston blinked and stared. The terrible keening wail had gone and the school sounded unnaturally quiet.

"Headache," he managed.

"I'll open up the classroom and you can sit quietly," said Mr. Blake. "If that doesn't take care of it, you can go and see the nurse."

He set off walking toward the form room and Preston followed at half-speed, dreading what he might see around the corner.

But there was nothing beyond the usual painted brick walls and buffed linoleum tiles; no dead caretaker or any sign that he had been there only moments before. Preston slowed still further, not from fear now, but confusion. Had he imagined it? Was it all in his head?

He considered this unhappily as he sat in the back of the classroom with his eyes closed.

"Drink this," said Mr. Blake. He had brought a ceramic mug of water.

"Thanks, sir," said Preston, seeing the kindness in the teacher's eyes and remembering how he had joined in with the others in laughing at him, torturing him, the day before, and on many other occasions before that.

Poor old Count, he thought bleakly. *Cursed with an accent and an ineffectual temper. Still, it could be worse. He could imagine seeing dead people in the hallways.*

"You don't want to go and see the nurse?" Mr. Blake pressed.

That was, Mrs. Watkins, better known – because of her preoccupation with head lice – as Nitty Nora the Biddy Explorer.

"No thanks, sir, "said Preston. "I'm alright."

In a manner of speaking, he thought. A bit, you know, *haunted,* but all right.

He tried to laugh it off, but as the buses arrived and the other pupils started filing in, loud and playful as ever, he couldn't help wondering not just why he had seen the ghost, but why the ghost could see him. Worse, why the ghost – if that was what it was – seemed so angry with Preston in particular. The man had died of old age. That wasn't his fault, was it? How could it be? So why had his eyes been so full of loathing, of blame?

* * *

For the rest of the week Preston avoided the school building except when class was in session. In the mornings he loitered around the car park or the bike sheds, keeping a watchful eye open for the wandering caretaker, but the spectre did not reappear, and by Friday Preston began to hope that the ghost had indeed moved on.

After tea that night Preston went up to his room and spent

a long moment staring at the freshly washed scout uniform hanging in his wardrobe, the green shirt with its achievement badges on the arms and the silver jubilee patch on the chest. He had hated it, but after wearing it for so long in the nine twenty-two limbo it had become strangely part of him, as if it knew all he had been through which he could tell nobody, so that for a uniform it had become oddly personal, private even. It wouldn't stay that way, not if he went to scouts tonight. Then it would lose all that secret magic and just make him another of the boys tying knots and standing at attention, but never quite part of the group.

He went downstairs in jeans and a jumper.

"You're going to be late for scouts," said his mother, looking up from the ironing board.

"It's fine," he replied. "I'm going like this."

His dad, sitting in the corner, his unlit pipe in his mouth, lowered his copy of the *Lancashire Evening Post* and shot his mum a quick look. In that instant Preston realised they had known this moment was coming, and that gave him the strength to push through.

"I'm going to tell the scout leader I'm quitting," he said. "Need to focus on my O-Levels."

That was the line of attack he had thought they would be most persuaded by. His mum became still, holding the iron up so it wouldn't burn the shirt she was pressing, then placed it carefully on the asbestos pad.

"What about getting promoted or doing your Duke of

Edinburgh Award?" she said. She was trying to sound composed, but her voice was a little higher than usual.

"I think my exam results are more important," he said, "and I don't think I'll get promoted anyway. My face doesn't really fit," he said with a bleak smile. Preston had been third in command of his patrol – the peewits – for as long as anyone could remember, and had been passed over for APL – Assistant Patrol Leader – twice. His mother flinched at the truth, and he read the emotion in her face.

"It's OK," he said, meaning it. "I'm not disappointed. I'm just . . . not the kind of person they want."

"Which is what?" asked his father carefully.

Preston shrugged. He didn't know that he could put it into words beyond saying that he wasn't sporty enough, but he thought of the golden boys at scouts, his classmates who were PLs and APLs and he knew he wasn't one of them. His sense of humour was not quite right. What he took seriously and what they did rarely aligned, so that he was both too clever by half and not nearly clever enough.

Preston sat down, calm, thinking. Then, in a measured, even tone, he said,

"Every scout meeting begins with the flag break. Everyone stands at attention while one of the patrol leaders goes up to the flag pole, pulls the rope to free the Union Jack which has been rolled and tied up at the top of the pole beforehand. Then he leads the troop in the scout oath while everyone salutes the flag. A few months ago, it was Austin Davis' turn. He goes up to the flag and pulls the rope, but nothing happens. He hasn't fastened it up right. Everyone is standing at attention behind him, waiting. He fiddles with it, adjusts the rope. Still nothing. Everyone is still standing there, stiff and quiet like. He unfastens a knot somewhere, pulls the rope again, and this time the flag just falls off the pole completely. It's still wrapped up so it sort of bounces."

Preston grinned at the memory.

"And you laughed," said his dad.

"Everyone laughed," said Preston. "For a few seconds. It was funny! But me . . . I thought it was about the most hilarious thing I'd ever seen. I don't know why. Because they took it all so seriously, I suppose. The flag fell off and I just cracked up. Everyone else stopped, but I couldn't. I was laughing too hard. Could barely stand. Eventually the troop leader walks over to me, while everyone else is back at attention, and without saying anything, he gets hold of my ear lobe and marches me to the front door and out.

"They came to get me about five minutes later – *assuming you're ready to control yourself* – and everybody went on as if nothing had happened. I felt bad, you know? Ashamed. But at the same time I kept thinking, *this is all so stupid!* And the truth is, most of them think it's stupid too. Maybe even the troop leader does. I don't know. But they pretend it's serious, important. I try, but they can tell I don't mean it, and I don't want to keep trying any more. I've done it for years, and maybe I'm a better person for doing it, but I'm not really one of them, and I think I've gone along with it long enough. There are other things I'm more interested in so I want to quit."

There was more to it, of course, other ways he wasn't cut out for scouting, but he stopped speaking and waited to see what they would say.

His parents looked at each other and something passed between them in that silent way they used so much, so that Preston was sure some version of this moment had been discussed before. He wondered if they were about to have a row about his attitude, his punk music, the teacher reports of inattention in class . . .

"All right," said his dad. "But if I were you I'd just tell the troop leader that you want to focus on your school work."

He glanced at his mother and she looked momentarily and bafflingly distraught, stricken by a paroxysm of grief which chased across her face and then was gone.

"It's OK," Preston said reassuringly. "Honest."

"You just seem so different lately," she said.

"Just growing up, aren't you son?" said his dad with a wide, and somewhat laboured, smile.

"Sure," said Preston. "I suppose so."

His mother nodded, but her sadness was still there, softer now, less intense, but that was almost worse. This was a sadness she was resigned to.

"Right well, I'm going to go round to my mum's," she said. "Your grandma's a bit poorly."

It was Preston's turn to nod and smile. As she left he half-turned to give his dad a friendly man-to-man grin – knowing and, in its way, loving – but his father was watching her go with an expression of pain that was almost as stricken as she had worn moments before.

CHAPTER TEN

On Saturday, Preston met Tracey in town. He hadn't planned what they would do because it had seemed enough to see her and do ordinary stuff, wandering around the record shops, maybe go down to Avenham Park. It was only as he was getting off the bus at the town's massive, futuristic and generally squalid bus station that he started to worry that he should have planned something. Perhaps they should wander to the Odeon or down to the ABC cinema and see what was playing, or really pretend to be grown-ups and go for tea at the grand café over the old Booths on Fishergate or at the snug but equally old-fashioned Bruccianis. Or was that trying to hard? Maybe Tracey would prefer something cheap and cheerful, more modern. Hadn't his mum mentioned a new Italian restaurant? They could go for pizza or something. That seemed the kind of thing to do . . .

"Hiya," said Tracey.

Preston came to with a start.

"I didn't think you'd be here yet," he confessed.

"Bus was fast," said Tracey, shrugging. "Is that a problem?"

"No, course not," said Preston, his mind racing. "Great."

What shall we do? What shall we do? What shall we . . . ?

"Fancy a coffee?" said Tracey.

"Right. Coffee. Yeah. Great. Fantastic. Coffee."

She gave him that patient/baffled/amused look he had seen before.

"Sorry," he said, then added, "wait. I thought you didn't drink coffee?"

"Figure of speech," she said. "Tea. Juice. Vodka. Whatever."

"Vodka?"

"Joke," she said.

"Right," he said, laughing suddenly and hollowly. "Good one."

She rolled her eyes, but when he looked down, blushing, she took his hand in hers. The gesture was so unexpected that he actually jumped a little so that she gave him another look, then led him down through the underpass which came out under the guildhall by Morrisons. It was a dour place, stained white walls and a black rubbery flooring, smelling of urine and wet leaves, but Preston was aware of none of it. He felt only the soft warmth of Tracey's hand and practically floated through the subway, eyes fixed sightlessly ahead, wafting on a cloud of astonishment and joy.

They emerged through the posh end of the guildhall past posters advertising concerts by groups like Hawkwind and

Camel – the kinds of bands his mate Dez loved – and wrestling matches featuring Big Daddy and Giant Haystacks. They walked out past the old post office and onto the flag market at the foot of the Harris Museum, but Preston didn't really see any of it. Tracey Blenkinsop was holding his hand and there was no room in his head for anything else. In this mood he drifted, breathless and silent toward Fishergate past the Victorian splendour of Miller Arcade.

"So," said Tracey. "Coffee?"

She was asking for a recommendation, assuming he – as the Preston lad – knew the town better than she did. Preston glanced wildly around and his eyes fell on another monumental shopfront and his brain grasped onto the helpful sign posted up by the roofline: café.

"Booths," he said, managing to sound confident, certain, though he had only been in once before, and that with his grandmother. Tracey gave him a sideways smile, not falling for the attempt at Sophisticated Adult, but going along with it anyway.

Good enough, he thought.

He briefly imagined telling his grandma that he had taken a girl to Booths, and had to repress an urge to grin, which is what his grandma would do: grin and say nice, supportive things, ask a few questions, perhaps, but nothing too nosy or probing. He should check in on her tomorrow. Take her some flowers or something maybe, since she was sick.

Tracey and Preston entered the impressive Booths building at the corner of Glovers Court and went up the broad, dark stairs, their free hands tracing the heavy, rounded bannister rail, shaped and burnished by tools, polish and time. There was a warm and pleasing smell of freshly ground coffee. Preston didn't drink the stuff but he liked the aroma; it felt sophisticated, as he might expect the streets of London or Rome to smell, so that he almost wished he liked the taste.

The café itself maintained the same slightly fussy but undeniably impressive ornamentation, white plaster ceiling mouldings, dark mahogany panelling and an air of – for want of a better word – Empire. The windows looking down onto Fishergate were vast and arched at the top, like they were modelled on some ancient abbey, and the tables were laid with starched tablecloths and precisely laid out silverware, porcelain and linen napkins. Preston felt a momentary return of his former panic, and wondered for a moment if he was underdressed. It suddenly seemed likely that a place like this might have a 'no jeans' policy, or something, and that he was about to be turfed out by the austere-looking man in the dark suit who was patrolling the place like he'd stumbled off the set of *Upstairs, Downstairs*.

"Grab us a table," said Tracey, releasing his hand. "I'm going to . . . er . . . *powder my nose*."

She said it with an ironic twinkle and Preston laughed a bit too loudly, not entirely sure if the half-joke was about the place, herself or him. If he was honest he wasn't entirely sure what even the first level of the remark had meant, let alone whatever was smirking from beneath it. Powder her nose? That meant 'go the toilet' in fancy old speech, right?

Right?

"Table for one, sir?" said a waitress in an old-fashioned bib apron. She was plump, middle-aged and kindly looking.

Preston blinked, trying to decide if this too was a joke at his expense, then nodded quickly.

"Two, please," he said. "By the window if there's one free."

He liked the way that had come out – very James Bond – and wished Tracey had been in earshot. Maybe he could say something similar when she got back. At least her absence would give him chance to study the menu and think of some suave remark, though he now realised he should have gone to the toilet at the same time she did. Maybe that 'powder her nose' thing had been a kind of coded invitation, offering to step away from prying eyes for their first private kiss . . .

"Posh here, isn't it?" said Tracey, sitting down. "I feel like I'm about sixty."

"We can go somewhere else if you'd rather," said Preston.

"Nah. It's good. Just a bit . . ."

"*Upstairs, Downstairs,*" inserted Preston. Not exactly James Bond, but at least relevant and, in its way, sophisticated.

"Yes!" agreed Tracey enthusiastically. "My mum used to watch that all the time. My dad was always extracting the you-know-what and ranting. *Suppressing the workers and glorifying a corrupt aristocracy.* That kind of thing."

"Oh," said Preston, smiling but a little out of his depth. "Right."

"Did you order?"

"Not yet, but I don't think we'll have trouble getting served."

The place was very quiet, almost deserted. Even so it was a different waitress who came out to see them, younger than the other and less formally dressed. She seemed surprised to see them, and couldn't – or couldn't be bothered to – mask the edge of her irritation when she came over.

"We usually like patrons to wait until we seat them," she remarked, pulling a notepad and pencil from her pocket. She had a hard, impassive face and stringy blond hair which looked dyed.

Preston scowled, but before he could say that he had been directed to this table by her colleague, Tracey's eyebrows arched and she replied, "because it's so crowded, you mean?"

"It's just . . . policy," said the waitress.

"Right," said Tracey, smiling sublimely. "Policy. So do you think policy will let us stay here or should we go out and come in again?"

The waitress's eyes narrowed fractionally but her response was professionally pleasant.

"You're fine where you are," she said. "What can I get you?"

"Pot of tea for two," said Preston, feeling he ought to be involved in this part of the exchange. He gave Tracey an inquiring look and, when she nodded, added, "something to eat. Cake? Scone?" He was trying to sound both casual and magnanimous.

"Just tea," said Tracey.

"Just tea," said the waitress, closing her notebook pointedly. "And nothing to eat."

Tracey made a vague wave of her hand.

"These aren't the customers you're looking for," she said, à la Alec Guinness.

A *Star Wars* joke! Preston grinned from ear to ear as the waitress scowled and, baffled and returning to her original irritation, walked away. They waited for her retreat back to vanish before giggling furtively, comrades in unbelonging.

They talked about the people they could see in the street below, Tracey speculating on what they were doing, which shops they would be visiting and what they would buy. Preston was quietly amazed at her imagination and wit, though a part of him wasn't in the least surprised.

"That's Vera," she said confidently. "Husband works for British Aerospace in Warton, strictly shop floor, not management, and he wants their six-year-old son to do the same, but she fancies he might be able to go to university and is scouting for educational Christmas presents."

"In September?" said Preston. "Bit early."

"Money's tight and she's organised. Hoping to spot some pre-season bargains."

"Smart lady," said Preston.

"Necessity is the mother of invention," said Tracey wisely. "That bloke there with the face like thunder was supposed to be on North End with his mates, but the missus dragged him along . . ."

"Can I get something for you, sir?"

Preston had been so entranced with Tracey's precise brand of whimsy that he hadn't noticed the waitress approach their table. It was the older woman in the slightly more old-fashioned frock who had shown him to the table in the first place.

"We're alright, thanks," said Preston. "Already ordered."

"Very good, sir," said the waitress, smiling and walking away.

Preston turned his attention back to Tracey but she was regarding him with a version of that confused amusement he had seen from her several times now.

"What?" he asked.

"I don't get it," she said.

"Get what?"

"What you just said about already ordering."

Preston's bafflement matched hers.

"I was just telling the waitress," he said, nodding to the woman in the starched apron who was inspecting one of the empty tables by the counter.

"She just took it a minute ago," said Tracey peering over to the doors communicating with the kitchen. "She didn't remember?"

"Not her. The other one."

"Other what?"

"Waitress!" said Preston, starting to laugh. "The one who just came over. The one standing right there!"

He nodded discretely to where the slightly grandmotherly waitress had stopped what she was doing and had turned to face them.

"Where?" said Tracey, turning from side to side.

"There!" said Preston, indicating with his eyes, then looking down at the table cloth. "Don't stare. She's looking."

"I don't know what you're talking about," said Tracey. "There's a bored looking family sitting over there, an old woman by herself at the table in the corner and literally no one else. No waitress."

Preston stared at her, then swivelled to face the waitress again. She wasn't there.

She hadn't walked away. She had just gone. Or had never been there.

"I need to go to the bathroom," he managed.

"I don't think I have a handle on your sense of humour yet," said Tracey, giving him a quizzical look. She looked confused and just a tad wary.

"Right," said Preston, getting hurriedly to his feet and trying to laugh. "Sorry. Not much of a joke, was it? Anyway . . . I'll just be a minute."

And he left, not actually running, however much he wanted to. He needed to be somewhere else, just for a moment. Get his head straight.

"Upstairs," said Tracey. "The gents."

"Right," said Preston again. "Thanks."

He managed to maintain a stiff walk till he reached the stairs and then broke into a stumbling trot, his mind racing. What was going on? Mr. Simpson was one thing, but here too? Because his instinct said that while the woman looked solid, normal, alive, she wasn't. Tracey couldn't see her. The other waitress showed no awareness of her. And now that he thought of it, that might work the other way around as well:

Table for one, sir?

That was what she had said. Which meant that the ghost, if that was what she was, had not seen Tracey. She had come to serve him alone.

The toilet was at the top of the stairs to the right of another door which Preston mistakenly tried and found to be locked. Now that he considered it properly it looked disused. The one next to it marked with the gents sign in faded white paint pushed open easily and he ducked inside, bolted it closed behind him, then ran some cold water into the sink. He splashed it onto his face, then gripped the chrome taps, as if wanting their cool solidity to anchor his own.

What is going on?

All this madness was supposed to be behind him. The word stopped him, cold as the water running down his face.

Madness.

He was losing it. Maybe he had been for a long time. Maybe the whole nine twenty-two nightmare had been some fever dream, a complex hallucination which wouldn't quite go away. Maybe there was something wrong with his head, a tumour or something that made him imagine things that weren't there . . .

No.

Every fiber of his being said that his memories of the limbo within which he had been trapped for that almost endless night were real. But even accepting that had all been real, it was over. He was back in the living present. How could this still be happening?

For a long moment he stared at himself in the mirror over the sink and then a further complication occurred to him.

Tracey.

Just how weird had he been just now? Was she sitting down there thinking she was going out with a lunatic? Only a half hour ago she had taken his hand. Was it possible that he had ruined things already?

He squeezed his eyes shut as he fought to get a grip on what to do. Then he opened them again, stared at his reflection again fiercely, and decided. He would go back down to their table as if nothing had happened. If she asked what he had been talking about, he'd repeat what he'd said before: it was a bad joke. He would drink his tea. As soon as was plausible and natural, they would leave this place and not come back. Ever. He would hold Tracey's hand and head down Fishergate toward the park. Maybe they'd swing by Brady's Records over the road . . .

And if he saw the waitress again?

The dead waitress.

He would ignore her. He would pretend he saw nothing at all. And maybe that would do it. Maybe it was all in his head and he just had to refuse to accept it, insist upon a more conventional version of reality, and it would all go away.

Maybe.

So he flipped the bolt on the bathroom door and strode out trying to look purposeful.

The door next to the bathroom, the one that had appeared disused and which had definitely been locked when he came up, now stood ajar. Through it he could see a wide open expanse which he suspected matched the footprint of the café below, though there was a wall which blocked some of his view.

He hesitated in the doorway, intrigued, peering in. He could see square pillars, panelled at the bottoms, holding up the ceiling, and the moulding work was less elaborate than the floor beneath, still classy but more modern. There was a stack of empty cardboard boxes and a few twists of brown paper and other rubbish. The striped wallpaper was grimy and peeling, giving the place an air of desolation. The corners of the room were dusty but there were little boxes against the peeling skirting board which looked incongruously new: poisoned bait for mice or rats, he guessed. Traps. He leaned in through the doorway, his eyes moving along the tall arched windows which were the only source of functional light, and he realised he was listening.

Something or someone was moving around in there, just around the corner. A rat? Preston hated rats. He had glimpsed them occasionally near the old railway lines, sleek and furtive with mean little eyes and those awful, bald tails that seemed to move by themselves. Horrible. Yet Preston took two steps inside, then stood quite still, focused and unbreathing, though he did not know why. He had planned to go straight down to Tracey who would be waiting for him, wondering what he was doing, Tracey who was suddenly and clearly the most important thing in his life. But here he was, drawn to this desolate space.

No, not drawn. *Compelled*. He had to see what was around the corner.

He took another two steps, moving carefully, silently, and now he could look round into the part of the room directly over where Tracey was sitting. The arched windows were slimmer than those underneath them, a little less grand, but this part matched the opulence of the café with its rich plaster mouldings shaped like clusters of leaves, swags of fabric and – strangely, startlingly, what seemed to be the heads of sheep, eyeless skulls with curled rams horns. It was the same as the room below, and had surely once been part of the same café operation, though it had long since been abandoned as anything other than storage. There was a counter, and though the tables were long gone, there was still a solitary waitress moving between them, serving people only she could see.

She had her back to Preston, but he knew it was the same one who had shown him to his seat downstairs. She had the same broad back, the same formal outfit, the same apron. She was half-bent over some imaginary table, busying herself with cutlery and napkins, and she looked to him quite solid, though he knew she was not really there. And now he realised that the sound he had heard was not simply movement, but a kind of low, tuneless humming. It came from her as she worked, half-snatches of a melody delivered imperfectly and in fragments, so that it took Preston several phrases before he recognised it. In that moment, as if she sensed his presence behind her, she put words to the lilting tune, words that filled Preston with disbelief and horror.

Oh don't deceive me . . .

And now the café wasn't abandoned, but full of tables and chairs, all set for lunch, though there was no one else present except the waitress, and the room still oozed an ancient and forgotten desolation.

Oh never leave me . . .

Then Preston was running, blind and terrified, sure that the door through which he had come would have swung silently shut, locking him in with the waitress, or whatever it was which looked like her.

But it was open, and Preston shot through it, stumbling into the wall as he found his footing on the stairs, descending three at a time, heart hammering. His terror was almost enough to drive him from the building entirely, but he went back to the first floor café where Tracey had poured tea from a fancy china pot into elegant porcelain cups and saucers.

"I'm sorry," he said, fishing money from his pocket and putting it on the table. "I don't feel well. Do you mind if we . . . ?"

Her smile faded fast and the look she gave him was first concerned, even anxious, then clear and decisive.

"Sure," she said, getting up. "I already drank most of mine anyway."

He was so grateful that he almost sat down again, but he thought of what was pacing the empty room upstairs, what might come back down at any moment, and he stayed standing. He swilled half his teacup down for the show of the thing as

Tracey slipped her coat on, and then they were leaving. Preston kept his eyes front, refusing to look round, determined to see nothing but the stairs and the door to the street till they were safely out into the bright autumn air and straggling crowd of Fishergate. He thought Tracey was watching him from the corner of her eye, but she said nothing, pretending everything was fine, that he wasn't strange or sick, that he wasn't scaring her.

CHAPTER ELEVEN

He had said nothing to Tracey. They had wandered around the shops, but Preston had been antsy, constantly alert for people only he could see in ways that made him furtive and jumpy. Tracey pretended not to notice but eventually asked if he was not having a good time and when he said he was, but couldn't explain his distracted mood, she said she should probably be getting back, though she had originally said she would be free for at least another hour. Preston escorted her to the bus station with a swelling sense of failure and misery which dominated even his fearful worry about where next he might see a ghost.

When it was time for her bus to leave she had just said, "bye, then," and gave him a sad little wave, before turning away. She didn't look back, and even though Preston couldn't blame her, the words held a finality that left him breathless as if Pete

Maddingly had punched him hard in the gut. He watched her bus pull away, looking for . . . he wasn't sure what. A wave from the window, perhaps. But there was nothing, and it took him a moment as the bus pulled around the vast forecourt and out of sight to process the idea that he could have ridden the same bus with her. The idea must have occurred to Tracey too, but she hadn't suggested it, and standing there alone as a sudden rain shower gusted against the glass of the vast station windows, he wondered if he would ever see her again. The thought seemed to hollow him out, so that in spite of his previous fear he rode home feeling only a kind of numb emptiness.

That evening, Preston watched *The Generation Game* with his parents while they ate hotpot with red cabbage in the front room, but the program wasn't the same without Bruce Forsythe saying "nice to see you, to see you nice," and "give us a twirl." Larry Grayson was OK, he guessed, but Preston's dad frowned every time he used his catchphrase "shut that door!" and his mum kept saying that the glasses he wore on a chain round his neck made him look like an old lady. Today was also the day his dad had decided to add herbs to the hotpot, something he had been threatening to try for months. It was the only meal his father made and he always made it the same way. Till today. The result pleased no one particularly and they agreed to return to the usual recipe in future, but while his parents shrugged it off, Preston felt a more profound sense of disappointment. What he had hoped would cement a sense of normality, eating familiar food and watching familiar telly with his mum and dad, left him feeling oddly disorientated, as if the world had shifted fractionally on its axis during his absence and couldn't now be brought back to the way it had been.

He had assumed that being home with his parents, and connected as a living person to Tracey – who had held his hand only a few hours before – would make him feel assured, safe and brimming with joy, but he felt almost as lost and afraid as he had done before his final battle with the Leech. The words of the song came back to him – *Oh don't deceive me, oh never leave me* – and a horrible possibility occurred to him.

Perhaps it had not been his final battle after all. Perhaps the Leech was still out there, still hunting him.

* * *

Tracey was sullen all evening, though she brushed aside her parents' inquiries – "you all right, love?" – with increasing irritation. She knew they meant well, and hated herself for being so snippy with them, so dismissive, but she couldn't help it, and that made her angrier still at Preston, so that she considered phoning him up just to tell him not to call her again.

But that too was stupid. And besides, her parents still thought the phone was a luxury to be used only for emergencies. If she talked for more than a minute her dad would appear in the hall and start tapping his watch pointedly. Maybe she should write Preston a letter, though what she would say she didn't know. She didn't understand why a friendship – for want of a better word –

built so quickly should cause her so much bitter humiliation and hurt, but there was no way she was going to put that down on paper. Words made things true, especially written words. There was nothing for her to say, except to accept Preston's apology when he got round to making it, assuming she was feeling benevolent and he had a good reason for his earlier behaviour. So she went to her room and, instead of playing music, flipped through books, in case the phone rang.

It didn't, and she went to bed angry, partly at Preston, but more at herself for caring.

Tracey awoke a little after three in the morning and lay still trying to decide what had pulled her from sleep. After a few moments of nothing she had started to drift off again, when a loud bang from below sat her up, all senses suddenly alert, drinking in the night. She wheeled her legs round, planted her feet in her slippers and got up. She plucked her dressing gown from the hook on the door – still closed – shrugged into it and belted it loosely in place, then stepped lightly out and onto the landing.

Probably dad: gone down for a snack, and knocked something off the kitchen counter . . .

Probably.

She hesitated, not wanting to wake her mother if her instinct was right, but determined to make sure. She moved across the landing and flicked the stair light on. The staircase was narrow and steep, yellowish in the glow of the single bulb fixture and somehow tight, limited, as if some invisible barrier was keeping the light in, so that the landing at the top and the hallway at the bottom still looked eerily dark. She wondered why her father – if that was who had made the noise – had not turned the lights on as he went. She gripped the bannister rail and, finding it curiously cold to the touch, turned to consider it, moving slowly as if still in a dream and watching herself from a distance. She took a step down, and then another, conscious that the cold seemed to intensify as she moved. She hugged the thin dressing gown to her and pressed on, aware now that her breath was fogging in front of her. Someone had left a window open. That must be it. But even so, this was a deep, January cold.

At the foot of the stairs she moved through the hall to the kitchen door and started abruptly as three loud bangs rang out on the other side of the door. *Crack. Crack. Crack.* Loud as rifle shots. She had reached out for the handle but now she hesitated as, for the first time since she had been woken, confusion gave way to real fear.

Something was wrong.

The phone was right there. She could pick it up, call 999, and whisper that there was an intruder . . .

But that felt wrong too. She had to see before she called, and not only because a part of her was holding onto the idea that it still might be her dad, blundering about in the fridge for something to put on a sandwich . . .

A wiser, older part of her knew it wasn't him, though she could not say how she could be certain, or why – unnerved at the strangeness of the thing – she proceeded to push the door open.

It was dark in the kitchen. She reached for the light switch and flicked it, eyes still focused ahead, but nothing happened.

A power cut, she told herself. Some consequence of the trade disputes that Prime Minister Callaghan was botching and which her father had so much to say about. But the stair light had been working. *A fuse, then.*

She flicked it back and forth, wondering if the power issue could somehow have caused the banging. Nothing.

She took a cautious step into the kitchen.

"Hello?" she said. "Dad?"

The silence stood tall in the darkness, hemmed her in on all sides. Hand outstretched she forced herself to take another two steps. Feeling for the edge of the counter with one hand and keeping the other out in front of her face, fingers splayed. Another step. Surely she should be at the counter by now. She thought she could make out the flat sheen of the window over the stove and moved toward it, the soles of her slippers rasping slightly on the tiled floor. She could feel the blood rushing through her throbbing fingers, her ears, her racing heart.

The bang which came next was the slamming of the door she had just come through. She spun round, almost losing her balance, gasping out a thin cry of panic, but when she stepped toward the sound she did not reach door or wall or anything, and now the floor was soft and gummy, rank with an odour of wetness and decay. She stooped into a crouch, one hand grasping her knees, the other feeling the slick ground.

Mud.

Or worse. As her fingers disturbed the surface a still fouler stench met her nostrils, an animal scent of corruption, of death. She swayed on the spot and put another hand out to steady herself but found that the expanse of the kitchen was gone. In its place was the slick dirt and clay, not simply below her, but rising up in a solid wall in front of her face. She turned and reached out to the point which had been behind her head but found the same thing: a yielding, vertical softness. All around her.

She was in a hole or a shaft, deep as a well, and stinking of corruption.

She screamed now, flailing, scrabbling at the walls of the pit, sliding in the foul dirt beneath her feet, terror finally overcoming her, so that for a moment she did not notice when the kitchen light came on.

It wasn't the full brilliance of the modern fixture her father installed, however. The light came from its little wooden arms with their neat, streamlined shades, but it was a strange bluish light, soft and thin as foxfire and little better than the darkness which had preceded it. But it showed the kitchen as it was, albeit deeply shadowed, and Tracey, squatting in the middle of it, not in a muddy grave – which is what she had decided it was – but on the chill, tiled floor with its cheerful pattern of stylised yellow flowers. Her house. Her kitchen. The tiles were hard and familiar. One had the corner cracked off where she had dropped a bottle of HP sauce on it months ago. The light was weak and eerie, and it was still unnaturally cold, but all was well. Strange, but well.

Apart from the smell which she now thought was rank,

animal, but touched with that strangely familiar and human scent she had smelled the last time. She had wondered about it since, unnerved by associations she couldn't pin down. She kept reaching for it with her mind, but just as she seemed to snatch hold of it, it always seemed to dance free. It was an ordinary smell, but one that bothered her nonetheless, perhaps because it didn't belong in her house. Smelling it again she wondered if there was more to it than that, that the smell itself was somehow worrying, alarming. It smelled sharp and alcoholic, but spiced like . . .

After shave.

Yes. And not just any after shave. It smelled like . . .

Hai Karate.

It was absurd and impossible, but she was certain of it, and with that realisation came other unpleasant associations. Mr. Goggins. The creepy PE teacher who watched the girls . . .

Hai Karate. Be careful how you use it . . .

A flicker of movement in the corner of her eye. She revolved on the spot to face it.

There, crouching up on the counter by the stove, and almost lost in the cave-like shade was a figure in a powder blue track suit, his balding head bowed so that the gold chain around his neck swung free.

It was him.

It couldn't be, but it was. Tracey tried to shout but her voice was gone. Instead her eyes flashed around the kitchen for a knife, a rolling pin, anything she could wield in her defence.

When her eyes came back to Goggins, the silent figure on the counter had changed, becoming something huge and hunched. It was blacker than the night and almost lost in shadow but she felt that it was covered in stiff bristle like an animal. Her eyes widened, sucking in what little light there was, still spellbound in her terror. The thing was filthy, with matted hair and hard red slits for eyes. Eyes which were locked onto hers. All trace of Goggins was gone now, save the discordant aftershave tang. It was big and shapeless, only as humanoid as a great ape, and it was hunkered down with its shoulders braced against the ceiling. As it moved toward her, Tracey had the impression of lolling jaws . . .

* * *

Her scream woke the house. Tracey's parents found her sobbing in the kitchen, shaking from head to foot and gibbering. A nightmare. She must have sleepwalked her way down – something she had never done before – turning on the lights as she went. But what she had dreamed about, she did not remember, or would not say.

CHAPTER TWELVE

Preston didn't want to go to church on Sunday. In truth he rarely *wanted* to go, but the episodes with the ghosts of the school caretaker and the waitress at Booths had left him wary of leaving the house at all. It was impossible to ignore now; he had survived the nine twenty-two no-place and come back to life, but somehow the experience had left him with this unwelcome gift.

He could see ghosts. All of them. And they could see him.

How this could be, he could not begin to guess and he tried various approaches to find a kind of explanation. Sometimes he thought it was something to do with the way he had shifted in and out of the past itself, that his experience with these new ghosts – which seemed to him quite solid and real – meant that he was somehow seeing back into the past as he had in that final confrontation with the Leech on the train, the one which had opened the loophole to his escape and survival.

But if he was seeing the past shouldn't he vanish from the present or something? Tracey had not seen anything happen to him when he had been talking to the waitress at their table. She just hadn't been able to see the ghost.

So maybe his experience in the land of the Merely Dead had caused him to develop some sort of spiritual affinity with those trapped in their own personal limbos?

That seemed more likely. But how was he supposed to live life like this, never sure if the person in front of him was really present and visible to everyone else, rather than the trapped spectre of some dead person? And what was he supposed to do about it? Help them? Find a way to uncover their stories in ways that would allow them to pass on to the next stage as he had with the brakeman?

All of them?

The world seemed suddenly crowded with ghosts.

And that itself was strange. When he had been dead, he had gone what felt like days, sometimes weeks, without seeing another ghost, and when he did it was usually Roarer. He had had to go out of his way to find other ghosts, but now they seemed to be everywhere he looked.

Coincidence, perhaps.

He had only been in the Booths café once before, so encountering the ghost waitress there was, perhaps, unsurprising now that such things were clearer to him, but the school caretaker was a stranger case. Roarer had suggested that ghosts were rare, that most of the dead passed on directly to the afterlife, whatever that was, without being trapped in their final moment beforehand. It had happened to both of them, he thought, because they had both been killed by the Leech whose spectral attack had stopped them from moving on. But if that was right, why should old Mr. Simpson be stuck at school and, more troublingly still, why had the old man's ghost pointed at Preston with such certain fury?

Like it was your fault.

In any case, the prospect of wandering around where he might encounter other ghosts unnerved Preston, and if he thought he could skip church without having to row with his parents, he would have done so. Another day he might, but he couldn't face an argument now. And besides, graveyards and churches were only haunted in films. He knew from personal experience that where your body finished up didn't determine the ground which attracted your spirit. Ghosts were drawn to and confined by the places they had been in life. The church was just another building full of living people. Plus, he'd be able to say hello to grandma who always went to this mass. Perhaps all would be well.

And at first it seemed like it was. Preston got to the sacristy, buttoned up his cassock and threw the cotta over his head, then made the necessary preparations for the service – filling the water and wine cruets, lighting candles, laying out the brass chalice and plate, lighting the thurible – and all was quite normal. The mass began and it was almost comforting in its familiarity: the same prayers and responses, the same choreographed ritual, the bell ringing, the movement around the altar, the closing of the gated rails across the front before communion. Preston had always assumed that the old dears who came alone to the lunchtime mass on week days must be super-religious, but now he saw that the sheer repetition of known things was appealing. It gave life structure and that made things feel reliable, safe.

The only niggling concern was that he saw no sign of his grandmother in the congregation, which was unusual, and suggested she was sicker than he had thought. He should go round to hers later.

At communion he escorted the priest down to the rail as the congregation filed up the central aisle and knelt on the lowest step which was carpeted in fading red and gold. Some of the old people had to stay standing, so he had to lean out with the golden plate, in case any crumbs of the host fell before it was placed on the communicant's tongue. Sometimes the host slipped from the priest's fingers entirely and it was important that the plate was properly positioned to catch it.

"The body of Christ," said Father Edwards.

"Amen."

The choir were first, so that they could get back to singing. Then the keenest who sat at the front, Nora Macintyre among them. Preston moved to the right and the priest came with him, to the next, and the next, and the next. Sometimes they were people Preston knew, even kids from school and Preston had to look down at the plate reflecting their chins, so that he wouldn't catch their eye and grin. Mr. and Mrs. Harding took communion, each rushing their Amens as if they were afraid that if they would be caught speaking as the priest tried to put the consecrated wafer into their mouths. Next came a West Indian family, dressed smartly in bright colours.

It was near the end of the line now: just a handful of those who sat at the back and would not return to their benches after communion, but would walk right out of the big front doors, saving themselves at least five minutes, maybe ten. There was a burly man in jeans and a denim jacket who looked a little embarrassed to be there at all, then three more old dears, the first one with a blacked-out lens in one side of her glasses. Preston waited at each in turn:

"The body of Christ."

"Amen."

Then on to the next. Three to go. Two. One.

He had already moved to the right and positioned the plate at the chin of the last one before he realised that Father Edwards had not come with him. Preston dithered, caught between wanting to call the priest back, baffled as to why he hadn't seen this straggler at the very end of the line, but then he turned back to the old woman kneeling in front of him. She was wearing black including a lacy veil and her hands, gripping the varnished wood of the rail, were gnarled and veiny. The tail end of her rosary beads dangled from one fist. He couldn't see her eyes properly, but he saw her mouth move, heard the whispered

"Amen," which she said as if the priest were there, then watched her thin lips part to admit the sacred wafer.

For a moment he stared, realising the truth.

She's a ghost. No one can see her but you.

And then she looked up and her reverence slipped first into confusion then rage. Her eyes locked onto his and she mouthed his name, extending a bony finger and pointing it at him.

"Preston Oldcorn!" she breathed.

Preston faltered then turned quick as he could, going up the steps in Father Edwards' wake, hoping no one had noticed. He returned to his place on the side of the altar and knelt down, closing his eyes in what he hoped looked like prayer, but not before he had flashed a searching gaze over the congregation, to see if anyone was sniggering at his error. The ghostly communicant was still there, standing at the rail now, still staring and pointing in silent accusation. And in the second row of the pews was Nora MacIntyre, her eyes fixed on him, her face rigid.

* * *

Nora had seen ghosts in the church before. *Seen* was perhaps too strong. She had sensed them, glimpsed them as flickers of a presence that was not quite there, felt them, even heard them, though rarely in any kind of clear or coherent way. She had always been what her mother called "sensitive" to such things, and the loss of her brother had intensified her gift, if that was what it was. Or maybe she had simply accepted her ability,

embraced it after Roarer's death in the hope of one day seeing him again.

What she saw today was new. She had felt an additional presence in the church as the communicants had lined up and, partly out of respect, partly because the feeling continued to unnerve her a little even after all these years, she had closed her eyes and prayed fervently.

May the souls of all the faithfully departed, through the mercy of God, rest in peace, Amen.

May the souls of all the faithfully departed, through the mercy of God, rest in peace, Amen.

May the souls of all the faithfully departed, through the mercy of God, rest in peace, Amen.

Over and over. She whispered the words into her hands, earnest and breathless, and it seemed to help. But then she took communion herself and felt the presence again.

It was different this time, and in so far as she could localise it, it seemed to come toward her from her right, moving along the communion rail with the priest. That made no sense, and she received communion in a state that was distracted, tempted to flee as it became strong and insistent, at the very moment that the host was placed in her mouth. She stiffened, bracing herself for worse, and then the priest moved on and the feeling was fading again.

She returned to her bench and knelt with her elbows on the back of the seat back in front of her, trying to make sense of what she had experienced. She was still there as the communion hymn was coming to an end and the last communicants were leaving the rail, and then she felt the original sensation again: a presence which was also an absence, different from what she had felt from the priest but related to it. It felt like an opposite, an inversion. There was presence and absence again, but in reverse proportions. Where the priest was present, this was absent, and where the priest was absent, this was present.

And then she saw the boy move to the communicant who wasn't there, saw the way he positioned the plate under the chin of emptiness, and she caught a flicker of a figure in a dark dress and veil. It lasted no more than a second, but it was an image she had half-seen before in the church and felt sure she knew who it was, or rather who it had been.

Her name was Josie Eccles, a devout church-goer who had come to mass daily as well as to confession and benediction throughout her sickness. She had been dead almost six years.

And the boy had seen her. More than that, he had tried to minister to her, so for him this was no half-glimpsed phantom. For him, Josie Eccles was there and as real as those who had lined up before her.

Only then did Nora realise that the curious interplay of presence and absence she had felt had not come from the priest at all, but from the boy with the plate at his elbow.

Preston Oldcorn.

And now she remembered meeting him in the sacristy the week before, the strange feeling which had gone through her as she looked at him, like someone walking over her grave.

Nora did not understand it, could give it no name, but she was suddenly sure; there was something badly wrong with Preston Oldcorn.

CHAPTER THIRTEEN

Preston was in his room alone that evening finishing up some reading for school which he should have done earlier, watching the last leaves fall from the pear tree in the front garden, and wondering whether to repaint one of his model spitfires in desert colours. He had some left over decals that would work, though they were really for a hurricane squadron. They'd look fine, but the numbers wouldn't be strictly accurate . . .

He sensed a shift in the light before he realised what was happening, and snapped his head around. Something was materialising in his room.

Someone.

Preston's first thought was a panicked desire to get out,

and he made for the door, but before he could drag it open, he stopped and stared as the figure – almost solid now – turned to look at him. Preston couldn't believe his eyes.

"Roarer!" he exclaimed.

The older boy grinned. He looked the same as ever, same Teddy boy quiff, same heavy-buttoned jacket, same swagger. Or almost the same. He looked calmer somehow, his smile soft, almost thoughtful. It was so good to see his old friend that Preston wanted to hug him, but he settled for a handshake, strong and rigorous.

"Your hand!" he exclaimed. "You have all your fingers!"

Roarer considered his hand absently, flexing it, his eyes vague as if he was half-asleep.

"That's right," he said vaguely. "I had lost them."

"To the ghost dogs," Preston agreed, grinning.

"Dogs?" said Roarer. "Yes, I think there were dogs."

"But now you are well," Preston encouraged him. "Is that how it is? Death? Is it, you know, good?"

Roarer seemed to consider this for a long time, frowning in the same dazed manner and eventually shook his head very slowly.

"I'm not sure," he said. "I don't remember."

"But there is *something*," said Preston. "You don't just disappear when you move on?"

"Something," said Roarer uncertainly. "I think so. I . . . I'm not sure. I think I was somewhere else and then I was here, and I think I will be somewhere else again when I'm done, but I can't say for sure."

He seemed neither happy nor sad, just resigned. But Preston seized on what he had just said.

"When you're done here? What do you have to do?"

"I have to tell you something," he said. "It's the only reason I could come back."

"What is it?" asked Preston, excited by the idea of learning some great truth from beyond the grave. "Tell me."

"The Leech was not the boy."

For a moment Preston just stared at his old friend, baffled and a little disappointed. He had been expecting some profound insight. This wasn't even accurate.

"No," he said, "it was. But I freed him."

Roarer shook his head gravely, and Preston thought he looked more sure of himself now, but sadder with it.

"You saved the boy," Roarer agreed, "but the boy was not the Leech. He was just where the Leech had come to live. They were . . . entangled, but they were still two, not one. You allowed the boy to move on and that unbound the Leech to go . . ." again the vague headshake, "somewhere else."

"You mean there's another ghost that the Leech is living in?"

"Not a ghost," said Roarer, and he looked urgent now, hunted. "Something else. But that's not what I came to tell you."

"What then?" said Preston, feeling a prickle of irritation as well as uncertainty.

"You were special," said Roarer unexpectedly. "As a ghost, I mean. You had power. You released the brakeman, the Bannister

Doll, Margaret Banks. All of them. Even the boy who was the Leech."

"Thanks," Preston began, but Roarer held up his hand.

"You don't understand," he said, and suddenly he looked pained, as if he was carrying some terrible weight, a weight he had to pass on against his will. "When the boy passed on . . ."

"To the Sincerely Dead," Preston prompted.

"The Sincerely Dead, yes," said Roarer with the flicker of a smile, "that was what we called it. I remember now. When the boy passed on, you didn't."

"No. The timeline where I died unravelled and I came back to life."

"Because you wanted to," said Roarer. "You could have moved on, become Sincerely Dead . . ."

"No. There was no gate for me."

"There could have been, but you didn't want it. You weren't ready."

Preston held his eyes for a long moment, then nodded once.

"I wanted to live," said Preston, knowing it was true.

"Yes. And all that power you had – all that made you different, special – slammed the door to the Sincerely Dead, and sent you back to your own time and to the world of the living."

"Yes," Preston said again, then – a little more defiantly – "so? There was no need for me to die. I had a whole life ahead of me, a life which the Leech had taken . . ."

"Yes," said Roarer and the pain in his face was softer now

and full of pity, like he was comforting a child. "But Preston, you closed the door for everyone."

Preston blinked.

"What do you mean?"

"I don't know if it's just around here, near this place, or what, but you closed the door to the place where the Sincerely Dead go not just for yourself, but for everyone else."

"You mean everyone is suddenly immortal?" said Preston derisively. "I doubt that."

"No," said Roarer, sad again. "They still die. They just can't move on. They are trapped in the moment of their deaths like we were. Forever. Going slowly mad and incapable of moving on. Your survival has made ghosts of everyone else who dies."

Preston stared again, horrified now. He wanted to laugh it off, or yell at Roarer as he had done before, argue with the boy who he had always secretly thought was, perhaps, not quite as clever as he was, but he couldn't. He knew in his heart with a sudden and burning clarity that what Roarer was telling him was true. He stared at his old friend, feeling a hot tear slide down his cheek.

"Why are you telling me this?" he said at last.

"You have to fix it."

"How?"

Roarer shrugged, suddenly looking like his old self.

"Sorry. I don't know."

"Then what use are you?" snapped Preston, crying openly now.

"The Leech is still here," said Roarer, unoffended. "You have to find it and stop it but I can't tell you how. It is not a ghost. It's something else. Something old but somehow connected to you."

"Where do I look?"

"There is a ghost," said Roarer. "Perhaps the first to die after you came back. Killed by the Leech. Find that ghost and you'll learn where the Leech is now."

"And defeating the Leech again will free the ghosts who died since I came back?"

"Perhaps," said Roarer. "I'm not sure. One other thing: you can trust my sister."

"Mrs. MacIntyre?"

"Nora, yeah. And Preston?"

"What?"

"I really am sorry."

And then he was fading . . . fading . . .

Gone.

CHAPTER FOURTEEN

Jed Atkinson drained his last pint and put the glass down rather more heavily than he had intended on the polished bar of the Corporation Arms. It wobbled dizzyingly and the barman snatched it up before it could walk off the edge.

"I'd be leaving my car overnight if I were you, Jed," he said, giving his customer a level, no-nonsense look.

"What? I'm fine. Be 'ome in two shakes of a lamb's tail."

"And not much more than that walking," said the barman meaningfully. "You plough into a tree and kill yourself, and it will be my license the police come for."

"I'm fine," Jed slurred, leaning back to make his eyes focus.

"Keys," said the barman, putting out a hand palm up. When

Jed just stared at the empty hand the barman snapped his fingers. The noise seemed to bring Jed to what was left of his senses, and though he scowled and muttered, he fumbled in his pockets till he found the keys to his Ford Escort and dropped them with ceremonial delicacy into the barman's hand.

"Good lad," said the barman. "Come by tomorrow, anytime after eight," he added, whisking the keys away before Jed could think better of it. "Mind 'ow you go."

So Jed left, a little unsteadily, shouldering his way through the front door and into the cool night. It had rained, leaving the road sparkling and a fine, cold mist in the air. It got into Jed's lungs, sobering him up a little as he blundered along Lower Road toward Knowle Green.

Jed was forty-five, single and like to remain so. He'd had girlfriends when he was younger but never for long. They always seemed to move onto people smarter, slicker, men with better prospects, or so he had told whoever would listen over the years. The women themselves told a slightly different story emphasising his sullen moods, quick temper and tendency to blame those around him for misfortunes crafted from his own laziness and stupidity, often with his fists. Now he lived alone in a rundown mill worker's cottage and worked ungodly hours up to his ankles in cow muck ploughing and haymaking. He'd still be drunk when he had to get up, but what did Jed care? It wasn't like they were his cows.

The road was quiet at this time. A couple of cars past him and he stuck out a hopeful thumb, which he replaced with a two fingered V when they didn't stop. Jed went on trudging along the weedy verge, flanked by overgrown hedgerows and skeletal trees. The damp seemed to muffle sound, so that in the absence of traffic on the road the place was deathly silent. There was no moon to speak of and the night was unnervingly dark, so that even though he knew the route like the back of his hand, he was conscious that he was moving slower than usual, and not just because of the beer. There were no houses along this stretch, and there was no movement from the fields around him, save where an occasional sheep stirred in her sleep.

The rain began again.

"Figures," Jed muttered as he continued his listless amble along Lower Road toward where old Agnes Tattershawl had dropped dead.

Good riddance, thought Jed, who had never forgiven the nosy old crow for reporting him – twice – for being – allegedly – drunk and disorderly. Well, she was gone now. Popped her clogs right here, and, to Jed's mind it were a bit of a let off for mankind in general and Joe Tattershawl in particular.

"*So here's to you, Mrs. Tattershawl!*" he sang drunkenly, borrowing from the old Simon and Garfunkle song that was in that weird movie when the bloke went into church on a horse. He raised an imaginary glass to the wet night and giggled to himself.

He wished he was back in the warmth of the pub, though he'd have a few things to say to the barman who had made him walk home. He had half a mind to go back now and give him what for, except that the pub would be locked up by now and while he would get some pleasure from throwing things at the windows and yelling at them till they came down, he didn't want to stand in the wet any longer than he had to. Plus, they might call the police.

Jed kicked at a stone irritably and sent it skittering into the road. He stepped out after it and kicked it again, calling out, "Nobby Stiles!" The stone shot along a wide, erratic arc, bouncing off the curb and up onto the pavement at the top of Written Stone Lane. It came to rest at the feet of a strange-looking woman.

Jed assumed it was a woman from the long dark dress, but he couldn't see her face which was turned away from him and hidden by an old-fashioned bonnet. Like the dress, the bonnet seemed to be made of some black silky material, stiff and formal and antique. She bore a wicker basket with a cloth over it in the crook of one elbow.

The stone Jed had kicked sat beside the woman's high-heeled boot like an accusation but the woman did not move or acknowledge his approach in any way, gazing away down the road as if waiting for a bus.

"All right there, miss," said Jed. The woman was in his way so some kind of greeting seemed appropriate as he went around her, but he was also curious. A woman out by herself on a night like this? Maybe she was looking for a little male company. Wasn't out of the realm of possibility, especially in Jed's drunk and self-serving brain. He leered inwardly to himself. Perhaps the evening wasn't a total loss after all.

"On your way somewhere, love?" he tried. "All dolled up 'n' all."

She looked somehow faint in the dark, as if he might be able to reach through her, but he stepped closer, keen to find her real to the touch. She turned to him now, but kept her head bowed so he still couldn't see under the rim of the coal-scuttle bonnet, and as he stooped to peer in, she turned demurely, almost coyly, he thought.

Playing 'ard to get, he decided. A warm anticipation was starting to spread through him, despite the chill night. For a moment the woman seemed to flicker in the mist, which annoyed and disappointed him, but when he turned around again, there she was, real and, if anything, more solid than before.

"Give you an 'and with your basket?" he offered. You never knew what women might give you in return for gallantry.

She seemed to hesitate for a second, then wordlessly pushed the basket toward him. She was wearing slim black gloves to match her dress. As he took the basket from her, remarking on how it weighed so little it barely felt it was there at all, she began to walk, not along Lower Road but up the overgrown track which was Written Stone Lane. Jed didn't pause to think, but went after her.

Maybe she knows a nice dry spot in't long grass, he mused, licking his lips.

She moved ahead of him, walking slowly and evenly, not making a sound, so that for all his excitement Jed began to get a little uneasy and spoke to break the mood.

"So, what's your name, love?" he said.

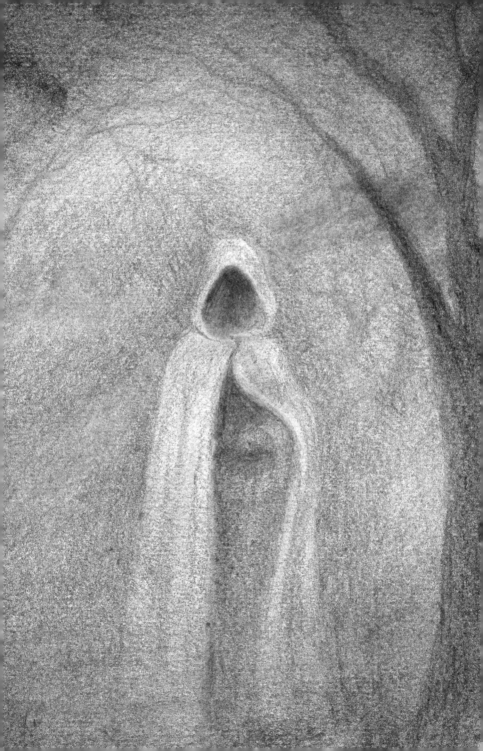

Still she walked between the dark, looming hedges and empty fields, saying nothing, drifting ahead, her long black dress trailing in the weeds.

"Where we goin'?" said Jed, impatient now, feeling the strangeness of the thing start to settle on him like the damp and cold of the misty night. "My place isn't far, unless you'd rather . . ."

He broke off. She had come to a standstill a few yards ahead of him, and from the slight tremble of her bowed shoulders he thought she had begun to cry. Not being good at compassion he faltered. Even in his beer-sodden state he knew this was all a bit strange, creepy even, and if he had to play nursemaid to her womanish feelings, he might be better calling it a night and heading for home. But then he realised that what he had taken for the tremors of grief were actually the opposite.

She was laughing. The sound was odd but he was sure of it, and as he stood staring at her back, she turned very slowly and inclined her head so that for the first time he could see into the deep shadows of her bonnet.

Except that there was nothing to see, just a black hollow. And now he realised that the strangeness of the sound was because it wasn't coming from her at all.

It was coming from the basket.

Horrified, he pushed the fabric aside and there, gazing up at him with gleeful malice, was a woman's face. Its mouth opened wider as her laughter built to mad hysteria, showing unnaturally bright and pointed teeth. The eyes were red and burning.

Jed dropped the basket like it was a snake. The head bounced out, righted itself on the ground and then leapt impossibly at him, snapping those awful jaws. He batted it away, caught between revulsion at touching the thing, and terror of what those teeth might do if he didn't, then turned on his heel and ran.

Wide-eyed and stumbling, gasping for breath, he blundered along the lane with the horror biting and laughing at his back, gashing the backs of his legs, tearing at his hair and the flesh of his ears. Jed screamed, running blind now, bursting out onto the road and into the path of a Ford Cortina driven by a Mr. Archie Clarkson, postman, on his way home to Clitheroe. The headlamps barely had time to strike Jed before the bonnet caught him full in the hip, sending him all the way over the front of the car and into the ditch on the other side.

Archie Clarkson braked hard but the damage was done, and by the time he had made it out of the vehicle and had run back to the point of the accident, Jed Atkinson was beyond any help Mr. Clarkson might have been able to give.

MRS T Blenkinsop,
Written Stone Lane,
Longridge,
Preston.

CHAPTER FIFTEEN

It was the same young policeman who knocked on the door of the cottage where Tracey's family lived, and they had almost the same conversation about another unexpected death. It was odd, they concluded, but not suspicious. Jed Atkinson had been, in the policeman's words, "the worse for drink," when he had blundered into the path of an oncoming motor vehicle, and though the car may have been going a little quick for these dark backroads, the driver had been alert and had reported the accident immediately, leaving the scene only to drive to the Corporation Arms to use the phone. The case was, the policeman said, "open and shut," delivering the phrase as if it was some highly professional classification, rather than something they might have heard on *Starsky and Hutch*. He was just there dotting i's and crossing t's, he said, making sure the neighbours hadn't heard or seen anything which might explain the victim's state of mind.

"His state of mind?" said Tracey's dad. "I thought you said he were drunk?"

"Aye," said the policeman, looking suddenly furtive, "but the driver of the vehicle in question suggested that Mr. Atkinson seemed to be running from someone or something. Came out of the lane like a bat of hell, he said. Got a good look at him right before the impact. Said he looked . . ." The policeman took refuge in his notebook. "Mad with terror. His exact words."

Tracey and her parents shook their heads and said they had heard and seen nothing, but Tracey felt her mother's eyes linger on her. For a moment, Tracey stared, terrified that her parents would start recounting tales of their daughter's nightmare-inspired sleepwalking to the local bobby, but in the end they just promised to call if they remembered anything that might be relevant and left it at that.

And *were* Tracey's nightmares relevant to the deaths of two people outside her house, she wondered?

How could they be?

It was just a coincidence, and not an especially strong one at that. People had bad dreams all the time. People died of heart attacks or in traffic accidents all the time. The two things were unconnected.

Yes, she decided with enough force to close the matter. *Just coincidence.*

On Tuesday Preston braved the bus from school again, but rode it all the way to town, listening to Eddie Kyd and Matt Singleton bickering amiably about which version of "Blame It on the Boogie" was best. There were two in the charts at the moment, one by the Jacksons which was driving and exuberant enough to get anyone dancing, and another by the improbably named 'Mick' Jackson, the white bloke from Yorkshire who had written the song. Eddie was mixed race and sported a serious Afro and the wide, loosely knotted tie that all the disco fans liked, while Matt's almost skinhead cut and tight, miniscule knot marked him out as a punk. Why he was bothering to make the – fairly obviously doomed – case for the songwriter's version of "Blame it on the Boogie" was anybody's guess.

While they jeered and taunted and mocked each other's sad renditions, laughing uproariously, Preston wrote a note of inadequate apology to Tracey, making sure no one could read his hurried scrawl, and keeping a wary eye open for Pete Maddingly who had gone upstairs. As soon as Preston got off the bus at the central station with its stacked half-pipes of modernist concrete, he sealed up the letter in a manila envelope. At the main post office overlooking the flag market, he bought a nine penny stamp with a picture of an oil rig on it, licked it and popped it on the corner of the envelope, posting it in the pillar box outside. From there he walked down Cheapside to Fishergate, crossed the street and, looking anxiously around, pushed through the corner door into Booths. He moved hurriedly up the stairs, his head down. He didn't want to have to deal with the hard-nosed waitress who would surely insist on seating and serving him when all he wanted to do was to go upstairs to the disused portion of the café.

Wanted was not remotely the right word, he thought bleakly to himself, picturing that desolate room with the sheep's head mouldings. Not the right word at all.

Still, it was what he'd come for. Roarer had said the Leech had not died with the boy in the railway accident. He said it had bound itself to something else, not a ghost, but what else was there? The spectral waitress was clearly not a recent victim of the Leech, but she may not be all she seemed, Preston reasoned. She had certainly hummed that awful song which the Leech's dreadful choir had droned in the nine twenty-two darkness. It made a kind of sense.

The café was quiet, almost deserted, so that Preston wondered how much longer the place could last. It had once been the height of sophistication in town. Now it felt jaded and a bit dingy, a remnant of a world which had moved on without it. The thought caught him mid stride and he faltered, remembering he had felt the same about himself, trapped in the twilight of his own death, while his school friends grew up, married and moved away . . .

But he was back. He hadn't been abandoned and forgotten.

I am alive, he thought defiantly trying not to think about what Roarer had said.

Still.

Could a building be sad? he wondered as he looked about. No, he didn't think so. It felt that way though, the dark wood and earnest plaster moulding hankering after a time when people admired such things. Maybe the waitress was like that, an embodiment of the café as it had been before.

He scanned the first floor quickly and headed up the stairs to the next level. If anyone asked, he had decided he would say he was looking for the bathroom. In truth, that was probably as far as he would get, since the door into the derelict portion of the café would probably be locked. He was ashamed to say that that would be a relief. He would have tried, given it his best shot: but if he couldn't find the ghost, that wasn't his fault, was it?

The door was open again, not wide open, but cracked. Preston stood at it, eyes closed, jaw clenched, fists balled. He didn't want to do this, wasn't even sure what he hoped to achieve. He could still go back down the stairs and out into the blessed ordinariness of Fishergate.

He pushed the door open.

It was dark inside, not the blackness of night but a stiff, grey twilight which bled in through the high, narrow windows and painted the dusty floor with the softest of illumination, like stripes of water colour which parted the pooling darkness. It felt empty and abandoned, and not just in the sense of being disused. It felt lost, like a ballroom when the dancers have all gone home: you could almost hear the silence, the absence of what had once defined it. Again Preston wondered if it was possible for a building to be sad, to feel a sense of failure, as if its closing was evidence that it had somehow let everyone down.

He stepped inside, moving around the corner and leaving behind the plainer more modern mouldings which were all line and geometrical shape for the more florid side which overlooked the main road, the plaster swags of fabric, the grape clusters and the unsettling sheep skulls with their curled, shell-like horns and empty eye sockets. Preston took another step and then stopped, looking around. There was no sign of anyone or anything out of the ordinary, and for a moment he felt it again, the relief that he had tried and failed, and could now go home.

But then there was a noise over his right shoulder, a thin, metallic scraping that set his teeth on edge and made the hairs on the back of his neck stand to quick attention. It stopped, then came again, very slightly different this time, with a burring rasp at the beginning and a silken whistle at the end. He knew what it was before he turned woodenly to see.

Someone was sharpening a knife.

The ghost waitress was standing in the room's deepest shadow. Preston could make out the pleating of her broad back and the white tape where her apron tied, but he only saw her arm when it moved, drawing back the long silver knife against the steel in her other hand. The metal sparkled coldly.

He should have researched the building, he thought wildly. Maybe there was a history of bloody murder perpetrated by – or on – a waitress decades ago. Preston took a breath and, for a second, considered just turning and padding quietly out before anything could happen . . .

"Hello?" he managed. He hadn't really decided to stay, to speak. It had just come out.

She did not turn around but stayed where she was, slightly hunched over her work, sharpening the knife with long, slow strokes which, in the gloom, seemed to sing the café's song of desolation and menace. "I know you," said the waitress, still not turning. Her voice was low, but without emotion.

Shing! went the knife blade and Preston winced, but did not run.

"I don't think you do . . ." he began.

"You are Preston Oldcorn," she said, and now he could hear her teeth in the words as she bit off each syllable.

"How do you know that?" he stammered.

"Preston Oldcorn," she said again, hissing his first name as she swept the blade along the steel. *Shing!* "The boy who wasn't there."

"I don't know what you mean," Preston tried, but she spun suddenly round to face him and her eyes seemed to burn with a cold inner light, like a fox in the darkness of a field, whose eye-shine is the only way you know they are there.

"Yes," she said, "you do."

Her hands stopped moving abruptly as if the knife was forgotten and she croaked out the first words of the awful song.

"Early one morning . . ." She took a step toward him and the thin light from the windows fell onto the long, slender knife so that it flashed.

"Stop," said Preston, taking an involuntary step backwards.

". . . just as the sun was rising . . ." Another step, eyes level and fixed on his.

"I said stop!" Preston shouted.

"I heard a maiden singing . . ."

"You are the Leech!" Preston roared back.

The words worked like a magic spell or a talisman. The old woman froze, the singing stopped, and her face rippled with confusion. For a long moment she just stood there and then, with growing certainty, she shook her head.

"No," she said. "My name is . . . ."

She seemed to search for it and changed tack.

"I'm a waitress," she said brightly.

"Yes," said Preston, feeling that this was important, "I know but . . ." He looked for a name badge on her uniform but there was nothing. "You have a name."

"Mabel," she said. The word came out automatically and it seemed to take a moment to register in her face. "Yes, Mabel. I'm a waitress."

Preston almost laughed at the sudden release of tension. It may once have been a common name, but where Preston came from it was a kind of joke: a cartoon name for a cartoonish old woman. He swallowed.

"Mabel?" he said.

"Mabel," she said again, sure now, and the former menace was quite gone. She seemed as she had been when he first met her, grandmotherly and ordinary. Preston breathed out and, in that moment, he realised that the derelict room with its rubbish and broken bits of abandoned furniture had changed. There were tables, all immaculately laid, and the peeling paint looked fresh and pristine. He was seeing the place as it had once been, as she remembered it.

"You're not the Leech," he said, already close to sure.

Her face creased into perplexity.

"I've told you," she said, slightly cross now, but with no hint of anything more sinister in her eyes. "I'm Mabel."

"A waitress," said Preston.

"All my life," she said, proud of the fact.

"Here at Booths."

"That's right. What is this about? Can I get you something?"

"No thank you, I wanted to ask you . . ."

"No one comes in now," she said, with a sudden, profound sadness that took Preston's breath away. "No one to wait on."

"I'm sorry. Roarer said . . ."

"Roarer? Where is that young scamp? I haven't seen him in yonks."

"You remember him?"

"Used to come with his sister, but she . . . moved away," she said, and some of the uncertainty was back in her manner when she spoke those last words. Preston thought he knew why. Nora hadn't died. She had indeed moved away, not in space, but in time. Roarer had stayed in death, in whatever version of the Merely Dead Mabel now inhabited. He wondered why Roarer had never mentioned her to him, but then he remembered why he had come.

"You sang the song," he said.

"Song?" she repeated, bland and bewildered now. "What song is that, love? I never had much of a voice for music."

"Early one morning," said Preston, disliking the feel of the words in his mouth. "Oh don't deceive me . . ."

"Oh, never leave me," she completed for him. "That one. Yes. I can't remember where I heard it."

"Or who taught it to you?"

Another head shake, and then a thoughtful frown. At last, like the headlamp of a distant train coming fast through fog, a memory came back to her; realisation dawned in her face, and then turned to fear and horror. She dropped the knife which clattered to the ground and put her free hand over her mouth. Her eyes were shining with unshed tears.

"I'm sorry!" said Preston, striding toward her. "I didn't mean to . . . What is it that you remember?"

"Another boy, not you or Roarer," she said, but then immediately shook her head and with a pained expression took back what she had just said. "But not really a boy. It was holding him, had eaten through him, lived through him, but it was not the boy."

"The Leech," said Preston. "When was this?"

Again her face clouded and he knew there was no way she could answer the question. When he had been a ghost he had not been able to track the passage of time at all. She probably thought it was still the 1950s or whenever it was she had died, some time before the upper floor café was closed.

"This . . . thing which was attached to the boy," he tried. "It told you who I was?"

"Told everyone," said the ghost of Mabel the waitress. "Preston Oldcorn, it said. The boy who shouldn't be. Said it was all your fault."

Preston swallowed.

"What was?" he asked.

Again her face clouded with perplexity and then her eyes lighted on the dropped knife and she scowled and stooped to pick it up. Preston flinched but, when she straightened, she was her old self again, as if their previous conversation had not happened.

"Need a good edge on a cake knife," she said, returning to her sharpening with a smile. "Wouldn't want a rough edge on your Victoria sponge, would you?" she said, shooting him an open-faced smile so wide and uncomplicated that she looked like a different person, a person full of hope and generosity, full of life. Preston agreed that he wouldn't, but he looked quickly away, because he was feeling it again, the sadness and desolation of the place.

"You sure I can't cut you a piece?" she asked, her eyes twinkling playfully. "No, thanks," he said. "I should be going."

"Well mind 'ow you go," she said, in a tone so like his grandmother's that Preston's breath caught. "And stay out o' Glovers Court."

Preston had half-turned to leave but the remark stopped him.

"Glover's Court?" he said. "Why?"

"You mark my words," said Mabel, raising the knife in a

cautionary fashion. "Bad lot they are down there. Trouble. You steer clear."

"Right," said Preston. "Thanks. Mabel?"

"Yes, love?"

"Do you like it here?"

"Where else would I go?" she said. It was a bleak, demoralised statement of reality. "I'm a waitress."

"You could leave. Go somewhere else. Move on."

"Out there?" she said, looking positively alarmed, even scared. "I told you, there's a bad lot out there. They don't come in here though. No one comes in here. I wish there were people to serve but at least *they* don't come."

"Who?" said Preston.

"Them," she said, glancing toward the windows and shuddering. "Them! Killers. Monsters."

"Killers?"

She shook her head, flustered and upset.

"I can't be talking about that," she said. "And I'm not going out there. Best I stay here where it's safe. Where I belong."

"Maybe there's somewhere different, better . . ."

She cut him off, her tone certain and final.

"I'm a waitress. At Booths."

"Yes," said Preston. "Course you are."

She smiled, her old self again.

"Now put wood in't thole as you go out, my lad. You could catch your death in 'ere."

CHAPTER SIXTEEN

Tracey was doing her biology homework – 'explain the process of photosynthesis' – at the kitchen table while Kid Jensen babbled between songs on the radio in the background. With a crash the front door burst open and her father came raging into the house, stomping his work boots on the floor and cursing under his breath. Noticing the creamy puddle collecting around his feet, he cursed again, louder this time.

"Language!" shouted her mother, bustling into the hall to see what the fuss was about. "What on earth is the matter?"

"That damn stone!" roared her father. "No matter how we shim and brace it, it won't stay steady. Six whole milk kits over turned! Milk everywhere. Ken is spittin' feathers, like it's my fault the bloody thing won't stay put."

"I thought you had it all straight and secure?" said her mum, absently wiping her hands on her apron.

"We did!" her dad retorted. "Swear to God. And all the churns set up nice as ya like. But as soon as we turn our backs it gives this almighty wobble and every damn kit is down and spilled."

"Well, there's no use crying over spilled . . ." said Tracey, but her father cut her off.

"Don't say it," he said, his eyes flashing. Tracey knew when not to push her luck and turned her gaze back to her biology textbook, but she wasn't really reading, and a moment later she glanced up as her dad, steeled now to return to the fray, rummaged under the sink for a mallet with a rubber head.

"Going to try again?" said her mum in an encouraging and sympathetic voice.

"Just needs adjusting," said her father. It wasn't an idea so much as a decision he was thrusting into the world by sheer force of personality. "It's just a stone. Has to be a way to get it level. Stands to reason."

Tracey almost smiled at her dad being so . . . him, but she caught the way her mother watched him leave, and she felt a prickle of unease. She looked out of the kitchen window, but the autumnal nights were fast getting short, and it was already quite dark outside. With the lights on indoors she could make out almost nothing beyond the black reflection of the window glass. The unease Tracey had felt a moment before bucked like a wild horse and she felt a sudden dread of the darkness outside, hemming in the cottage, surrounding it.

Tracey got to her feet and went quickly to the door.

"Dad," she called after him. "Dad!"

He was halfway down the path already and turned in what she thought was surprise, though his face was lost in shadow.

"What's up?" he said.

"Leave it till tomorrow, eh?" said Tracey. "It's too dark to work now."

"There's a light in't dairy," he said.

"Still," she replied, a little desperate now. "It's nearly tea time. Mum'll go spare if she burns the crust on the hotpot."

He hesitated then, as if sensing something under what she had said, and Tracey bit her lip.

"Just gonna give it a quick look," he replied. "Come get me if we're getting close to tea."

He turned and walked into the dark.

* * *

So, Preston thought, *Mabel isn't the Leech.*

But the Leech had touched her somehow, reached out to her and put Preston's name in her head, along with that song. That was worrying because it meant that the town's other ghosts might know him too, and what had come with that knowledge? Something of the Leech's hateful malevolence? Perhaps. He would need to be careful. Mabel had been harmless, it seemed – just another spirit trapped in a sense of what mattered, old habits and activities she couldn't let go of – but the knife she had held had seemed to Preston absolutely real. Was that because she could handle real things when she was in her environment, or because the knife was also a kind of ghost, an echo of her world, her time, which he had somehow stepped into in the same way that he had really been on the train with the Leech? If she had attacked him, would that ghost blade have passed through him like so much air, or would it have left him lying on the dusty floor of the derelict room in a pool of his own blood? It seemed at least possible.

Whatever gift his experience with the Leech had left him with, it seemed that it had made him vulnerable to ghosts in ways other people weren't. For all the spookiness of the ghost stories they had told after scout meetings, he had always – in the cold light of day – dismissed ghosts as a threat, because even if they were real he didn't see how a bit of vapour and memory could hurt a living person. Or rather, he hadn't until the Leech's spectral hand had closed around his heart at the foot of Stuart Road . . . And now things were worse. He didn't understand it, but it was probably wise to assume that – in his current state – ghosts could do a lot worse than frighten him.

Back outside on Fishergate he hesitated in the gathering gloom of the early evening, wondering if he should try to release Mabel to the next world and how he might do that. He turned idly and his gaze fell on the clock bridge that connected the upper story of the Booths building to the building across the road, his eye lingering on the street sign: Glovers Court.

"*Bad lot they are down there,*" Mabel had said. "*Trouble. You steer clear.*"

165

Which meant what? A link to the Leech? Something he should explore, or a needless danger? She had been scared of what she had called killers, monsters, and Preston knew from personal experience that there was good reason to fear ghosts even if you were already dead. He considered the side street which was broad and brightly lit.

Killers? Monsters?

The clock said it was after six which meant he should be getting home, but he wondered if there was more to be learned. He turned away, gazing down the main thoroughfare in the direction of Winckley Square, Avenham and the railway station. The days were getting shorter and in the low light the street looked dingy, untidy, the trendy sixties renovations already looking decrepit and cheap. Preston looked down, saw that his shoe was untied and dropped into a crouch to fasten it.

He didn't notice the change till he had finished tying the bow, registering it first in the near silence. The traffic noise had dropped to nothing. It was darker too. And the ground . . .

Preston stood up suddenly, still staring down. The flagged pavement was the same as it had been, but the road surface which had been pocked tarmac was quite different.

Cobbles or, more accurately, sets. Regular stones shaped and set into mortar, all pale with frost . . .

He looked up. The busy street was gone. The shape of the place was roughly the same, but it felt ramshackle and uneven. The clean lines of the modern buildings had vanished entirely and in their place were lurching, irregular constructions with

sagging roofs and walls of soot-stained brick, some high and implacably business-like, some low and rustic-looking. Glovers Court had all but vanished, turning into a narrow underpass through a grimy and austere building, its frontage blank and cheerless. A thin mist filled the air and the streets which had been bustling with people and cars, were empty.

"No," Preston gasped. "No. It can't be."

Because though he had never seen the town look like this, the stillness felt eerily like the nine twenty-two no-place in which he had spent his half-death. He turned woodenly, taking it all in, one hand drifting to his chest where his heart was.

It was beating hard, and that was a very reassuring sensation. It meant he was alive, not a ghost trapped in time.

Because that was what it felt like. He had fallen into the past, or a version of it, and not his own past. This version of the town had vanished long before he was born. There was no Booths on the corner of Fishergate, no clock, and when he moved cautiously out into the silent street and looked around he saw almost nothing that looked familiar, just lurching brick buildings, mostly three-storied with shallow pitched slate roofs. Even the parish church whose tower was just visible up the road looked like a different building entirely. The air smelled of wood and coal smoke and the tang of something sour like stagnant water or marsh.

Preston peered down through the narrow, square tunnel which had been the entrance to Glovers Court and saw, lounging against a wall, a solitary figure smoking a long-stemmed pipe. He was maybe fifty yards away, a slim, sinewy man, and even at this distance his dark clothes looked coarse and baggy, worn but oddly formal. He wore a tall hat, and as he sucked on the pipe its bowl glowed amber and the shadows rearranged themselves on his face. It was dark in the alley, but Preston thought he had a heavy moustache and side whiskers of the kind he had heard his grandma call mutton chops. His movement was slow and careless, languid, but he seemed to be looking at Preston, and after a moment when their eyes seemed to have locked, he pushed himself away from the wall and began to walk away, down the cobbled slope of Glovers Court.

Preston stared. There was no one else around and he could hear the man's heavy boots on the stone sets, echoing in the cramped alley which had been a broad, modern street only moments before. Then, feeling almost magnetically drawn to the mysterious figure, Preston followed him into the dark.

As he passed under the stark, brick building which faced onto Fishergate, the light dropped still further and air became dank and chilly, and though he emerged from the other side and could see the sky again, the cold seemed to increase as he moved further down the street. It was like stepping into a low spot early in the morning, where mist had pooled. He was heading toward the river, but surely he was too far from the bank of the Ribble for that to make a difference? He had a vague idea that the river had been diverted at some point before the docks were built, though that must have been further downstream.

And maybe the cold has nothing to do with anything natural. None of this does.

The man ambled lazily down the narrow street with an odd, rolling gait, swaggering and slow so that it was easy for Preston to ensure he didn't lose him. Midway down the street he turned extravagantly to his right, then glanced over his shoulder, gazing back up the street. For a moment his face, which had been lost in the shadows, was caught in the amber glow from the adjacent windows, and though his eyes were still mere sparks, Preston felt sure the man was looking at him. For a moment he just stood there, first leaning slightly back, then slightly forward, like a sail in a shifting breeze, then he opened a door and stepped unsteadily inside.

The pause had seemed odd, deliberate, as if he was waiting for Preston to follow, but that clumsy swagger suggested a less mysterious explanation.

He's drunk!

That made sense. The building had even rectangular windows, a fanlight over the door and, a little further down the road, a broad arched gateway. Even without the sign hanging over the street which read 'The Wellington', Preston would have recognised the old coaching inn for what it was: a pub. It should have been noisy, he thought, a place of drinking and merriment, but in the curious, dream-like condition in which he found himself, it looked like everywhere else, silent and empty, save for the strange man who had gone inside.

Preston hesitated. Mabel had said the ghosts around here were a "bad lot." He might have put that down to their being boozers, but the waitress had been more than disapproving: she had been scared.

Killers. Monsters.

Was it possible that the thing the Leech had fastened onto, when it was driven from the boy Preston had freed on the train, was in that pub? He shivered at the thought and glanced wistfully back up the cobbled alley and through the dingy underpass to Fishergate. He could turn around and go, but to where?

Or, more particularly, when?

He hadn't chosen to be in this inexplicable flashback and he didn't know how he might get out of it. When he had been a ghost he had understood the rules. He had known where he could go and where he couldn't, how – with skill and effort – he might force his way into the living present. He had understood the way spectres simplified and reduced over time until they could barely recall who they were. But now he was alive, not a ghost, but somehow still able to see them, vulnerable to the way they pulled him into their pasts, and with no clue how to stop it. When he had spoken to Mabel, the abandoned café had reverted to the way it was when she worked there. Now the streets themselves felt old: Victorian, perhaps, or even older, as if the figure who had stepped into the pub had caught him in a memory of days long past. Who knew what awaited him inside?

Preston sucked in a freezing breath, then opened the door and stepped into the inn.

He had expected noise to hit him as soon as he crossed the threshold, but the pub was ominously silent. It felt strange being there. His parents weren't big pub-goers and Preston had always felt they were strange places outside his experience. The last time he had been in one, he thought with a jolt – the Plough in Grimsargh – he had been dead. It was almost funny when he put it that way, though he didn't feel like laughing.

Nowhere close to it.

There was a flicker of fire light on the wall, but the pub felt unnaturally cold still, no warmer in fact than it had felt outside. He moved silently through into a porch and looked around. There was an open area which seemed to be the main bar, but to his right was a smaller room of the kind he thought they called a snug, though it was quite empty. He moved into the heart of the inn where the floor was tiled, and passed another little room on his left, also full of tables and chairs, also empty. He followed his feet, knowing somehow where to go, moving toward the back of the building and a door which looked to lead into the stable yard, but turned left before he reached it into another snug.

It had a pinkish marble fireplace with smoky pictures over it. The drunk man was lingering in the doorway, but as if sensing Preston behind him, he stepped in and sat abruptly at a table in the corner by the fire. Feeling again as if he was inside a dream, Preston followed him in. Only then did he notice that someone else was already there, a broad-shouldered man who was nursing a glass of some dark spirit. He turned to watch the newcomer with undisguised malice.

The Leech?

It was possible. The man's eyes were full of the firelight but they burned with more than reflection from the hearth – loathing, perhaps, rage – and Preston instantly felt the dread of imminence. He didn't know what it was, but something was about to happen. Something bad.

* * *

"Hot pot's ready," said Vivien Blenkinsop, getting the piccalilli and red cabbage out of the pantry. "Get your dad, from 't dairy, will you, love?"

Tracey stiffened in her seat, her eyes locking onto the black windows.

"Tracey?"

"Right," she said. She didn't feel right, but she couldn't say that. She couldn't say she was afraid of going outside. "Where's that torch?"

"Torch?' said her mother. "What you want a torch for?"

It was true. Tracey had made the short walk to the dairy later then this a hundred times. But the darkness sat around the house like the coils of a snake or, she thought – recalling the almost dream she had had in this very kitchen – something ungainly and covered in black, bristling fur. She felt momentarily stupid and ashamed, wanting to take a light with her but incapable of thinking of a reason that wouldn't stoke questions and concern, then shrugged it off.

"Fine," she said, knowing she sounded petulant and refusing to look her mother in the face.

"You alright, love?"

"I said I'm fine," said Tracey, opening the door and stepping into the cooling dark of the lane. She did not look back, but walked briskly to the right cutting between the cottage and the Shakeshaft house into the farmyard.

Go fast. Get it over.

The dairy, set behind the cottage and screened by a copse of trees, was accessible from the pasture, and she opened the gate with practiced, if unsteady fingers. The gloom of the evening sat heavy on the fields and its coal black trees, which were already silent as if in the dead of night. It occurred to her, that the dairy windows should be bright, the dusk full of the sounds of whatever her father and Ken Shakeshaft were doing in there, but the long, low shed looked eerily dark and she could hear nothing from within.

Something was watching her.

She felt it before she saw it, then looked up and found it.

A solitary crow was perched on the roof of the dairy directly over the door. It was large and black, and so still that it was almost lost in the night, but she could feel its eyes on her. She matched its quiet stillness, suddenly on her guard. The bird was only a few yards away but it showed no sign of fear, and now that she thought about it, there was something oddly unbirdlike about its unflinching motionlessness. It was like a totem or some heraldic statue overlooking ancestral grounds, a sign of age and the ownership of all it surveyed.

It was a curious thought and she immediately tried to laugh it off. The crow was probably just sleeping.

And watching you in its sleep? she thought.

An unhelpful idea. She hadn't put her coat on to come

outside and it now felt unseasonably cold. She wrapped her arms around her thin chest and hugged herself, her eyes still fixed on the crow which sat like a finial or a weather cock. She couldn't see its eyes, but also couldn't shake the sense that they were fixed on her.

This was stupid. Her dad had obviously left the dairy, shut the lights off and gone into the house through the back door. There was no point in standing out here by herself.

She was about to turn when the crow gave a guttural caw and spread its wings. The call was too loud and the wings too large. Even though the fields were dark and the bird was only a bird, she felt the shadow of those wings fall over her, plunging her into the deepest darkness imaginable, and in that moment she saw that the bird was not a bird at all.

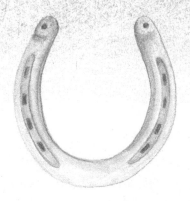

CHAPTER SEVENTEEN

The drunk who Preston had followed into the pub was, in spite of the old-fashioned facial hair, a youngish man, probably in his thirties. He had strong-looking hands, but was slight of build, and now that he sat down he looked small and half-asleep, showing no awareness of the other bloke who was glaring at him with such ferocious intensity. This other man was bigger, broad and red-faced, and though he looked at least a decade older he was a powerful, bull-like presence who seemed to fill the little room. He leaned into the smaller man and growled.

"You've got some nerve coming in 'ere, Alderson," he said. "Owing me as thee does."

The other man did not respond at all, and sat gazing vaguely ahead as if unaware of the other's presence.

"You 'ear me, Alderson?" the big man bellowed, getting so close to him that his spit flecked the other man's face. "I'm talkin' to thee, Alderson. One penny piece, you owes me! Did you think I'd forget?"

Still the man called Alderson ignored him, and with sudden fury the big man got abruptly to his feet and swung a meaty fist into the other's face. Preston gasped and stepped back as the smaller man was thrown backwards off his stool and crashed to the floor.

Then it was as if the bigger of the two was responding to people only he could see. He turned toward the bar and roared, "He owes me money!" But whatever he saw or heard next seemed to put him on the defensive and he was pushed back against the wall by unseen hands. He shrugged out of whatever grip had him, made a wave of his hand which was both dismissive and a kind of threat that everyone should keep away from him, then he snatched up his glass and, still standing, threw back the contents. With a last scornful glance at Alderson, who was hauling himself up from the floor, he marched out – or was ejected, it was hard to be sure – and banged the inn door closed behind him.

Preston stood where he was, his mouth open. At no point had either man made eye contact with him since he had stepped into the bar, and he was no longer sure that they could see him at all. For a long moment he wondered what he should do, try to communicate with the mysterious Alderson who had gone back to sitting quite still on his stool, or go after the man who had hit him.

"Hello?" said Preston. The man didn't turn or acknowledge him in any way. "Excuse me, sir?"

Still nothing. Preston waited and then, as much out of embarrassment as anything else, muttered "fine," and turned on his heel.

Back out in Glovers Court, the big man was still just visible as he lumbered down the long incline of the street toward Frenchwood. It seemed even colder now, frosty, and Preston's breath plumed before him. Not knowing what else to do and feeling like he had to let whatever strangeness he was caught up in play out, he gave chase.

Where Glovers Court became Glovers Street the man walked on, occasionally grumbling at no one, but loud enough to be heard, so that Preston hung back, loitering for a moment in the shade of some great round gas or oil tanks which he was sure he had never seen before. On Avenham Lane he took a left, past the top of Russell Street and made a right onto a road Preston had never heard of: Pleasant Street, a featureless terraced brick row of two-up, two-down houses, all with the same stone window ledges and lintels, the same clay chimney pots.

Factory housing, thought Preston, *or built for labourers*.

The pavement was flagged and the road cobbled, and in spite of its optimistic name, the street felt functional and dour, a place in which to exist rather than to thrive. Again Preston wondered if they were getting close to the river, and peering ahead the bottom of the road seemed to end in trees as if the town just stopped there. He didn't like the idea of leaving the area he knew and worried again about how he would get back, but then the big man was unlocking the door of one of the terraced houses and shutting it firmly behind him. For a second there was the sound of the lock being turned, and then there was nothing, but the cold, still night.

Preston stood there, but being unsure of what exactly he was waiting for, wondering if Mabel had got it wrong after all and there was nothing really to be afraid of from these long-dead men. He decided to go back to the Wellington, but had just turned the corner onto Avenham Lane, when he saw a slight and familiar figure coming along the street toward him.

Alderson.

Instinctively, Preston hid, ducking round a corner and squatting behind a rusting iron drainpipe. The man came on, and Preston thought that while he still looked glazed and unaware he moved with a greater sense of purpose. He turned into Pleasant Street, weaving slightly, and made toward the other man's house, but at the last moment, he crossed the street, opened an entirely different door and disappeared inside.

What was going on? What – more to the point – was Preston supposed to do? In spite of the strangeness of his predicament and the fear he had felt when the fight – if a single punch could be called a fight – had taken place in front of him at the Wellington, Preston realised he was getting both irritated and bored. He had got this wrong. These men might be rough, but they were not the monsters Mabel had feared they were. He needed to find a way out of this pointless little glimmer of history, a way back to his own time, his own life. There was no sign of the Leech and nothing to be gained by . . .

Alderson's door cannoned open and the drunk man came striding out, hatless now, crossing the road and seizing the latch of the other man's door. He rattled it and, finding it locked, kicked at it, shouting, "Bell! Come out. I want to pay you for what you've done to me at the Wellington."

Preston was suddenly overcome by a sense of foreboding. The feeling of something dreadful, looming and inexorable, which he had felt in the pub returned full force. He advanced on the man, telling him to stop, to go back home, but Alderson still showed no awareness of his presence, and continued to shout and rattle the door. It was coming now, something awful. Preston could feel it, getting nearer like a train in a tunnel.

* * *

The wings of the crow filled the night, the world. Tracey staggered back, gasping as if the air had grown mountain top thin. She tried to see the dairy, the house, but there was only the impossible bird blotting out everything else: raven black feathers against her face, reptile feet and sharp little claws in her hair, and the eyes – hot, and red as coals in the heart of a fire – burning into her own.

"Radcliffe," it said in its crow-but-not-crow voice. "You are mine."

Tracey flapped at it, shrieking in panic and revulsion, her mind empty as the night. There was nothing but the not-bird. It was bigger than the dairy, bigger than the field, and she was nothing, a newborn lamb, its eyes moist and shiny, there for the taking. She shrank back, arms over her head, and then she was falling, not so much knocked off balance as overwhelmed by the terror and madness of the moment.

"Mine," screeched the crow, its beak slashing the night like a razor, opening up the fabric of the world.

* * *

"Cut it out!" Preston shouted. "Leave it!"

But the door of the Pleasant Street house was suddenly open and there was the big man – Bell, he supposed – hunched over, his face dark and set like an ape's, a knife in one hand, the other balled into a fist.

"Bring me my money or get off 'ome," he warned, raising the blade and pointing with it.

"I've come to teach thee a lesson," said Alderson.

"I'll do for thee," Bell replied. "You see if I don't. Step one more foot toward me and I'll run this through your heart."

"I'll try thee for that," shouted Alderson, and flew at him. Seizing him in a violent embrace and slamming him against the door jamb. For a moment the two men were locked in a kind of awful waltz as they fought to contain each other's hands, stumbling clumsily about. Alderson got a fist free and lunged at Bell, who took it on his chin, crumpled for a moment, then surged upright, lunging with the hand which held the knife.

A terrible change came over Alderson. The two men became statues, then the knife slid out of the wound it had made, and Alderson crumpled to the cobbles, bleeding heavily.

Preston put his hands to his face in horror, biting at the knuckle of one of his own fingers to stop himself from screaming, and then the killer, for the other man was clearly dying, snarled, "he deserves all he got."

Preston turned away, heart thumping. He knew they were ghosts, that this incident had happened over a hundred years ago and that the pooling blood on the street in front of him had been scrubbed and washed away long since, but that didn't seem to matter. It was too horrible and he could stand it no longer.

He had to get out of here.

"Wait," said Bell. "It's you."

Preston looked again and now the knife man was glaring directly at him as if he had just seen him. Preston took an involuntary step backwards. Bell's eyes seemed to swirl with fury and madness. He raised the dripping knife and pointed it at Preston as he had pointed it at the dead man.

Killers. Monsters.

Mabel had been right after all.

"Preston Oldcorn!" he growled, taking a long step forward. "You owe me a penny piece!"

* * *

The soft earth cushioned Tracey's fall but the impact drove the air from her body. Above her all was blackness though whether that was the vast wings of the impossible crow or the night itself she was momentarily unsure.

"Radcliffe!" whispered a voice. It was harsh and low, a rasped sound that was the voice of neither bird nor man, but had elements of both. And then there were the eyes, red and burning but similarly indistinct. They seemed to flicker in size and shape, sometimes bright and round as a deer or a cow, sometimes narrow and with a slit for a pupil like a cat. That made a kind of sense, because though the creature was clearly nothing as simple as a cat, it was certainly a predator, a stalker of prey. A killer.

And then it was the thing she had seen on the kitchen counter, hunched and covered in black animal bristle but also man-shaped. It knuckled toward her, looming, swelling as it grew close and she thought she saw those awful eyes crack open lengthways. They split wider and wider and she realised that what she had taken for lashes were really teeth that grew up and out as the two mouth-eyes opened to swallow her up. And suddenly there was the smell again, earth and animals, but also the sickly tang of aftershave.

Tracey kicked wildly, horror and revulsion giving her unthinking strength.

She didn't think she really hit it, wasn't even sure there was anything to hit, but the swiftness of her resistance, the grim determination which drove it, seemed to unsettle the thing. In its moment of surprise and indecision she was up and sprinting back to the cottage.

She had no weapon against such a monster, but she felt sure she was safer indoors, dreams or no dreams.

* * *

"What?" Preston sputtered. "A penny? No!"

But the spectre of William Bell was coming, stumbling murderously toward him, the bloody knife smoking in the cold air.

Preston ran. In fact he stumbled as he turned, slipping on the icy cobbles and nearly going sprawling, but he righted himself and began sprinting back the way he had come, up Pleasant Street and toward Avenham Lane. He didn't know the area so the smart thing was surely to go back up Glovers Court to Fishergate where the nightmare had begun. He rounded the first corner and began heading up the increasingly treacherous incline to the Wellington and on. Outside the pub he hesitated to get his breath and looked back, half-expecting to see an empty street or, at worst, the older man wheezing a couple of hundred yards back down Glovers Street.

Bell, knife in hand, was right behind him, only a few yards away, running hard but silent after him. Preston gasped in shock and, gripped with a new terror, threw himself into another stumbling run. Against all the odds, the older man had gained on him and was somehow and, in spite of the incline, maintaining his original speed with long, pounding strides. Wide-eyed with horror, Preston set his sights on the underpass where Glovers Court met Fishergate and ran hell for leather, his mind full of an awful truth: he was tiring, slowing. But he remembered all too well that he hadn't felt anything like exhaustion when he had been a ghost. Unless he had broken a bone, he could have run forever, hours and hours at a flat, cruising dash . . .

And so could the knife-wielding killer behind him.

It wasn't the Leech. It didn't need to be. A knife was a knife was a knife. Who or what plunged it into his back didn't really matter.

So Preston ran, along Glovers Court and up to where the road narrowed like a bottle neck, squeezing under the blank walled building above the corner where Booths would one day stand, and then – with a surge of frantic, panic-driven dread – he rushed through the cold shadowy passage and burst out into Fishergate like a champagne cork fired from the bottle.

He collided with a big woman in a pink mac.

"Oy!" she snapped. "Watch it!"

It was a fraction lighter. Evening rather than midnight. The street was . . . his street, the way he knew it. Booths and the record store on the corner of Cheapside, and cars honking and a big red Ribble bus, and . . .

"What?" he sputtered. "Oh. Right. Sorry."

The woman's face froze just as she was about to unleash some withering retort but she caught something in his eye.

"You all right?" she asked.

Preston glanced back toward Glover's Court – wide now,

a real road and not just a passage – and saw milling shoppers, a family with a push chair, a man in a striped butcher's apron going into Booths, but no spectral killer, knife in hand.

"Yeah," he said, amazed and delighted. "I'm fine."

But he glanced back at Booths, thinking of the ghostly waitress. It was no wonder she was afraid to leave the safety of the cafe.

* * *

The boggart hissed its fury as the girl reached the cottage door and vanished inside. It heard the slam, the snap of the bolt across, and it knew it had missed a chance. She wasn't safe inside. Not entirely. But she was harder to reach there than she was out here in the damp night, amidst the grass and cows, the brook, the hedgerows and the ancient sandstone bedrock. This was the boggart's haunt, where it had begun and such things still defined its essence however much it had borrowed from mankind over the centuries. Inside the house the girl was surrounded by more than walls. There was the horseshoe over the door and the holly that surrounded the pit where the written stone had lain. But there were other things that shielded her, things whose power was known to none of them: the familiar pots and pans, the family photos, holiday souvenirs and other traces of half-forgotten happiness and shared experience. They were small, insignificant things, but together they were humanity writ large and they interlocked like the bars of a cage to keep the boggart out.

They would not last. It was getting stronger by the hour, and feasting on the old woman and the drunk had accelerated its slow awakening to full power. It could already manifest inside the cottage, though only with difficulty, and what it could do there was limited, but even in defeat it was strengthening. The girl had got away, but she had left behind her fear and despair pooling like sweet and heady wine in a fine goblet, like the blood pooling around a carcass.

The boggart sipped.

And grew.

CHAPTER
EIGHTEEN

Tracey received a letter in the first post on Thursday. Her father laid it on the table with her Ready Brek – "Central heating for kids!" – and gave her a questioning look which she pretended not to understand. Suspecting it was from Preston, she deliberately didn't open it till she had gone up to her room and closed the door behind her.

It was written in blue-black fountain pen, like he was doing a school assignment and trying to look posh. There was a smudge on the top right-hand corner and a perfectly formed bluish thumbprint on the envelope. It looked like the contours on a map. She read it quickly once, then again more slowly. It read as follows.

Sunday, September 24th

Dear Tracey,

I'm sorry about yesterday. I don't really know what happened. I got sort of freaked out but it wasn't your fault. I just didn't really know what to say or do, because I thought I would look stupid. Ironic, eh? To be really honest, I'm not used to going out with girls, which I suppose is what we were doing though we never really said. Are we still? I really like you. Sorry for being an idiot.

   Preston

She considered sending him a one-word answer in a letter – no, if she wanted to win the point, yes, if she was going to do what she really wanted – but then it would be after the weekend before she heard back, which seemed both absurd and unbearable. She asked permission to use the phone when she got home from school and her dad – albeit frowning and thoughtful – said, "just keep it short."

When Preston answered she got straight to the point.

"I got your letter," she said.

"Oh. Right," said Preston, eloquent as ever.

"As an apology it was OK I suppose," she said, "though it was rubbish as an explanation." She had landed on this useful distinction at lunchtime while clearing her tray in the school cafeteria. "And yes, we are still going out, but no more café freak-outs; deal?"

"Deal," he said.

Even in that one word she could hear his relief, his joy, and that made her feel both a little sorry for him and pleased, because it was how she would have reacted if their positions had been reversed. It was that curious mutuality that made her add,

"good. There's something I want to tell you."

She refused to say what it was over the phone, partly because she didn't want to be overheard – particularly on this subject – but also because she knew she would need to be able to see his face to determine just how much she was going to say. They both had homework, and Preston was supposed to see his grandma on Friday, so that meant another Saturday meeting. It felt like a long time off, but Tracey agreed that it would be best, and hung up.

That night she watched *Top of the Pops* hosted by Dave Lee Travis, whose mid-Atlantic manner she always found a bit naff. It included the Ramones doing "Don't Come Close" in the studio, shaggy-haired, their guitars slung low and their legs spread wide and stiff in drainpipe jeans. She thought it sounded live, the music rough and muddy and the vocal occasionally a little flat, but she liked it. It felt real and unpolished, which suited them and was a welcome break from all that *Grease* slickness. Blondie was on too doing "Picture This," but that was a video. She wanted to call Preston to discuss it all, but that would have to wait, and thinking of him and what she had planned to tell him made her anxious again.

She was afraid to go to sleep. The house had been quiet since her "nightmare" in the kitchen and the strangeness outside the dairy, but Tracey knew it wasn't over, and she had the beginnings of an idea why. It was a mad idea, one she could not bring herself to speak.

Since Tuesday the business with the milk kits falling off the stone in the dairy had happened twice, though they were only using it to store the empty churns so they had lost no milk. She had mentioned it in school because having to help clean up had made her late, and, worst luck, it was for PE. The loathsome Mr. Goggins, dressed as always in his sky blue track suit, had scolded her for it, and said she would have to make up the class. He had said it with a private little leering smile and Tracey – already exhausted – caught the scent of his Hai Karate aftershave – "be careful how you use it!" – and shuddered, trying to shut out the memory of the hairy thing squatted on her kitchen counter.

"See me in the gym before you go home," he said.

"Can't tonight, sir," Tracey had responded with dogged certainty. "Mi dad is coming to get me. Family event."

Goggins' predatory eyes narrowed, but he withdrew.

"Later in the week then," he said. "Don't forget, Miss Blenkinsop. I won't."

He flashed her his ferrety smile and she walked away, careful not to breathe till she had escaped the smell of him.

On her way to History – where they were trying (un-successfully to her way of thinking) to make sense out of the causes of the First World War – Jeanie Martin had caught up with her and gave her a disapproving stare. She was a pale, skinny, black-haired girl, odd and belligerent in equal measure, and not what anyone would call academic. She was a classmate, but not a friend, and Tracey had barely spoken to her in weeks.

"What you skennin' at?" said Tracey.

"You oughtn't to have moved that stone," hissed Jeanie.

The girl spoke in a tone that was something between conspiratorial and as scolding as the teacher had been, and though it took Tracey a second to realise what she was talking about, her response was indignant.

"I don't see that it's any business of yours," she said.

"Written Stone Lane," said the girl significantly. "'ow long have you lived there?"

"Eight months. What's it to ya?" Tracey returned, still defiant.

"Long enough to know better," said Jeanie.

She huffed off, shooting Tracey another disapproving glare over her shoulder as she went, so that Mrs. Perry – the terror of the corridors – roared at her for not watching where she was going.

The girl's dire remark stayed with her, and Tracey asked her mum about it when she got home.

"The stone?" said her mother, who was getting the chip pan going. "I only know what it says on it. Anything else is a bunch of superstitious rubbish, why?"

"But you've heard stories?" Tracey persisted.

"When we first moved in there was some mad old biddy who stopped by to warn us."

"What did she say?"

"I don't remember. Didn't pay it no mind. Something about

not moving it, I suppose. Why? Someone been filling your head with nonsense?"

"Just something I heard," said Tracey, looking away.

"Village like this," said her mother wisely, "people have nothing better to do than make up stories. Ignore it."

"But we moved the stone. It said we shouldn't, but we moved it."

"It had already been moved, hadn't it? Your dad is just putting it to good use for once."

"Right," said Tracey. "Yeah."

But her dreams, if that was what they were, were still in her head – the smell, that thing crouched right there on the counter – and her mother's answers didn't put her mind at ease. Jeanie Martin's taunting comment – "long enough to know better" – had got under her skin. When Tracey felt something niggling at her she wanted – needed – to deal with it, preferably by consulting a book. So she decided to go to the one place her parents never questioned: the library.

Since it was almost tea time, she would have to wait till after school tomorrow, and that meant another restless night, but the strangely vivid nightmares did not return, and she woke only once to find the room colder than it should be and her bedroom door open. She closed it decisively, refusing to go out onto the landing to investigate that now unpleasantly familiar odour of dirt, decay and the scent of the PE teacher's watchful presence.

Eyes like mouths . . .

The local history section of the library on Berry Lane was small, and smaller still when you ignored the books that were really about Preston, or Lancashire generally, and apart from the idea that Written Stone Lane was once part of a Roman road – which she thought pretty cool – there was nothing much to say. That was hardly surprising, given the fact that the road as it was now was little more than a track between farms, and a part of her was pleased to find nothing to substantiate Jeanie's dark hints. Still, Tracey was Tracey, and that meant she didn't give up on a thing till it was properly finished, so once she had replaced the last relevant volume, she went over to the checkout counter where a young woman with long straight hair was sitting.

"Can I help you?" asked the librarian.

"I was wondering if that shelf there is all there is on Longridge," said Tracey, trying not to sound like she was finding fault: the woman probably took a personal pride in what the little library had to offer, "or if I should be looking somewhere else."

"Hmm," the woman, shaking her head slowly so that her hair swung. She had remarkable dark, beautiful eyes. "I think that's all there is. What were you looking for?"

"Something on a particular road. Written Stone Lane."

The woman's face lit up.

"Oh, well you might want to try folklore," she said, beaming.

Tracey's heart sank.

"Folklore?" she echoed emptily. "Why?"

"Oh, you know. *Written Stone Lane*," said the woman, smiling and giving a mock shudder.

"No," said Tracey, sharper than she had meant. "I don't. And I live there."

"Oh," said the librarian, backtracking. "I'm sorry. But, well, yes. There are legends about the stone."

"I know that," said Tracey, recovering. "About not moving the stone, right?"

"And what happened to those that did."

"You mean it's been moved before?" said Tracey. Instantly she saw the impact of that last word move through the librarian's face and she kicked herself for saying it.

"Someone moved the stone?" asked the woman. She sounded curious, interested rather than spooked, and Tracey relaxed a bit.

"A car hit it, I think," she said, covering. "And now they are using it to put the milk churns on in the dairy."

"And?"

"What do you mean?"

"Any spooky events since the stone was moved?" said the librarian with a playful twinkle.

Tracey shook her head and tried to look nonchalant.

"Nah," she said with a kind of mature scorn which she knew was overdoing it, but which she hoped concealed her mounting trepidation. "Why, what happened last time?"

"Well," said the librarian, leaning forward, enjoying herself, "it's all just stories of course, and I don't know why the stone was originally laid, but they say that a farmer wanted to use it just as you are doing now: in the dairy! Apparently, it took nine horses to move it, and once out of position all manner of terrible things happened. First it was just that things wouldn't stay on the stone, so a lot of things got broken, but then it was worse: the milk turned to blood and other awful things. Eventually they moved the stone back, and this time it only took one horse to move it. I don't know much more but I'd be glad to help you look. Sounds like a fun project."

"Yes," said Tracey, whose mouth felt very dry. "Fun."

* * *

Preston had used every strategy he could think of to avoid being alone on the school grounds before or after classes for fear of encountering the wrathful spectre of the caretaker. For several days he had insisted on taking the bus instead of riding with his dad, but that meant more opportunity for Pete Maddingly to bully him. It hadn't become physical. Not yet. Maddingly generally preferred to threaten violence and rely on the occasional slap or discrete thump, rather than risking anything that might get him in real trouble. But the effect was the same or worse: when he was around him Preston felt a constant, low grade dread of what might happen, the fear of which was – in some ways – worse than the pain of the thing itself. On the double decker blue school buses, on which Preston was enough of a rarity to attract attention, and without teachers to restrain him, Maddingly was in his element. Mostly it was leering, taunting and pushing, brandishing a punch which he didn't deliver but got enough of a flinch out of Preston to generate gales of laughter. Preston tried to join in, tried to get inside the joke rather being the target of it, but that never worked for long.

"Oldcorn, ya big puff," Maddingly remarked casually as Preston climbed aboard on Friday, "who said you could ride with us today?"

"Get lost, Maddingly," said Preston, trying to push his way past. This had happened before. Usually Maddingly just laughed the matter off, glad of the chance to torment Preston for the whole ride back to the Cromwell Road stop. Today he set his shoulder and stopped Preston cold.

"No briefcase boys on this bus," he snarled under his breath, just low enough that the driver wouldn't hear. "Not allowed."

"Don't be a pratt, Maddingly."

"You calling me a pratt?" said the bigger boy, shoving Preston so that he lost his balance and stumbled. "You could have given me what I wanted when I came to't tuck shop, but you wanted to be the teacher's pet. Worse, the teacher's *son*. Now you're calling me a pratt? Better get off now, before I decide to smash your face in."

"Yeah?" said Preston, suddenly angry. "I'm not scared of you, Maddingly."

"That right?" said Maddingly, leaning in.

"I've seen things you only see in your worst nightmares," said Preston.

It should have been a chilling dramatic moment. Maddingly

should have seen the seriousness in Preston's face and been cowed by the truth of what he had said. But Pete Maddingly didn't listen and had no imagination, so Preston's words fell meaninglessly around him and the bully reverted to type.

"Well in *your* nightmares," he said, "there's me."

And however much Preston hated to admit it, that was also true. He shouldn't matter, this boy. He was just another kid: a bit bigger, certainly meaner and stupider, but just another kid. But in spite of all the real horrors Preston had survived, Maddingly was still in his head, still scary.

"So, what's it going to be?" said Maddingly. He wasn't playing now.

Preston hesitated. It was more than just bluster on Maddingly's part. He looked angrier, meaner than usual. Maybe he'd been pushed around by someone else. Maybe he'd been given bad grades or had a letter sent home. Whatever it was, he was looking for an excuse to beat someone up, and his stop was the same as Preston's. Even if he survived the journey unscathed, he would have to deal with Maddingly after the bus had left and there were no witnesses.

Preston glanced at the driver, but he was reading the *Evening Post* as the engine idled, and Preston wasn't about to say anything. That wasn't how things were done.

"Go on," said Maddingly, putting a fat index finger in the middle of Preston's blazer pocket and giving it a jab. "Off."

Feeling stupid and ashamed, defeated, Preston turned around and climbed down the tall steps at the front of the bus.

"You not coming?" said the driver, finally noticing him.

"Nah," said Preston, his face burning, hating the driver almost as much as he hated Pete Maddingly. "Just remembered I have stuff to do."

He walked away quickly, not looking back, knowing that Maddingly and his mates would be making faces and flipping him the Vs through the bus windows. He crossed the bus park blindly, heading for the main school building and the playground with its bike sheds and the teachers' car park beyond. He wasn't trying to go anywhere. He was just going away.

It had begun to rain.

Of course.

Without really thinking about it, he cut inside where the boys' toilets led into the main school hallway which was only a few doors down from the staffroom. He would wait around there and catch his dad as he emerged from his meeting. He pulled the outside door open and stepped onto the tiled floor. The interior door was closed, and the bathroom which opened to his left had a hard, institutional feel, echoey and sharp with disinfectant.

The dead caretaker stepped out from round the corner as if he had been waiting for him, his eyes levelled on Preston, his head bent forward like a bull ready to charge.

All Preston's anger at himself, his sense of smallness and failure, his fear of Pete Maddingly went out of his head in an instant. He stepped instinctively away from the ghost and hit his shoulder on the wall. The soles of his shoes slithered on the polished tiles.

"You!" said the caretaker.

"Mr. Simpson!" Preston gasped.

"Preston Oldcorn," said the caretaker, tasting the words in his mouth as he stepped closer. He looked, as before, quite solid and normal, but there was a wild gleam in his eyes. "This is all your fault."

"I'm sorry!" said Preston. "I didn't mean to hurt you! I didn't know I had done."

"But you did," said the ghost with undisguised menace. He paused for a second, then took another step toward him, and as he did so, he began to hum absently under his breath.

"Early one morning, just as the sun was rising . . ."

"No," muttered Preston pleadingly. He reached for the door he had come in through and tugged at it, but it merely rattled in its frame.

Locked.

"I heard a maiden singing . . ." croaked the caretaker, a reptilian smile spreading across his face as he shambled closer.

"I'm sorry!" Preston sputtered. "I didn't know the Leech would survive. I didn't know it would get you."

The dead man took another step, and then something seemed to flit across his face: a thought, an impression. The droning song dried up and the caretaker's old work boots halted their slow and menacing approach. Preston felt sure this moment of confusion would not last and that he had to exploit it, though there was no reason to think the other door would be open. Even if it had been, there was something he needed to know.

"The Leech *didn't* get you?" he said.

The caretaker's confusion seemed to deepen.

"Get. Me?" he said, his voice as faltering and as unsure as his face.

"How did you die?" Preston asked.

The ghost's eyes strayed for a moment, grew vague, then focused again.

"Yul Brynner," he said.

Preston blinked.

"The actor?" he said, baffled.

"Magnificent," said the caretaker, his face lighting up.

Something snagged in Preston's memory: his grandad planning his evening's TV viewing. It had been that same Saturday.

"*The Magnificent Seven*," he said. "You were watching telly when you died."

The caretaker nodded.

"And that's all you remember?" said Preston.

The old man's right hand crept across his chest and his face clouded with distress. The open palm moved over his heart to his left arm.

"You had a heart attack," Preston said. "It wasn't the Leech. You just . . . died."

"And am trapped here forever," said the caretaker, his gaze hardening again. "Because of you." He took another step toward Preston who flattened himself against the wall. The ghost was close enough to touch him now.

"I will make it right," Preston said earnestly. "I promise. I don't know how. I don't know what happened. But I will . . ."

The internal door snapped open, its latch gunshot loud in the silent bathroom. Preston twisted his neck and saw his father standing in the doorway.

"I thought you were going home on the bus?" said his dad.

Preston flashed his gaze around the bathroom, but the caretaker had vanished.

Not moved on, he reminded himself. *Just disappeared. He'll be back.*

"Preston?"

"What? Oh. No. I changed my mind."

His dad looked momentarily baffled, but then his hands were patting his pockets for his keys.

"Well, I'm ready to go home if you are," he said.

CHAPTER
NINETEEN

So, Preston thought as they drove home, the Leech did not kill Mr. Simpson. He died of natural causes, but had still been trapped in the world of the Merely Dead, something for which he blamed Preston. That must have come from the Leech, that special, targeted bitterness, as had that dreadful song.

O, never leave me . . .

But precisely how the Leech had touched the caretaker's ghost was less clear. As the Leech had been separated from the boy killed by the train, it had lashed out, left some little malice which had attached itself to all ghosts in the area, so they would all know Preston's name. In that same moment the doors to the world of the Sincerely Dead had slammed shut, so more ghosts were appearing daily, all convinced that their timeless prison was Preston's fault.

And they were right.

Roarer had said as much. Preston's desire to hold onto life had somehow – coupled with the vengeful spite of the Leech – sealed them into that static no-man's-land between life and death. Roarer had also said that if he found the first victim of the Leech's new identity, Preston's path to the Leech would be clear. He had dodged the implications of this for a while, but Preston had eventually confronted the person he felt sure had been that first victim, only to find that the old man had died in front of the telly watching a Western.

So now what? Find the person who really was the first victim to fall to whatever form the Leech had bound to this time? He supposed so. But he didn't know how to do that, and the project suddenly seemed both dreadful and pointless. He had beaten the Leech once already, but the monster had just found a new home, a new soul to steal, and corrupt, a new heart to blacken and mould to its own terrible purposes . . .

"Where are we going?" Preston asked, snapping out of his reverie as they drove past the top of Stuart Road and kept going along Ribbleton Avenue.

"Well, since you have no scouts to fill your evening," his dad replied, eyes carefully on the road, "we thought we'd have tea at your grandma's house. She's still not well so your mum's gone round to cook."

A buffet, it turned out, with some salad, boiled ham, and

a cake tin crammed with mushroom vol-au-vents, to which his aunt Bridget added two of those party hedgehog things: grapefruits wrapped in tin foil and stuck with little sausages, pieces of cheese and pineapple chunks on cocktail sticks. A trifle – made, thank God, *without* jelly – for dessert.

Preston was a bit baffled at all this. It was the kind of thing they did on Sundays or at Christmas, and as they were getting out of the car he found his mum waiting in the drive, her hands clasping and unclasping.

His confusion swelled and turned into something else which his mum read in his face.

"She's having a hard time cooking," she said. "So we're rallying round a bit. Till she's back on her feet."

She turned to consider the house's green trim as if appraising whether it needed redoing but Preston was sure she was avoiding his eyes.

"What do you mean?" he said. "What's wrong with her?"

His grandmother was the unshakable loadstone of the family. She was never sick. She was who you went to when you were sick, or short of money, or depressed about school. The idea that she was more seriously ill than Preston had thought sent a tremor of alarm through him.

"We don't really know yet," said his mum, her voice low, her eyes flashing to the front bedroom window, her hands and words fluttering. "Went in to see the doctor last week and then back for some tests yesterday."

"What for?" said Preston. "What kind of tests?"

"Now, don't take on," said his dad. *For your mum's sake*, his look added.

"Why did no one say anything?" asked Preston, his voice low. *You knew she was ill*, he accused himself. *You should have visited.*

"Well your mum has been talking to your uncle Bob and aunt Bridget . . ."

"To *me*!" Preston shot back. "Why did no one say anything to me?"

"Well," said his mum, "you've got school and what have you . . ."

And you've been weird and jumpy and secretive . . . Preston added the unspoken words in his head, feeling suddenly guilty and stupid. He had known she was sick and should have realised it wasn't a bit of a cold or something when she wasn't in church on Sunday. He took a steadying breath.

"What's wrong with her?" he said.

"I told you, we don't . . ."

"I mean, what are her symptoms?" he clarified.

"Well, she's been dizzy and that has made her stomach upset, I think. Has to stay sitting down. Or lying down. Been getting a bit confused as well, seeing things that weren't there . . ."

"Double vision," said Preston without thinking.

His mother shot him a shrewd look.

"Yes!" she said. "How did you know that?"

"I saw her a week last Saturday," he said, kicking himself for never mentioning it. For never following up for almost two weeks. "She was having a hard time reading . . ." He broke off at the stricken look in his mother's face. "I'm sorry," he said.

"I didn't realise. She said it was just that she needed a new prescription for her glasses. Is it . . . I don't know. Serious?"

"I wouldn't think so," his father cut in, getting a box of Peek Frean's Family Circle out of the back of the Cortina. "Just needs a bit of a rest. It's not easy looking after grandad now that he can't get around so well. We'll be helping out a bit more till she's feeling up to it."

He was trying to sound upbeat, as if it was something and nothing that would blow over, but – though she tried to hide them––there were tears in his mother's eyes. When they got to the house and his uncle Bob had tried to lighten the mood with a 'Get Well Soon' card that said 'Hope your double double vision vision's getting better' but she didn't laugh.

What did double vision mean if it wasn't about tiredness or eye strain? he wondered. Nothing good.

His grandma was upstairs in the front bedroom, a part of the house Preston had barely ever been in, alone in a vast bed heaped with blankets. She smiled when they filed in but she didn't seem entirely sure who was there, and drifted off to sleep after a few minutes.

"It's the drugs," said Preston's dad confidingly as soon as the others had gone back downstairs. "They've got her on the strong stuff to help her rest."

"Drugs?"

"Some sort of opiate," he said.

He patted his son's shoulder awkwardly and Preston knew that his father had seen the shock and panic in his face. An hour ago his grandmother was a bit under the weather, or so it had seemed in Preston's head. A tummy bug or a bit of flu. Now she was on opiates for the pain?

"It's just so fast," Preston said. The words immediately sounded stupid and inadequate. "I mean, I *just* saw her! How can she be so sick so quickly?"

"That's how it goes sometimes," said his dad. "'Specially when you are getting on." He framed a sad smile.

"Well, when will she be up?" asked Preston. Another stupid question. His mum had said they would help out till she was back on her feet, but that suddenly looked like a dodge at best. At worst, a massive self-deception. Preston stared at her, silent and somehow shrunken in the bed. The transformation since he had seen her last was staggering. She looked old and tired beyond imagining. It suddenly seemed almost impossible to see her back to her usual self, humming as she pottered about in the kitchen, slicing ham from the shank and dropping it into a bubbling pot of green split peas, the quick and gentle smile when she caught his eye . . .

"Is it a tumour?" Preston asked quietly.

His dad looked ready to bluster, to shake the possibility off and tell him all would be fine, but he faltered and seemed to collapse in on himself, as if he had only been looking the way he usually did by some great internal effort. He glanced over his shoulder, then pursed his lips.

"Probably," he said. "We're waiting to hear."

* * *

Tracey went to Preston's house after lunch on Saturday. She had insisted upon going there because she didn't want to be near her house, or – as she was starting to think of it – near the written stone, but she also didn't want to wander around town or fields. Preston hadn't seemed quite comfortable in either environment and he would need to be comfortable if she was going to tell him what had been going on. Better speak on what he would consider home turf.

She hadn't decided how much she was going to say, only that if she was going to tell anyone, it would be him. She was private at school and had deliberately kept her distance from the other girls once it seemed clear her family were going to move, but they hadn't, and her carefully maintained distance merely left her isolated and, as far as the other kids were concerned, standoffish, probably a bit weird. That was mostly OK, but with what had been going on at home weighing on her sleep-deprived mind, she missed having a friend to confide in. She loved her parents very much, but there was no way in hell she was going to be telling them about this. They'd pack her off to Whittingham, the local mental hospital.

No, she thought, rolling her eyes and grinning, *they wouldn't*.

They'd try to talk to her out of it. Her dad lived, he liked to say, close to the ground. He wasn't a fan of psychology or any of the kind of abstract thought he assigned to "boffins." He was neither unintelligent nor unsophisticated, but he liked ingenuity to have practical application of the kind you could see and touch. It occasionally put him at odds with his "book smart" daughter, though he did his best not to speak the words which lurked behind his frown at the time she spent on her essays for English. He wanted her to be an engineer, and as a kid had bought her Lego and Meccano sets, the fancy kind they couldn't really afford which had motors and winches. She had loved them too, and she was – like him – rigorously logical and practical, even if her tastes leaned in more esoteric directions these days. If she talked to him about spooky noises and apparitions in the kitchen, he'd think she'd lost her mind, or that he'd lost her, which would almost be as bad. Her mum was more even keeled but her faith in the power of O-Levels to change your destiny was terrifying to behold, and she would not countenance anything which deflected Tracey's attention from her school work.

Which left Preston, the odd boy she barely knew but who she thought maybe – just maybe – might listen without laughing.

"Let's go for a walk," he said, as soon as she arrived.

"You'd not rather we just . . . I don't know, went to your room or something?"

Preston frowned, and the fractional glance over his shoulder told her that that idea had been floated unsuccessfully with his parents already. She bridled inside, but it wasn't her fight, and she didn't want him on edge.

"OK," she said. "Not into town though, eh? Not Booths."

He grinned ruefully at that.

"Nah," he said. "I'll show you the delights of Ribbleton."

It was a brisk, cool day and the pavement was clogged by the yellow-brown leaves of the horse chestnuts and sycamores.

"Ok," she said. "Which way?"

"We could go up Cromwell Road and through Brookfield Park?" he said musingly. "There are sand cliffs up above the brook where we go sledding in the winter. When I was little it felt super high and steep." He grinned at the memory and then caught himself as if he had given something away. "But you're a country girl."

"Meaning?"

"You've seen grass and trees before."

"That," she admitted, "is true."

"Okay, then," he decided. "This way."

He led her up out of the residential block where he lived, pausing only to throw a glance down to where the little street dead-ended in a fence.

"Behind there is the railway line," he said, as if this was somehow significant. "The one that runs up to where you are in Longridge. Or used to. The actual line stops behind my school now."

"Oh," she said. "Right."

"Just goods now," he said, playing tour guide. "Used to be a passenger line too but," he hesitated for a fraction of a second as if considering something just out of sight, "not anymore."

They crossed Ribbleton Avenue and she realised they were not far from the house her parents had been considering a few weeks earlier, though they had decided it was too small and pricey for what it was. She didn't say this, and certainly not that her mother had been unhappy at the prospect of moving to

Ribbleton from Longridge. It wasn't till they entered the high, formidable iron gates, their black paint shining with last night's rain, that she processed where they were going.

"The cemetery?" she said. "This is your idea of a nice walk?"

"It's calm," said Preston with a shrug. "There are benches."

"And dead people," she said. It was supposed to be a joke, but he just nodded thoughtfully and she wished she hadn't said it. She wondered if the environment would make what she had to tell him seem even more ludicrous, like they were in a *Scooby Doo* episode . . .

"My grandma's sick," said Preston. He didn't look at her and there had been no preamble, and she immediately knew he didn't mean she had a cold or something similarly trivial.

"What is it?" she said, taking his hand. It was cold, but he didn't flinch as he had last time.

"Not sure yet, but it might be cancer. In her brain."

She looked at him and he tried to smile but his face seemed to crack and buckle. He blinked and cleared his throat.

"Are you close?" she asked.

He nodded but didn't speak, and she felt a wave of tenderness for him that she didn't know how to convey. In the end she squeezed his hand and leaned into his shoulder, so that he pushed back a little in a playful sort of way and shrugged.

"I'm sorry about before. In town," he said. "I was just . . ."

"It's fine," she replied. "Forget it. I just thought you'd, ya know, lost interest or something."

"In you?" he said, turning to her, shocked into something

which could only be honesty. "No! Of course not! I mean . . ."

But he was shy again, and didn't know what else to say. Tracey smiled and said again "it's fine," because it was.

They had walked up a broad, tree-lined avenue and circled a kind of roundabout on which a bushy copse was planted, and only now was the full scale of the cemetery visible. The place was huge, far bigger than anything in Longridge, a mass of monuments and headstones of various kinds, most of them fairly new looking, many of the graves carpeted with green glass stones. She saw a water supply tap and there were wire baskets for dead flowers which breathed foully on them as they passed.

"My grandma lives over there," said Preston, nodding toward the high perimeter wall. "When I were little I used to be terrified of sleeping in the back bedroom because you could see into the cemetery."

Tracey's heart pounded as she sensed an opening.

"See any ghosts?" she ventured.

Preston looked almost dreamy for a moment, then shook his head.

"Nah," he said. "Sometimes thought I heard stuff but . . . no. In the end the cemetery is just a place for bones, isn't it?"

Tracey nodded her agreement, but she faltered inside.

"You don't believe in life after death?" she tried. "I mean, you go to church and all, right?"

He gave her a rueful grin.

"Catholic agnostic," he said.

"Which means?"

"I'm not sure," he said. It was almost a joke.

"And ghosts?" she pressed. "You believe in ghosts? Spirits? Things that go bump in the night?"

He seemed to wince as thoughts or feelings chased across his face, and when he spoke he sounded cautious, watchful.

"Maybe," he said. "I mean, I can't say for sure..." He frowned and this time the little twist in his features seemed pained as if he was more than dissatisfied with what he was saying. "I mean, scientifically speaking..." he tried, but that didn't seem to make him feel any better. "Yes," he said suddenly, and seemed to relax as if getting the word out was a huge relief. "I can't explain why, and maybe it's stupid, but yes, I believe in ghosts."

"Have you ever seen one?" Tracey asked, sharing his relief. "Felt a weird presence or something?"

He seemed to consider this and then became guarded again.

"No," he said. "When I was a kid I might have convinced myself that I had, but no, not really. I don't think so."

"But you still believe in them?"

He seemed uncomfortable now, and glanced away into the trees as if to hide.

"I mean, we want to believe that death isn't the end, right?" he said, stooping to one of the graves by the curb and picking up one of the little ornamental stone fragments. It was green as the sea and looked like a rough, uncut diamond. "That we don't completely lose the people we love. That we don't lose ourselves."

Tracey wondered if he was thinking about his grandmother, and decided to change the subject, but he dropped the stone back onto the grave and considered the writing on the headstone.

In loving memory . . .

Closeby a stone angel clung to a funeral urn, her weeping head in the crook of her arm.

"What about you?" asked Preston suddenly.

Tracey was caught off guard.

"What about me?'

"You believe in ghosts?" he asked. He said it calmly, interested to hear her thoughts on a real subject, like he was wondering how long the Labour government would last and whether Margaret Thatcher, the loathed leader of the Tory opposition, would ever be prime minister. It was the way he asked that, in spite of all her misgivings, made her answer frankly.

"If you'd asked me that a couple of weeks ago, I would have said no."

He turned to her sharply and his gaze was searching.

"Why?" he demanded. "What happened?"

Again, the honesty of the question, its utter lack of skepticism, disarmed her, and made her answer in kind.

"Not entirely sure," she said. "Strange noises in the night. Smells."

"Smells?" said Preston, clearly surprised.

"And the blankets keep being stripped from my bed," she said, blushing. "Bedroom door opening and closing by itself. It's weird," she said, deliberately, cautiously, noncommittal. "And I know this sounds stupid but you remember I said there was a creepy PE teacher at my school? Mr. Goggins?"

"Yes," said Preston, cautiously. "The Hai Karate bloke."

"Exactly!" said Tracey, as if his remembering that detail would make what she had to say more plausible. "When I wake up, my room smells of him. And something else, like animals and soil, but that aftershave for sure."

"You think he's actually . . . ?"

"No," said Tracey. "He's not really there. The doors are locked and all. But it's like something is watching me like he does and my brain is making a connection. Or maybe the ghost, or whatever it is, is making an association with my real life . . ." Her voice trailed off and she smiled and half-shook her head as if not really meaning any of it. "But one thing is for sure: the stone – the big old one outside the house, that we sat on when you came to visit?"

"What about it?"

"It was moved. Which it's really not supposed to, because there's a carving that says it shouldn't," she said, considering his bewildered face then added, "The night Agnes Tattershawl died right on the road by the lane, that's when the stone moved. And then Jed Atkinson was hit by a car. Drunk, but terrified, running out of the lane and right into the road. And then . . ."

She bit her lip.

"What?" Preston asked.

"The other night, right? I heard something downstairs. I went into the kitchen and . . . it's hard to explain, but I felt just awful. Miserable and terrified at the same time. And there was something on the counter."

Preston became very still.

"Something?" he echoed.

"A shape," she said, the words tumbling out of her as if she was an upturned bottle and someone had removed the cap. They spilled out and she couldn't stop them. "Big. Like a man but not. And the smell. Dirt and death and animals. It had eyes. And claws. And teeth. But it wasn't an animal. It wasn't alive. Wasn't really there . . ."

He reached out to her then, a steadying hand responding to the tears in her eyes, and she stepped into the half-embrace until it became real. She shuddered as a single gasping sob rippled through her, and then she was alright again. For a moment she stayed where she was, her face buried in the fabric of his coat, her eyes flicking around over his shoulder to see if anyone was watching, then she stepped back and looked at him frankly.

"You think I'm a nutter?" she asked. "It's OK if you do. A few weeks ago I would have too. But I'd like to know."

"I don't think you're a nutter," he said seriously.

"My parents think I have a vivid imagination, though – again – they would never have said that till a few weeks ago. Is that what you think? That I'm stressed from work and lack of sleep and am seeing things that aren't there?"

His eyes narrowed with thought, but he shook his head.

"No," he said. "I believe you saw what you think you saw. I don't understand it, but I believe it."

She was so taken aback by this, though it was what she had most wanted to hear, that she couldn't hold back one last honesty.

"Why?" she asked.

"I don't know," he said, looking down. "I guess I just think of you as trustworthy."

It was the first thing between them that day which didn't feel true.

Let it go, she told herself. *He said he believes you. That was what you wanted.*

But she couldn't.

"You *have* seen a ghost," she said. "Why are you lying to me?"

He blinked and looked away again but she grabbed his chin and made him face her.

"Preston!" she insisted. "Tell me the truth or I'm going home, and this time I won't come back."

"Ok," he said, twisting out of her grasp. "Ok. I have."

"Why didn't you say so?"

"Because it sounds stupid."

"I just told you I'd seen something!" she retorted, fury driving away her previous anxiety as if it had never been. "It's fine for me to look stupid but not you?"

"I said I believed you!" he replied, catching some of her heat.

"You didn't say why. You made me feel like I was the crazy one and you were doing me a favour when all the time . . ." She considered him shrewdly and gave up. He looked hangdog and shame-faced. "So, tell me. What did you see?"

Again the blink, the look of panic in his face, the open-mouthed stare. Tracey sighed, met and held his eyes, then nodded.

"Ok," she said. "Either you don't trust me or you are lying. It doesn't really matter which."

She turned on her heels and began walking back toward the cemetery gates, eyes squeezed tight, shutting everything out, and everything in.

"The waitress."

Preston had jogged up behind her and grabbed her by the arm. She spun to face him, defiant, daring him to acknowledge the tears in her eyes.

"What waitress?" she demanded.

"At Booths," he said.

"In the café?" she said, scorn and disbelief blending. This was the worst attempt to satisfy her he could have come up with and she was suddenly furious. "Goodbye, Preston."

"I mean it," he said, keeping hold of her arm even as she tried to wrench herself free. "It was why I freaked out. Not the waitress you spoke to. Another one. I thought she was a real person but she wasn't. And it's not the first time."

It was his turn to look earnest and upset. Tracey's fury stalled and she looked into his eyes, seeing immediately that he meant every word of it.

"You're serious?" she said. "I'm serious, Preston; I don't want you to make something up just to make me feel less alone in my . . . whatever it is."

"I'm not."

She gave him another silent, appraising look.

"You're not messing about?" she said at last. "Honest to God?"

He nodded.

"I see ghosts all the time."

CHAPTER TWENTY

Less than ten miles away the boggart stirred. It was too light for it take shape or move in the world and it was now no more than a cold and inexplicable shadow under the boughs of a crab apple tree on the edge of a field. A person might walk right past it and not know it was there: except, perhaps, for a sudden chill, a sourness in the air or some other vague and wordless instinct to move hurriedly away. They might feel watched. They might feel strangely lonely. They might feel a sense of foreboding, or see faces in the gnarled bark of the old tree.

But they would not see the boggart.

It was not seen till it wanted to be, and then it picked the shape of that appearance from your own unconscious fears melded with the forms it knew best. In daylight it rested, sucking energy from the ground, the trees, the water all of which, in time, would stifle and die unless it moved on to other haunts. It avoided the holly and the iron which was strewn about the farmyard – old troughs, cattle grids and pieces of discarded machinery – sensing them like the drone of some deep, rumbling sound which became unbearable as it grew close. The boggart rested and it thought, stirring its memory like a hog foraging under leaves, turning them over and over to see what emerged. It pictured the girl and remembered Radcliffe, the death cheat, and – as from another life – the Oldcorn boy. The boggart Leech twisted in its mind, turning snake-like in on itself, trying to recall what they had been to it, these humans who had – albeit briefly – bested it. It saw Ralph Radcliffe, still somehow alive even after being dead and buried, exploiting some catch, some technicality as the Oldcorn boy had done. He had returned to his family a hero, victorious over the old fear which stalked his fields.

But the boggart had revenged itself upon him and his family, snaffling them up and swallowing them down one by one, till the old man begged for mercy.

Mercy!

Radcliffe should have known better. And at last he changed his tune, making, instead, the kind of offer he thought would appeal. In its mind's eye the boggart saw the old man, pleading for the life of his family, offering himself in tribute.

The boggart had agreed, but both had been lying. For its part, the boggart meant to go right on ravaging the old man's wife, children and servants long after Radcliffe had made his futile sacrifice. The game played out and Radcliffe died a second time, but even there he proved slippery. Slippery as an eel. He had arranged the laying of the stone even as the boggart fell to its victory meal, and before it had realised what was happening, the boggart had been trapped. Many a long year it had lain under the stone. It remembered that all right.

But it was out now and would not be bound again. It was out and would be revenged most horribly on all who lived there, Radcliffe or no. It thought of the girl and for the briefest of moments someone passing might have seen a curious flicker in the shade beneath the tree, as if for the merest blink of an eye a monster had stirred beneath the branches, licked its slathering lips, and then vanished once more.

* * *

Preston sat Tracey on a bench under a copper beech and told her about the ghosts of the waitress, the caretaker at school, and the woman who had come to communion in church. He gave a detailed and breathless account of the two men who had met in the Wellington where they had quarreled over a loaned penny, fought in Pleasant Street, the sole survivor pursuing him, knife in hand, all the way to Fishergate. He was specific and frank, and she listened with rapt attention, silent and stricken with something like dread.

"There was another ghost," he said. "Worse than the others."

Worse than the lot put together. They call it the Leech because it feeds off other ghosts, and off the living too, I think. I thought it was gone but . . ." He remembered what Roarer had told him and a cold knot of dread settled into his gut like a stone. "Now, I'm not so sure."

He did not tell her about his time in the nine twenty-two no-place, that he had been a ghost himself, a dead person, because that would have been too much, too frightening, and he thought she might run from him. He wouldn't have blamed her. Preston was used to feeling like an oddity, an outsider, but for people to know he had been dead and had made it back to life on a kind of technicality, was too strange. It made him, what? Not an ordinary boy, that was for sure.

That wasn't the only thing that made him keep the truth to himself. If he'd told her everything about the nine twenty-two no-place, he would have to say he had known her then, even though she didn't remember any of it. That would be creepy, him knowing a part of her life which she didn't, a part which had not happened. The Tracey he had got to know had been two years older than this one. Even if she believed it, it would mess with her head and make him feel like . . . what? Some kind of weirdo like the teacher who wore Hai Karate, spying on her, learning about her without her knowledge. It would be like he had read her diary. It *was* creepy, he decided, and would frighten her off.

So he left his strange ability to see ghosts unexplained and presented his macabre 'gift' as both new and inexplicable, and Tracey seemed to put all he had said together with her own recent supernatural experience, finding a kind of strange and suggestive coincidence.

"Why now?" she mused. "What has happened that has suddenly made us both see these . . . things?"

He noted the way she dodged the word, but then her experience hadn't sounded like any ghost he had seen. The nocturnal noises, the cold, the sense of being watched, he could square with ghostly activity, but the thing she had seen, dark and hairy, smelling of animals and – almost but not quite comically – aftershave? That was another matter entirely. She told the story several times and he felt only increasing bafflement and a sense of nagging anxiety.

Why now? Indeed.

One positive thing emerged from this uncomfortable discussion, however. Their former awkwardness and hostility which Preston had felt sure was about to separate them forever, was lost in a shared spirit of secret knowledge, of mystery, even adventure. When they had told their stories and left them to sit awhile in the autumnal chill of the cemetery, Tracey had turned to him with new purpose and her eyes were alight with something like excitement.

"So, what are we going to do?" she asked.

"Do?"

"Yes, do! This changes everything! I didn't believe in ghosts, in life after death. Now I can see the proof! So, what do we do?"

Preston couldn't help but grin at the enthusiastic earnestness, and had to remind himself not to begin his answer with "Well, last time I dealt with ghosts . . ." or "When *I* was dead . . ."

"Don't laugh!" she exclaimed, punching him playfully. "I'm serious."

"I know," he replied, smiling more tenderly. "That's why . . . I mean, I like it. That's all."

"So, what do we do?"

He nodded thoughtfully, liking the sound of that 'we.'

"We help them move on," he said. "Everything I've heard says that ghosts are souls trapped in some defining thought or act which has swallowed them up and taken away their sense of who they are. *Were*, I should say. We have to help them remember, and then they can move on."

Tracey stared at him in amazement, and Preston instantly thought he'd said too much. He began trying to come up with where he might have heard this, a book or TV show, but he didn't need to. The truth of it registered in her face.

"That makes total sense!" she said. "I mean, it's mad, and there's no way we could ever know if it was accurate, but it feels right, you know? So . . . what? We research who the ghosts were and then confront them with whatever we've learned?"

"Something like that, yeah," said Preston. "And make sure they don't kill us," he added, half-joking.

"Nah," said Tracey. "They can't hurt the living, surely? I mean, they're just spirits."

"Not so sure about that," said Preston. "The knife in that bloke's hand looked pretty real to me."

"Because you were in his world, kind of," said Tracey, who had obviously been paying close attention. "But that's not the way it happens to me. Maybe that's why the thing I saw in the kitchen looked different from your ghosts. We have different skills."

"Skills?" said Preston, not liking the word.

"Well they sure as hell aren't gifts," said Tracey.

"Agreed."

"So where do we start?"

"We should go to your house," said Preston. "That sounds like it's getting more serious . . ."

She cut him off with a pointed shake of her head.

"Not my place," she said. "I want to steer clear of Written Stone Lane as long as a I can, and besides, my mum and dad are home. I couldn't deal with them looking over our shoulders and asking us what we are doing."

"Ok," said Preston. "Then where?"

"Your Booths waitress," she replied. "I'll bet we can find out who she was."

"Mabel," he said.

Tracey raised an eyebrow.

"Mabel what?"

"She didn't say. To be honest she barely remembered that much. Kept saying she was just a waitress. Offered me cake."

For a moment Tracey gaped at him.

"A ghost offered you cake?" she said.

Preston shrugged and smiled.

"She seems quite nice," he said. "And it's not like she's an axe-wielding maniac. Just a waitress."

"Just a waitress," Tracey repeated thoughtfully. Her face lit up. "Just. She's trapped by her job. She lost her identity in the service of others. Happens to women a lot," she added sagely. "You ask me mum."

She got to her feet as if the problem was solved.

"Wait," said Preston. "That's it? A second ago you'd never heard of her and a bit before that you didn't believe in ghosts and now you've got it figured out?"

He was half-joking but a tiny part of him had enjoyed being the expert with first-hand experience and he felt like she was taking over.

"I might not know anything about ghosts but I know about life. Feminism isn't all bra burning, you know, Preston."

Preston flushed, suddenly inexplicably and absolutely out of his depth.

"Oh," he said. "Right."

"Come on then," Tracey answered taking a few steps back toward Ribbleton Avenue and then turning to him expectantly.

"You sure you wouldn't rather go to your house? See if we can see anything there. Figure out what this thing is that . . ."

Tracey shook her head emphatically.

"I said. I don't want to go home till I absolutely have to. And maybe dealing with these other ghosts will show me how to deal with mine. Besides, I have a plan for freeing your waitress."

"Telling Mabel she's not just a waitress won't allow her to move on," Preston shot back.

"You don't know that."

"I do!" he said. "But say you're right. Say she needs to

remember that she's not just a waitress. What's the best way to turn that into a choice, an action that might give her control of what happens next?"

Tracey frowned, but only for a second.

"Get her to walk away from the café!" she said.

"Right," Preston agreed. "But she won't, and not just because she thinks of herself as a waitress. She's terrified of leaving the building."

"Because of the other ghosts," Tracey realised. It was amazing how easily she was rolling with the strange logic of a world she had only just discovered.

"Exactly," said Preston. "And with good reason."

"So, we have to get those other ghosts, the ones you saw at the Wellington, to move on first. Once they've gone, we'll be able to go back to Mabel . . ."

"No way," said Preston, cutting her off. "I'm not going down there again. They're . . . Killers. Monsters."

And they know my name, he didn't say.

She looked like she was about to protest, but changed tack.

"Maybe I could do it," she said.

"You can't see them."

"I might."

"You didn't see Mabel."

"No, but I can see whatever is in my house. Maybe things have changed. Maybe *I've* changed. Let's go and see. You don't have to go all the way. And if you get pulled into their world, I'll get you out."

"What if you're pulled in too?" asked Preston, not liking this strategy at all.

"I suppose we cross that bridge when we come to it."

CHAPTER
TWENTY ONE

Nora MacIntyre popped into Stevens, the newsagents on the high street, to pick up a *Lancashire Evening Post*, then went into Forshaws, the bakery which shared premises with the post office, for butter pies and a couple of vanilla slices. She'd rather have a custard tart, personally, but the vanillas were Father Edwards' favourite. She was still at the counter when she caught – through the aromatic fog of bread and pastry – the scent of *eau de cologne*.

4711.

Nora would recognise it anywhere, because her mother had always had one of the little green labelled bottles with its name in curly italic script in her bathroom cabinet. It was her one concession to decadence and sophistication. The aroma took her back, as such things often do, and for a second she was standing on white tile, not tall enough to reach the sink, and her brother Barry, who called himself Roarer, was tugging at her dress to go and play. She could almost feel it, the memory perfect for a second or two, though what came before and after it, she had no clue, so that she felt happy and sad at the same time.

Not many women wore *4711* anymore, and compared to Charlie and the other stuff on the perfume counter at Marks and Spencer's, it seemed old fashioned. *Pre-war*, was the phrase that sprang to mind, for some reason: a world away. It was a delicate aroma edged with flowers and citrus, though whoever was wearing it now had really gone to town. It was dense, almost overpowering, and Nora turned, instinctively expecting to see old Mrs. Sanders, who always wore so much of the stuff that you could practically see it steaming off her.

But Mrs. Sanders was dead. Her funeral was first thing Tuesday morning. It would be a small affair, since the old lady had no surviving family.

Nora looked around. There was no one else in the shop, though now she thought of it, it had been one of the places she had seen Mrs. Sanders most. She had kept a Post Office Savings Account and was often to be seen – and smelled – standing there at the counter, the account book clutched in her claw-like hands.

Just association then, Nora told herself. *Your mind is playing tricks on you . . .*

And then she glimpsed her, out of the corner of her eye, a

bent, huddled woman in an ancient camel coloured coat and tea cozy hat, stick in hand.

Just for a moment. Then she was gone, leaving only a trace of *eau de cologne* in the air which, a second later, was caught by a draught from the door as Mr. Dewhurst came in, his arms full of parcels, and blown away.

Nora frowned.

Something wasn't right.

* * *

Tracey was only able to convince Preston to return to Pleasant Street, where the murder had taken place, by suggesting they took a route which wouldn't go past the Wellington Inn, but when they walked down Fishergate to Sweetens, the book shop, and looked at a local Ordnance Survey map they could find no trace of the road at all. They continued examining it until a shop assistant with a face like she'd been sucking lemons for thirty years stomped over and said, "you buying that or not?"

"We were just looking," said Preston.

"Not a library, you know," said the woman.

"True," said Tracey. "But you know what is?"

"What?" said the woman reflexively.

"The library," said Tracey.

"Ya what?" said the woman, as they hurried out giggling.

They walked back up Fishergate on the other side of the street and it was obvious that Preston wanted to keep his distance from

Glovers Court. As they got close to Booths he kept throwing furtive glances down the side street under the clock bridge but saw, apparently, nothing unusual. She had assumed he would be relieved to get inside the dark, cool grandeur of the Harris Library and Museum, but even there he seemed jumpy, shooting a searching glance up the heavily ornate staircase.

"What?" she demanded.

He jumped, but shook the question off.

"Nothing," he said. "There's a painting that used to bother me." He paused and added, afraid he looked soft, "when I was a kid."

"Last week then," Tracey shot back, grinning. Preston flushed pink and she said, "Kidding! Keep your 'air on. OK. Local history section. Where would that be?"

As they hunted, Tracey watched Preston out of the corner of her eye. He seemed jittery, on edge, and though she was sure he was glad of her company and help, he seemed scared. Of the ghosts he had told her about, she wondered, or something more? If so, it was something he did not want her to know about. That bothered her, not least because it raised the uncomfortable possibility that everything he had told her was a lie, a joke at her expense or – more likely – something he had invented after she had told him about the thing which haunted Written Stone Lane. If she found out he had made all this ghost stuff up to stay on her good side, to seem sympathetic or get closer to her, she'd never speak to him again. The alternative possibility, that he was crazy and actually believed what was really a load of rubbish, was sadder but would probably produce the same result. Either way it went, Tracey was on her guard and watchful.

She got him to show her the painting which he had been scared of, half-expecting it to be some old black and white photograph of creepy Victorian children or something, but it turned out to be a portrait of a woman in a yellow dress with a fluffy lapdog. It wasn't frightening, though the woman's gaze was disarmingly direct, but Preston was obviously still terrified of it, and stood well back, fists balled, eyes locked onto the subject of the painting as if she was about to climb out of the frame.

"You all right?" she asked.

"Yeah," he said.

A lie if ever she heard one.

Not good, thought Tracey. *Maybe my boyfriend is a bit . . . unstable.*

And that, she reminded herself, marvelling at the way her brain had conjured the term 'boyfriend,' was coming from someone who saw spectral ape men in her kitchen and crows with eyes for mouths which smelled of Hai Karate. She was going to have to be a little careful around Preston Oldcorn, at least until she was more sure of him and his stories.

But a partial confirmation of what he had told her came almost immediately.

"It looked like this," said Preston, showing her a gloomy looking black and white photograph in a book. "This is Fishergate from Glovers Court. See how much narrower it is. Not a real road at all."

Tracey leaned in to read the date.

"1913," she said.

"Yeah, but this office with the wires coming from the roof – the telegraphic exchange – wasn't there then and that was built in the 1880s, so what I saw was earlier."

"OK. So, we're looking for a nineteenth century killing on Pleasant Street," she said, "involving a man called Bell and another called Alderson. That ought to narrow it down. And we can look up the Wellington where the quarrel started. How old is that and how long has it been a pub?"

That last one was easy because it turned out that the building concerned had been constructed specifically as an inn and, more conveniently still, had been known as the Wellington since it opened its doors.

"You think this is that really awful ghost you mentioned?" she asked, feeling a tremor of fearful exhilaration. "The Leech?"

Preston frowned.

"Might be," he said. "I think it's connected but I'm not sure how."

She considered this, taking in the brooding dread in his eyes.

"How do you know about this Leech thing?" she tried.

"Just . . . something I heard," he said, avoiding her gaze.

Another half-truth at best, she thought.

"But this was a historical event," she said musingly. "A quarrel over a penny that escalated. The pub opened, when?"

"1838," said Preston, consulting his notes.

"Tell you what," she replied. "I have an idea. Why don't you stay here and see what you can find and I'll be back in an hour."

"By myself?" he said, wide-eyed again.

"You'll be fine, Preston," said Tracey calmly.

"This is an old building," said Preston. "There could be ghosts anywhere here."

Even in the context of their search it was such an odd remark that for a moment she just looked at him. He looked stricken, young and fragile. He wasn't faking to make her feel better. He really believed what he had just said, and that might just be worse than him lying.

"I won't be long," she said. "Forty minutes max. All right? I'll meet you in the foyer downstairs."

He nodded, but looked miserable.

Again, she thought, *not good.*

She pointed him toward the reference desk and left him. She headed briskly back toward Sweetens but took a right on Lune Street, down past Mears, the toy shop with the model trains her dad had loved to show her when she was small, to Fleet Street. Finding the place she wanted she studied the shop window, checked her purse to see what she could afford, and went inside.

* * *

Preston was waiting for her outside the library, and though he seemed to be skulking in a corner, he was positively cheerful.

"I found it!" he said, offering her a sheet of paper covered in scribbled notes, and pleased as Punch.

"Gist?" she replied.

"New Year's Day, 1839," he said, consulting the paper, "not long after the Wellington had been built. Two neighbours, both joiners, got into a quarrel in the pub which turned violent at home. Bell killed Alderson on Pleasant Street, but that road was demolished as part of sixties slum clearance between Frenchwood and Oxford Street."

Tracey was impressed, though she immediately saw why Preston seemed so much more content.

"So, we can't actually go there," she said. "But that's OK. The sequence you described began in the pub, and that's still there."

Preston's composure evaporated.

"You want to go to the Wellington?" he exclaimed. "How would we even get in without an adult?"

Tracey rolled her eyes.

"We'll think of something," she said.

And she did. When they reached the pub, having made their cautious way down Glovers Court, Preston looking ready to bolt like a spooked horse at any minute, Tracey pushed on the door and, as it swung inside, turned quickly to him. "Pretend you belong there. Like, maybe we're with our parents or something. And if anyone asks, just say we're looking for the toilets."

"Not exactly a Blofeld-worthy master plan, is it?" said Preston with a wan smile.

"Who's Blofeld?"

"James Bond's nemesis."

"The one he always escapes from and beats?" she clarified.

"Think I'll stick to my own plans, thanks very much."

"Fine," said Preston. "The Great Toilet Quest it is."

They went inside.

It was warm and close. Tracey wrinkled her nose at the smell of stale beer then drew herself up a little and looked around imperiously. She didn't know much about pubs. There was one her family went to occasionally near Chipping that served food, but this looked more about serious drinking.

"You lost, love?"

It was a blonde woman in slacks and a chunky sweater with a heavy necklace of glass beads. She had a white cloth in her hands and was moving around in a business-like fashion. Barmaid then. Or landlady.

"Hiya," she said. "I was wondering if we could ask you a couple of questions."

She felt Preston bristle and shoot her a hard, inquisitorial stare. This was not the Great Toilet Quest.

"Oh yes?" said the woman, reserving judgment. "About what?"

"Ghosts," said Tracey flatly. "Strange noises at night or weird events or . . ."

"Oh, you want my daughter," said the woman, as if nothing could be more normal. "I'll see if she's in the back. School paper, is it? Club newsletter or something?"

"Something like that," said Tracey. Preston stared.

The woman went behind the bar and pushed through a door roaring, "Gillian!"

Preston pushed deeper into the pub, amazed at how much of the rabbit warren of little rooms seemed to have survived largely unchanged. Tracey caught his eye.

"Look familiar?" she asked.

"Almost identical," he said. "The furnishings are different, the wall paper. But the layout is pretty much the same as it was. The room we want is through there. Same fireplace. Even some of the same pictures."

His eyes seemed to stray to the corner beside the hearth.

"That where it happened?" she asked.

He nodded.

"Might have been the same table," he said.

"Hello?"

The speaker was about their age, slim and blonde like her mother. She had a wide, flat face with a downturned mouth which moved cow-like from side to side as she chewed her gum.

"Hiya," said Tracey, not missing a beat. "Gillian, right? We wanted to hear about the ghost."

The girl's mother hovered for a second.

"I think it's all rubbish," she said, scowling at her daughter. "Old wives' tales and kid stuff. I've never seen owt."

"Don't like the cellar though do you mam?" said the girl with an arch look.

"That's just common sense, isn't it?" said the landlady. "Dark and cold, and you could come a right cropper on them stairs."

"That's not why you don't like though, is it?" said Gillian, pausing in her gum-chewing to send her a still and steely glare.

"Stuff and nonsense," said the woman, though she had hesitated for a fraction of a second before speaking, and in that narrowest of windows a shadow had passed over her face. It was as if she knew something her mind could not accept, something that scared her. "Talk to your friends, but make it snappy. Place'll be packed in a half hour."

As the woman left, Tracey took the initiative and motioned them into the snug, selecting the very table Preston had indicated. There was a portrait of Queen Victoria on the wall, looking dour, and a painting of what Preston took to be the Battle of Waterloo. The girl sat with them but immediately went into a kind of retreat, leaning back and chewing her gum with unnecessary ferocity.

"She thinks ghosts are bad for business," Gillian confided, referencing her mother's vanishing rear end. "There've always been stories about the pub: noises, spilled drinks, cold spots. But I'm the only one who's seen 'im."

"Seen who?" Tracey asked. Gillian was looking proud of herself.

"The old fella," she said, as if it were obvious. "Bloke in a long black coat. Seen him walking around the pub and up on the landing. Big as life. Mam says it were probably just a drunk or a dosser, wandered in. First time, I thought that were exactly right. Thought they'd opened early and let someone in off the street. But when I asked mam about him, she said the doors were still locked. We searched upstairs and down but there was no one there." She had leant in and held Tracey's eyes as she spoke, letting the words hang between them in all their delicious mystery, then she leaned back again with a self-satisfied look, as if she had just played a winning hand of cards. "Seen 'im a few times. Once, right here. We were told there were a murder, yonks back. 'appen it's him, the dead bloke, haunting us."

"He wasn't killed here," said Preston absently. Tracey could see his mind working frantically. Gillian grew still again and gave him an odd look.

"How'd you know that?" she asked.

"You've seen him several times?" said Preston, ignoring her question as some of his anxiety fell away and a light of excited earnestness flared in his eyes.

"Yep," she said, resuming her chewing. "Four or five times. No rhyme or reason to when or whereabouts. Like I said, sometimes here, sometimes in't main bar, sometimes on't stairs. Like he's wandering, looking for someone maybe."

"Or something," said Tracey, putting her hand in her pocket.

"Older bloke, you said?" said Preston. "Not small and slim, maybe thirties with old-fashioned side burns?"

Gillian shook her head.

"Nah, he were older than that. No beard or nothing. Big fella though. That were't first thing I noticed. From behind, when he were on't stairs he could barely go up without brushing his shoulders. He were that wide across his back. Not fat, mind. *Broad.*"

Preston's mouth fell open and the fire in his eyes kindled still further.

"It's not Alderson," he gasped. "The bloke who was killed.

244

The ghost is Bell, the murderer!"

Tracey felt a prickle of fear.

"Not the victim?" said Gillian. "Why would the killer be the ghost?"

"Because this is where it started," said Preston, snatching the page of notes he had made. "He was arrested and tried in Lancaster, but he wasn't convicted of murder because Alderson had started the scuffle in Pleasant Street and there were no good witnesses for how the fatal blow occurred." He was almost quoting, but in a rapid, almost frenzied manner as he joined the dots he could see in his head. "He was convicted of aggravated manslaughter and sentenced to transportation for life."

"Transportation?" said Gillian. "What's that?"

"Deportation," said Tracey.

"To Australia," said Preston, checking his notes again. "William Bell, one of 230 convicts transported on the Woodbridge, 10 October, 1839. Arrived in New South Wales, Feb 26, 1840. There's no record of what happened to him but he was a convict, bound for a life of hard labour. He would never have made it back to England, never seen his family again. All because of what happened at this table."

It was Gillian's turn to stare, first at Preston, then at the table.

"Here?" she said, her voice low and faltering.

"Here," said Preston with certainty.

Gillian raised her hands from the table top with a look of revulsion and then held them there, elbows tight to her body like a chicken.

"We need to move," said Gillian. Tracey thought she meant move from this table, but her horror was deeper than that. "I have to tell mam. I can't live here with a murderer wandering around the place. A *dead* murderer!"

"I may have a solution," said Tracey, fishing in her pocket. She laid a single copper coin on the table. It was large and dulled by time, its relief lines softened by use, and in parts stained almost black. Tracey had bought it for fifty pence at the dusty little shop on Fleet Street, picking it out quickly, decisively, while the other customers – all older men – scrutinised stamps and other collectables in reverent silence. She hoped this would work. She'd have got change for four pints of milk from fifty pence.

"What do you want me to do with that?" said Gillian.

"Leave it for the ghost," said Tracey. Preston looked doubtful so she explained, "you said the fight began over a penny which Alderson owed Bell, right? So, if the penny is here, maybe the fight doesn't happen. This penny is from 1827," she said, pushing it across the table top toward him. "See? George the Fourth. Perfect."

Preston shook his head.

"But I wasn't just seeing the past," he said. "I was seeing ghosts repeating the past. You can't avoid the fight. They are dead. They'll stay dead. We can't change the past from the present."

"But if this man Bell is still here," said Tracey, "as a ghost, I mean, he's looking for something, the something that changed his life. What did the trial records say about him?"

"That he was bad-tempered and disliked," said Preston.

"But you said he was convicted of manslaughter, not murder. No one saw the killing blow and Alderson initiated the fight in Pleasant Street. Bell sounds like an unpleasant and dangerous person, but he wasn't entirely responsible for Alderson's death." Tracey continued, pleased with herself and holding Preston's eyes, barely aware that Gillian was still there. "Bell spends the rest of his life smashing rocks or something in Australia, cut off from his family on the other side of the world, thinking back on the moment when his life came apart. It wasn't the moment of the stabbing itself, because he wasn't entirely responsible for that. It was the chain of events leading up to that second when Alderson rushed him, and that began here with the quarrel over the penny. So now the ghost comes back here, night after night, hunting for the one thing that might have made the difference in his life." She put the tip of her right forefinger squarely onto the big, pre-decimal coin and pushed it into the middle of the table. "We leave it for him, and maybe that releases him. He breaks the cycle and moves on. If he's the Leech . . ."

"The what?" said Gillian.

"Nothing," said Preston with ferocious intensity and a meaningful stare at Tracey. For whatever reason, he did not want them talking about that.

"You want to just leave the penny here for a ghost to collect?" he said.

"Some buggar'll nick it," said Gillian with dour certainty.

Preston and Tracey both looked at her.

"You're right," said Tracey.

"Unless they don't know it's there," said Preston. "You could stick it to the underside of the table."

"Will the ghost see it?" said Tracey.

"He might . . . sense it," said Preston, and there was something in his manner which Tracey thought was very slightly furtive, as if he wasn't comfortable with what he was saying. "Maybe the thing itself, being from his period, will be more visible to him. And, if you're right, he is actively looking for it."

"I could get mi dad to screw it to't table," said Gillian helpfully. "Drill it like: bolt it down."

"I still don't know if the ghost will see it," said Preston. "Or how he'll pick it up. Or . . ."

"I'm open to better ideas," said Tracey firmly, "and I see no harm in trying this one. I mean, if it doesn't work, what's the worst that can happen?"

CHAPTER
TWENTY TWO

Tracey's dad cracked the oven door, peered in and tutted. He was straightening up and wiping his hands absently on his floury apron as the kitchen door opened and his wife came in.

"Bloody useless, this oven," he remarked. "Doesn't heat evenly. How are you supposed to bake a proper loaf if you can't . . . ?"

He caught something in her face, that slightly strained smile that she put on when she was under pressure and didn't want to show it.

"Jim?" she said with false brightness. "Ken's here."

The smile expanded as if the corners of her mouth were being tugged by cables. She knew how much he disliked their landlord and employer dropping by unannounced. But he got something else from her wary eyes and it silenced him. She sort of slid sideways and Ken Shakeshaft sidled into the room, gave Tracey's dad a nod that was both uncharacteristically apologetic and shaken, and dropped heavily into one of the wheel-backed chairs at the kitchen table.

"All right, Ken?" said Jim. "What's up?"

"Summat wrong wi't herd," said the farmer.

"The cows?" said Jim. "Which ones?"

"Best I can tell, all of 'em."

And now Jim understood the man's demeanour. If there was a serious issue with the milk cows, the blow to the farm could be devastating.

"What's wrong with them?" asked Jim.

Shakeshaft shook his head slowly and shrugged, a slow and massive gesture which spoke of more than anxiety.

"Never see owt like it," he said at last. "I'll get 't vet in, but . . ."

Another glacial shrug.

"What is it? Not foot and mouth?" said Jim. "Tell me it's not that."

Shakeshaft buried his face in his hand for a moment, then blew out a long breath like a steam gasket. He got slowly to his feet.

"Better see for yourself," he said.

Jim shot his wife a look as Shakeshaft led the way out. She looked distraught, but in response to his glance she also shrugged and gestured vaguely: she didn't know. Outside they turned not toward the outer fields where the cattle stood, but toward the dairy. They picked their way across the damp, cowpat-spotted ground, and shouldered the metal gate open. It scraped and rang out under the corrugated roof. Jim was used to the smell of the animals and the sourness of old, spilled milk, but among those familiar aromas there was something else on the air. The scent was familiar but somehow worrying, dull but with an edge that was almost metallic. The cows in the stalls were unnaturally quiet and still and their great black eyes seemed wider than usual, as if afraid.

They moved to the loading area where they had set the written stone, but the churns were strewn around it, tipped over and rolled about the slick, wet floor.

"Not this again," muttered Tracey's dad.

"That, mate," said Shakeshaft, with a dark and mirthless grin, "is the least of our worries."

And that was when Jim realised that the dark pools around the stone were not mud and the effluent of the animals. It glistened as it set, but the colour was unmistakable. It was a deep crimson, and as Jim's eyes fought to make sense of what he was seeing, he traced the horrible streams, the spatters and rivers and little pools back to their origins in the unsettled churns. And now he knew what he was smelling and why the cows were so spooked.

"Jim!" exclaimed his wife in disbelief and horror. "It's the milk! The milk has turned to blood!"

* * *

"Are you still here?" said the Wellington's blond landlady. "You'll get us shut down!"

"We were just leaving," said Preston. He got to his feet and gave Tracey an expectant look. Their plans had made no further progress and he knew she was annoyed at him for not wrestling with the matter any longer. She was pouting comically, or as close as her thin lips would let her, and her eyes were bright with an electricity he knew could turn to lightning. He didn't care. He had spent too long in this place as it was. The ghosts did not wait for nightfall. Whatever drove their curious cycle through their final moments could restart at any moment. Preston wanted to go home. Or see Tracey home, all the way to Longridge and away from all this. He was tired of being afraid.

"Fine," said Tracey, standing up abruptly. "We'll go."

"Tell you what," said Gillian, the landlady's daughter. "How's this for a short-term solution?"

So saying, she snatched up the oversized penny with one hand and licked the fingers of the other. Then she plucked the irregular wad of chewing gum from her mouth. Though Tracey looked about to protest, Gillian stuck the gum to the back of the coin, reached under the table and pushed it into place.

"There," she said, pleased with herself. "The only person who will find that is him what's looking for it."

Tracey looked almost as dubious as Preston felt, but she shrugged and said "fine," again. Before she made for the door though, she stopped and turned back to the broad-faced girl who looked quite different now that she was wasn't chewing constantly.

"Thank you," she said. "I hope it helps."

"Just a bit of fun, eh?" said Gillian, grinning. "Check back in a week or two and I'll tell you what happens."

Preston hesitated.

"One sec," he said. "Bathroom."

"Ah," said Tracey. "The Great Toilet Quest lives."

"Through there to the back and on your right," said Gillian helpfully.

Avoiding Tracey's eyes, he made his way through to the gents, glad of a moment's solitude. He wondered dimly how he had come to be here with Tracey, about her tale of strange spectral beasts haunting her house in Longridge, and about Roarer's suggestion that it was in some way his fault that ghosts were being trapped instead of moving on. Whatever they did here wouldn't change that. These were old ghosts. They might know his name, but it was the new ones who had reason to curse him. He thought of the school caretaker and the old woman in church, pointing at him. And he thought of his grandmother, going in for more tests . . .

He washed his hands and left the bathroom, but all was not as it had been. Instead of being in the brightly lit pub hallway, he was outside in a cobbled stable yard at night. He was still in the Wellington, but this was a much older version of the inn, and as Preston gaped about him, eyes wide and heart thumping, he saw the figure of a large, broad-shouldered man emerge from the shadows of the arched coach entrance.

William Bell, knife in one hand, the forefinger of the other pointing squarely at Preston.

"You 'is bird, then?" said Gillian.

Tracey raised an eyebrow.

"I'm nobody's bird," she said.

"Does 'e know that?"

"We're just mates," said Tracey, patting her pockets absently.

"Oh," said Gillian with a knowing look. "Right."

"Right," said Tracey, shooting her a pointed look.

"Pardon me for living!" said Gillian. She half-turned as the door to the toilets crashed open. "'Ere he comes now. Is he alright?"

He didn't look it. Preston looked wild-eyed and frantic with terror. He lunged through the door into the bar but something seemed to hold him back. There was nothing to see, but it was as if some great force had hold of him and was dragging him backwards against all laws of physics. His shoes scrabbled on the tiled floor and his hands flailed for purchase on the door jamb. Tracey hesitated and then Preston cried out.

"The penny!"

It's got him! The ghost of William Bell . . .

"Is he muckin' about or what?" asked Gillian. She looked confused but also afraid.

"The coin!" yelled Tracey. "Get it."

Gillian flipped the table over with a crash and tore the penny from the chewing gum holding it in place.

"What in blazes is going on in there?" bellowed a voice from the bar. Gillian's mum. But Gillian didn't hesitate. She took two long strides and slapped the sticky coin into Tracey's hand just as Tracey – like a relay runner receiving the baton – made for Preston. Again she saw his face and flinched. It was a mask of horror.

* * *

There was nothing spectral about Bell's grip. He had hold of Preston's collar with one massive hand. The other was still clutching his knife, but the blade was pointing down from his fist and Preston hadn't been cut too badly. His shirt had been slashed through as Bell fought to hold him, and he had felt the hot sear of the knife scoring his flank till the blood ran, but he hadn't been stabbed. Not yet.

He could tell from her face that Tracey couldn't see the ghost, and that made it somehow worse, but just as Bell got him contained, thrusting him to the ground and pinning him down with a knee in his chest, he saw the flash of old copper in her hand. He reached out desperately as the long-dead convict reversed his grip on the knife handle and brought it up.

"Preston Oldcorn," Bell hissed through clenched teeth.

It all felt absolutely real and solid, a fight like one on the playground, all hurt and terror and madness and no other thought in his head. But he saw the coin and he reached for it.

She put it in his hand, and as he closed his fingers around it he thrust it into the knife man's snarling face. Still the blade drew back, ready to stab down, to end him.

"Your money!" Preston gasped. "The penny you lent to John Alderson!"

William Bell's crazed eyes seemed to flicker. The knife hand relaxed, tensed again to make the lethal plunging cut, then relaxed, for good this time. The man's eyes focused on the penny, rage turning to confusion and then to something else entirely which changed his face. Tears swam in his eyes and he took the coin with faltering fingers, sitting back against the wall and clutching it to his chest. He sat there in anguish, eyes squeezed tightly shut, as Preston wriggled free of his bulk, and backed clumsily away. To the big man the coin seemed more than the possibility of escape from the murderous cycle in which he was trapped. It was an alternative past which was almost as good as forgiveness.

"You see this?" he gasped to Tracey.

"Sort of," she replied, her face blank and pale. "And not till just now."

"What is going on here?" bellowed the landlady from the bar. "You kids need to move on out right this minute!"

"I see 'im," said Gillian, staring, aghast. "I seen 'im before."

"It's ending," said Preston. "Look."

Because there was a door where that had been only a wall, a heavy thing of rough hewn planks with large, age-blackened nails.

"That's for you," said Preston to the phantom which had been William Bell.

The ghost looked unsure, and the fury in his face was not

entirely gone, even as he got awkwardly to his feet and reached for the latch.

"Preston Oldcorn," he growled, leaning into Preston's face, his lips drawn back from his teeth like a dog. "You have much to answer for. And answer for it you will, lest you make all well again. And not just you. All those who hold you dear will learn to curse your name for ever for what you've done. Fix it."

"I don't know how," Preston managed.

"You do," said the ghost. "Or leastways, you will."

And then he dragged the door open and stepped through it.

* * *

"It's all rubbish," said Tracey's dad. "We heard all that folktale nonsense when we moved in. I won't countenance it."

Mr. and Mrs. Blenkinsop were standing on the lane outside their house with one of the strangely corrupted metal milk churns in front of them. He had insisted on bringing it out "into't light" as if that would have made a difference to what they found inside. It hadn't, of course, but he was not budging on any kind of supernatural explanation. He wouldn't countenance it.

His wife was used to quailing before him when he used that phrase. Not countenancing something was what Jim did when he had reached the non-negotiable stage. It was what the trade union bosses said before they walked out, and in Jim's mouth it was as close as he came to the kind of statements of faith made by martyrs before the pyre was set alight. She was used to it, and it was how their biggest quarrels ended.

Not today.

"Now you listen to me, Jim Blenkinsop," she said, taking a step toward him and meeting his eyes. "That stone has been nothing but trouble since it was moved. You might not like it, might not have room in your head for it, but something about it is wrong and in your gut you know it. Strange noises in the night. Visions and I don't know what. Tracey! It's affecting our daughter, Jim! You know it is. She's scared *all the time*. Now this with the milk."

"It's something wrong with the cattle . . ." he began, maintaining his principled defiance.

"No, Jim, it's not. And you know what? I don't even care about the damn milk."

"Well some of us have to! Some of us have to keep our heads screwed on and focus on the real stuff, the practical stuff which puts bread on our table . . ."

She didn't let him finish. With a cry of fury the like of which he had never heard from her, Vivien Blenkinsop kicked the milk churn over. It landed with a clang and rolled, scarlet fluid belching from its neck. It gushed into rivulets, pooled in the potholes of Written Stone Lane so that the place looked like a slaughter house.

Jim Blenkinsop stared, speechless and aghast. They stood for a moment, and a crow broke the silence with a harsh caw. The blood would draw them, the crows.

"It just makes no sense!" he said, his voice low now, confused, even sad, as if the strange events had upset his version of the world, kicking the certainty out from under him, leaving him swinging and powerless.

"That's as maybe," said Vivien. "But we have to think of Tracey. I don't understand it either, but that doesn't mean it's not real. You love Tracey, don't you Jim?"

He nodded then, mute, his eyes suddenly bright with tears.

"Then let's put the stone back where it came from."

"What about Ken?" he whispered.

The farmer was as at least as stubborn as her husband.

"I'll deal with Ken," she said.

And she did. She went round to see him right away, was admitted by Pearl, his mousey wife who always seemed to be making jam in church-like silence, and told him they were moving the stone. She didn't request it or make the suggestion. She informed him they were doing it.

Ken Shakeshaft was taken aback by her manner, but he didn't push his luck, and Vivien thought he was relieved that someone else had made the decision for him. Perhaps he thought that for him to reverse course on the stone was some kind of weakness . . .

Men.

In the end he just nodded curtly.

"I'll get 't tractor," he said.

Then, and only then, did Vivien see the flicker of a look between the farmer and his silent wife in her immaculate apron.

"Anything odd happen lately?" she asked. "Apart from the milk kits, I mean?"

There was a loaded silence in which Pearl stared at her across the stove, then Ken said, "No, can't say that there 'as." They avoided her eyes, and the lie hung in the kitchen between them like spilled milk.

Or blood.

CHAPTER
TWENTY THREE

Gillian was well impressed, Tracey thought. Neither of them had seen much of anything when Preston had first come back from the bathroom, when the phantom had been fighting to subdue him. But as he pressed the coin into the spectre's hand, what Tracey had seen as little more than a shimmer in the air and a curiously localised sense of cold, as if from a badly sealed window in winter, had become a man, solid and real. The adults in the bar who had come running to see what all the noise was, still couldn't see it though, and the three teens had immediately and tacitly decided to waste no breath trying to explain what had happened. The tear in Preston's shirt and the gouge that ran from just below his ribs on his right side to his waist was real enough, however, and Gillian's mum insisted on cleaning and dressing it before they left.

"How on earth did you do that?" she demanded, as she dabbed at the wound with cotton wool soaked in Dettol.

"Caught it on a nail," said Preston.

"Where?" said Gillian's mum.

"It was sticking out of the wainscoting in the hall, wasn't it?" said Gillian with a significant look. "I saw it the other day."

"Yes, that's right," said Preston.

"I'll get my dad's pliers," said Gillian brightly. She vanished round the bar, then re-emerged implausibly quickly saying "done!"

"Let me see the nail," said her mother. "If it's rusty he might need a tetanus shot."

"No, it was fine," said Gillian hastily. "I threw it away."

"I think we should go," said Tracey.

"Happen you should," said the landlady who looked both skeptical and anxious.

"They're all right," said Gillian.

"I don't want your dad seeing them in 'ere," her mother replied. "The North End just lost 5-1 to Brighton and he's not best pleased. If Alex Bruce himself comes in tonight, he'll feel the back of my hand."

"I'll see them out," said Gillian quickly, ushering them into the porch with a fixed smile at her dubious mother.

Out on Glovers Court, the girl took a long breath and grinned.

"That was brill," she said.

"Thank you," said Preston. "Both of you. A second later and I might not have made it."

"You think he'll be gone now?" said Gillian. "No more ghost?"

Tracey couldn't say.

"I think he moved on," said Preston shrugging, "but who knows?"

"What did he mean when he said you had much to answer for?" said Gillian.

"You heard that?" Preston replied quickly. He looked surprised and abashed.

"Yeah," said Tracey. "What did he mean?"

Preston shrugged again, but Tracey felt sure that he was being evasive again, and though Gillian seemed to accept his response at face value, it didn't make her any happier.

"Well," Gillian said, "I wouldn't want anyone saying that to me, alive or dead. Watch yourself, Preston."

"I'll be fine," he said with a confidence he was clearly faking. "But yes, I'll be careful."

Gillian's eyes narrowed and fixed on Tracey.

"You see that he is," she said.

Tracey wanted to say that it was impossible to protect someone who wasn't straight with you about what the danger was, but she let it go. When Gillian had said her farewells, shaking them formally by the hand and pronouncing their visit to the Wellington "the most interesting thing that had happened to her all year," she went back inside, leaving them in the rapidly dimming light of the autumn afternoon.

"Now what?" said Preston. "Home?"

"One thing first," said Tracey.

* * *

Preston didn't want to go back to Booths, but he didn't think he could argue with Tracey. She had just saved his life after all. And besides, if there ever was a reliably safe and benign ghost, it was Mabel. As they walked up to the corner of Fishergate, Preston found himself glad of anything that would get his mind off William Bell, his knife, and his dire warnings. He also thought that Tracey was watching him out of the corner of her eye as if she suspected . . . something. A part of him wanted to tell her everything, about their past which she didn't remember, about his having died, but it was all too much. He swallowed hard as they ducked into the corner door of Booths and moved hurriedly up the stairs.

"Oy!" called a woman's voice as they reached the first floor. "Where do you think you're going? We're closing."

It was the hard-faced waitress who had served them when they had been in a week ago.

"Bathroom," said Tracey. "Emergency."

"Both of you?" said the waitress, hands on hips, eyes fixed and flinty.

"Only be a minute," said Preston. "Promise."

There was a tinkle of broken china from the kitchen and the waitress's ferocious gaze swivelled like the beam of a baleful lighthouse. She was already moving toward the noise when she replied,

"See that you're quick. I'm locking up in five minutes and believe me when I say you don't want to be stuck in here after dark."

It was an unexpected remark, and so not the threat he had expected, that for a moment Preston stood there with his mouth open.

"Come on," Tracey muttered, tugging at his elbow.

She half-pulled him up the back stairs, but faltered at the top, moving clear of the steps with sudden wariness, glancing about her.

"Where to?" she asked.

It was darker up here than it had been when Preston had come before, and though he felt sure they were in no danger from Mabel, the place – thick with shadow and the desolation of abandonment – felt ominous.

"Through there," he said, nodding to the door which was very slightly ajar. Tracey considered the door, but did not open it, and stepped fractionally out of the way. He pushed it open, and it produced a geriatric creak, rising in pitch and unnaturally loud in the silence. The bustle and clatter of the café below was quite lost to them. Trying to look braver than he felt, Preston stepped inside.

The empty café was slashed by pale greyness from the narrow windows, but that merely cut swatches into the deep shade of the room. The tables with their white cloths were gone, and the blackness around him was featureless. There was no sign of Mabel.

Preston inched into the room feeling Tracey so close behind him that they were almost touching and he could hear her rapid, shallow breathing.

"Mabel?" he tried.

No response. Preston waited, then turned, shrugging, to Tracey.

The ghost of the waitress was immediately behind them. Her face was impassive and she stood quite still. The cake knife was in her right hand, its blade flat against her apron just below her hip.

Tracey gave a tiny, fractured scream and stepped back.

"Preston Oldcorn," said Mabel. It was a thin, reedy voice, vague as if speaking words only half-remembered, and it curled out of the darkness like smoke. "Didn't think you'd be back."

"I told you I would," said Preston, managing a hint of defiance. "I told you I'd return when it was safe."

"Safe?" the ghost repeated. She looked solid, but washed out, all the colour gone from her so that in the gloom she was mere shades of grey.

"You said you couldn't go out because there were other ghosts," said Tracey, apparently forcing herself to speak. "Dangerous ghosts." She shot Preston a look as if looking for help.

"A bad lot," you called them, he agreed. "On Glovers Court. Killers. Monsters. William Bell and . . ."

Mabel looked stricken. Her eyes widened and she seemed to contract in on herself as if lanced with sudden pain.

"It's OK!" Tracey said. "They're gone now."

Mabel shook her head.

"They are!" said Preston.

"Just now," said Tracey. "Swear to God. They are gone."

Mabel considered her with slow confusion as if her mind had been caught in some disorienting current which turned her around and around. Her eyes faltered, closed for a moment and then opened again, a new thought dawning, one which cleared her countenance and brought a cautious smile to her face.

"Gone?" she said.

"Gone," said Tracey.

"You can go now," said Preston.

"Leave the café?" said Mabel, as if she hardly dared to believe it. "But I am a loyal Booths employee. A waitress . . ."

"Not just a waitress though," said Tracey with a conviction that surprised Preston. "You are your own person. Not just what you are paid to do."

"Someone has to cut the cake," said Mabel. "Pour the teas, polish the cutlery, take the table cloths for laundering . . ."

"There are other waitresses," said Tracey. "You've done your part. It's time."

"Time?" said the waitress uncertainly.

The word hit Preston like inspiration.

"Time to retire," he said. "All those years of service got you noticed, Mabel. Mr. Booth himself said so. You can go."

He thought she might respond to the name of the company's owner, but it was her own name that stirred her.

"Mabel," she said musingly, then again, the smile returning. "Mabel."

Her hands moved and Preston's eyes flashed to the cake knife, but she handed it to him, reversing the handle and blade in her grip as she did so. He took it gingerly and her hands went behind her back. It was a moment before he realised what she was doing. Her apron flapped loose about her and she lifted it over her head, then turned and hung it on a tiny hook on the wall which Preston hadn't noticed until that very moment. She sighed as she did so and it was as if a great weight had been lifted from her shoulders.

She smiled again, wider than ever, and a door appeared in the wall, plain and flush to its surroundings: it was a servants' door, a door designed to blend in, to go unnoticed until it was needed, like the people who used it. Mabel stepped toward it, but as she put her hand on it, she half-turned back to them.

"Thank you," she said.

"The bad ghosts," said Preston unable to contain the impulse. "Bell and Alderson. Were they the Leech? I thought it was gone but then thought maybe it had fastened onto some other spirit. Was it them?"

He knew his manner was intense, desperate, and he hated to ask the question in front of Tracey. She was clever. She would surely realise that he was hiding something from her.

Mabel shook her head sadly.

"They were touched by it," she said. "By the thing you call the Leech. Touched by it, infected by what it knew and wanted, by its hatred for you. But the thing itself is somewhere else. I don't think it's a ghost."

Tracey was staring at him, confused and wary, but she didn't let this last remark go unchallenged.

"If it's not a ghost, then what?" she gasped.

"You are Tracey," said Mabel. Tracey gasped but she said nothing, merely nodding slowly once. "I'm sorry. It knows you too. It's watching, growing ever more powerful. I do not know how you can stop it, but if you cannot, if it reaches its full power . . ." Her voice trailed off and she shook her head.

"What?" stammered Tracey. "Can it kill me? Is that what it's going to do?"

"It can kill and it will," said Mabel with a sad and pitying look. "But not just you. I wish for your sake it would just be you."

And then she was through the door and gone.

* * *

Tracey's mum stood in the farm yard chewing her lower lip as she watched her husband, under Ken Shakeshaft's gruff direction, looping the chains around the stone and, pronouncing them secure, attaching them to the tow bar on the back of the tractor. Ken turned the tractor's engine over and set the thing into throbbing, roaring life, then twisted in the seat to monitor what happened as he rolled the rumbling vehicle forward: just a yard at first, taking up the slack of the chain.

"Ready?" Ken shouted back, juddering in the metal seat which had been polished bright by years of rough use.

Jim gave a thumbs up, then studied the chain where it met

the stone. They had set it on old wooden railway sleepers which were still lashed to it with cable. That would help it slide on the rough ground, a precaution designed more to protect the farmyard than the stone. The tractor rocked another foot and a half forward and stopped. The chains were taut now, tight enough to sing under the strain. Ken Shakeshaft frowned, looked backwards, and gave the engine a bit more thrust, so that its dull growl went up a notch and the exhaust pipe belched back smoke. The massive rear wheels did not move. He pushed it further still, and the nearside tire – huge and ridged – spun suddenly in place, smoking and filling the air with the acrid tang of burned rubber. The tractor lurched and slid sideways a foot so that Vivien stepped quickly back, but the stone did not move forward.

Jim waved both arms and shook his head.

"Stop!" he roared over the racket of the overworked motor. "It's not moving."

Ken shut the engine down, sliding out of the seat and down to the ground, his face twisted in bafflement and irritation.

"Makes no sense," he muttered. "Same bloody tractor moved it here in't first place. Now it's ten times heavier?"

Jim gave his wife a look, and though he said nothing, Ken spotted it.

"What?" he demanded. "Don't tell me you believe all that rubbish about not moving the stone so the boggart don't get us."

"Course not," said Jim, looking shifty. "But there's no denying some strange stuff has been going on round here."

"If this were about 't legend, it would a been 't other way round," said Ken with an arch grin. "Last time they said it took nine horses to move the stone in't first place but only one to pull it back when't farmer had 'ad enough."

"You knew about that?" said Vivien. "All this time, you knew?"

Ken met her eyes and shrugged.

"Old wives' tales," he said.

"Right," she shot back at him, "well, speaking as an old wife, I'm telling you to get on that tractor and shift it back where it belongs."

* * *

Tracey was trying not to think about what Mabel had said, even as the bus took her back toward Longridge and the house she had come to dread, but her mind was full of dreadful possibilities. This Leech thing that Preston was so afraid of knew who he was. Who she was too. How was that possible? She wanted to ask him more, but he was sullen and silent. There seemed a great gulf between them, an unbridgeable chasm which she filled with chatter so unlike herself that she began to wish the journey was over.

They were travelling on the smoky upper deck of the bus that went through Ribbleton and would drop Preston off at the top of Moorfield Drive. He had been quiet since Booths, thoughtful and anxious, frightened even. Tracey had tried to be upbeat for both of them, celebrating what they had achieved today on Glovers Court and the ghosts they had set free, Mabel in particular, but Preston still seemed preoccupied, his mood increasingly dark.

"You said two people died near your house?" Preston said without preamble.

"Yes. Agnes Tattershawl and then Jed . . ."

"When?" he demanded. "The first one."

"The night we met. Heart attack, apparently. She was on the heavy side. Over-exerted herself and . . ."

Her voice trailed off. Preston didn't seem to be listening. He had turned in on himself and looked somber.

"What?" she pressed.

He just shook his head. Nothing.

"Why can't you be glad for what we've done today?" she asked at last as the bus passed the sombre walls and turrets of the prison and rumbled along Ribbleton Lane. "Mabel. Even the Wellington ghost! We set them free."

"Because we have more to do tomorrow and I don't know how to do it," said Preston.

"Cross that bridge when we come to it," said Tracey, quoting her mum with forced brightness.

"Did you not hear what she said?" Preston returned, annoyed by the platitude. "You are in danger. Your family too. We've spent all day chasing ghosts but the Leech is something entirely different and I don't know what to do about it. It might not even be connected to the ghosts."

"It is," said Tracey. "It must be. It's too much of a coincidence otherwise."

"And the thing that is watching you? What's that?"

"It's about the stone," said Tracey. "I'll get my dad to move it back," said Tracey. She could hear the shrillness in her voice, the failed attempt to sound like she didn't care.

"Too late," said Preston in a low, defeated voice. "Whatever was in there is out. You can't re-seal it just by replacing the stone."

"You don't know that," she said, getting annoyed now.

"I do!" he shot back, matching her anger, so that an old woman three seats ahead of them half-turned to look at them. "Don't ask me how, but I do."

"Don't ask you," she said, unable to keep the bitterness out of her voice. "What aren't you telling me, Preston?"

He held her eyes only for a moment, then looked away.

"Nothing," he said, adding, as if the distinction was important, "nothing that matters."

"You think that this Leech you are so worried about is connected to whatever is going on at my house?" she said.

The question seemed to surprise him, widening his eyes as realisation dawned. He *did* think exactly that now, but it had been her question which had put the idea in his head.

"How?" he said.

"I don't know."

"Then don't think about it," he said, clearly pushing the idea away because he didn't know what to do about it. "The Leech was a ghost, or was connected to a ghost, a boy who died a long time ago. But he's passed over now. What you have been experiencing is something . . . different."

"Then what do we do about it?" she replied, eyes wide, willing them not to leak the tears she felt building. "You're the expert, but it's my house. I'm the one who has to live with it. How do we stop it?"

Preston stared at her, then half-closed his eyes and shook his head. His shoulders twitched in a one-sided shrug and he glanced down, his face both apologetic and defeated. He looked as close to tears as she was, and taking pity on him she leaned into him, her temple against his ear, her cheek against the side of his neck. He smelled faintly of rain and a hint of soap. In spite of everything, that made her smile.

As the bus crossed Blackpool Road she felt his tension building. He said nothing, but the stillness of him, the heat of his motionless hand against hers, told her he was feeling the same heightened awareness of her as she was of him. As they neared the top of Cromwell Road he reached across her and pushed the bell ribbon above the window, but instead of pulling away he lingered there for just a second longer than he needed to and she knew what was in his mind. She turned her face up to his. Their eyes met briefly, then closed.

He kissed her once, pulling back and away as he felt the bus slow for his stop. She caught a glimpse of his blushing face as he turned into the stairs and shot her an embarrassed half-smile as he vanished into the lower deck. She heard the squeal of the brakes, felt the inertia rock her forward, caught the hiss of the pneumatic doors, and turned in her seat to look back and down as he got off and looked wistfully up.

Only then as the bus pulled forward and on, past Mary Magdalene's and up the hill to Gamull Lane, did she put her fingers to her lips, not with the pleasure she had imagined when she had speculated on what that moment would be like, but with confusion. Confusion and something else, something a little like dread. Even horror.

Because Preston Oldcorn's lips were as cold as his hands, and though she did not know why she thought so, she was sure it was an unnatural cold. She had kissed him, and it had been like stooping over the face in a coffin, like kissing the lips of a corpse.

CHAPTER
TWENTY FOUR

After Mass on Sunday, Nora MacIntyre waited for Preston to finish clearing the altar and went into the sacristy just as he was hanging his cassock on the row of wall hooks. He looked gloomy, preoccupied, and there were dark circles under his eyes. She bustled for a moment, caught in two minds, and when she started fussing with the box of long, waxed tapers, showily seeing how many were left before replenishing them, her hands were unsteady. He was almost out of the door when she turned impulsively and said, "Preston? Do you have a minute?"

The boy stiffened, then shrugged with a kind of forced nonchalance. He looked wary.

"Sure," he said. "What's up?"

She responded in kind, nodding at a stack of hymn books

then reaching behind her back and lacing her fingers together so he wouldn't see the way they trembled.

"Give us a hand with those, will you?" she said.

"Where do you want them?" said the boy, stooping slightly and straightening his arms so that he could get his fingers underneath the stack and pin it in place between his elbows.

"The choir loft," she said, turning away, but not before she saw the flicker of surprise in his face. Surprise, and something else, she thought, that cautious look, like a rabbit sensing the snare or the dog. She led the way out of the sacristy and down the side aisle of the empty church without looking back except to prop the door for him. Then she went on ahead, not wanting to catch his eye, still unsure exactly what she was going to say and how she would say it. They filed past the painted carvings marking the stations of the cross – Jesus is condemned to death, Jesus takes up his cross, Jesus falls the first time, Jesus meets his afflicted mother – and it was like they were on a journey, long, dark and full of peril.

They passed the railed baptismal font and walked down to the foyer. Down by the great front doors the church was always dark, and the tight staircase up to the balcony always a little unnerving. It was worse today. She gripped the rail and hauled herself up the high steps, pivoting as the square sided staircase turned back on itself and led her to the loft. This too felt precarious because the floor sloped down toward the balcony rail and the great barnlike emptiness of the church. From here the altar looked miles away, a stage model in a box, the lights out and the great brass candlesticks remote and unfamiliar. She moved carefully down to the front row of pews and sat staring straight ahead to where the massive wooden crucifix hung dark and silent over the altar. Behind her, Preston said, "Just leave 'em here?"

She pivoted then and nodded, but added,

"Come sit down for a minute, Preston."

Again she sensed his hesitation, even in the gloom, the tall stained-glass window above him making him backlit so his face was impossible to read. He might just make a run for it, she thought, and then what would she do?

But he didn't. He came, albeit haltingly, and perched on the edge of the bench about a foot to her left. A silence fell between them, a silence made wider and deeper by their sitting in the huge, dim emptiness of Blessed Sacrament, and for a moment she closed her eyes. For a long moment he did not speak and at last, still with her eyes shut, she said,

"Tell me about the ghosts you see, Preston."

He did not scoff, protest that he didn't know what she was talking about, or storm off in a blustering swirl of denial but she felt him stiffen in his seat.

"What do you want to know?" he said at last.

She relaxed a little then. It was out in the open, admitted, accepted, a truth between them that let her turn to face him.

"I see them too," she said. "Not like you though. For me it's mostly glimpses, impressions. A scent or a familiar sensation when it's someone I knew. But it's not like that for you, is it?

You see them like they are really here. Solid. Present. Inseparable from ordinary, living people."

He gave her a wide-eyed look and she thought he was going to express amazement at her gift, but he said,

"How did you know?"

"Mrs. Eccles" she said. "At communion."

"You saw her too?"

"Kind of."

"I thought maybe Roarer . . ." he began, but caught himself when he saw her face. Nora had gasped, and for a moment speech was completely beyond her.

Roarer was her dead brother. Long dead. But no one called him that. His name had been Barry.

"Where did you hear that name?" she managed at last.

His mouth opened and closed and he looked away again, so she grabbed his wrist and spoke his name, urgent, demanding.

"He told me," the boy admitted. "Your brother. He told me."

The tears she had managed to hold back came then, brimming from her eyes and running silently down her face.

"So he is a ghost," she said. "I thought so."

"He was," said the boy. "He's passed on now."

"Passed on?" she echoed, hardly daring to trust what he had said.

He nodded considerately.

"I think so," he said, "yes."

"So, there's another . . . ?" she began, but couldn't find the word. "Another place? Another state of being?"

"After being a ghost, you mean?" said Preston Oldcorn. "I'm not sure. I think so, but I don't know what it is."

Nora looked at him, but she was still thinking of Roarer.

"Why do some become ghosts and others . . . ?" she tried, but he shook his head, as if unwilling to get into it.

"I don't know," he said. "Sometimes, it just happens. I don't know why."

"But lately," Nora began, starting at the quick, hard look he gave her, but pressing on regardless, "it seems to be happening all the time. Like, it used to be once in a blue moon I'd get the feeling that someone was there, someone who wasn't, you know, alive, but now it's practically all the time. And I know them. There's Josie Eccles who you saw at communion. And Mary Warrington who passed a week ago. Old Mrs. Sanders. She was in the post office. Harold Carstairs. He died on Wednesday but I could have sworn I smelled his pipe yesterday as I was meeting with his daughter about the funeral flowers. It's almost like everyone who dies these days doesn't really leave."

She hung the phrase there between them but Preston said nothing, and his face looked wooden. Nora waited, holding his eyes, and eventually he shrugged microscopically and glanced down into the empty church. He looked guilty, she thought. He did not dispute what she had said and she had the powerful sensation that he felt responsible, though how that could be she had no idea. She changed tack.

"Your gift," she said, ignoring the bleakly amused sneer he couldn't suppress at her choice of word, "why do you have it?"

Another long silence. He looked paralysed, as if it was taking all his strength not to run or scream or weep. Nora reached over and put her hand, calloused from work, on top of his, leaning in so that she could whisper.

"What happened to you, Preston?"

He swallowed and his eyes filled with tears. She gripped his hand tighter but kept her gaze on him. He tipped his head forward as if in feverish prayer, half-closing his eyes so that the tears spilled out and dropped to the floor of the choir loft. He took a deep, shuddering breath that made his entire body tremble, and then in a cracked voice he said simply,

"I died."

She had almost known it was coming and she felt the truth of it, but her rational mind couldn't let the statement go unchallenged. She found herself shaking her head.

"You can't have," she said. "You're here now. You can't come back from the dead."

"He did," said Preston, nodding down the church to where the great crucifix hung over the altar. Nora gasped, genuinely shocked.

"Are you saying . . . ?" she began but he shook his head again.

"No," he said quickly. "It were nothing like that. I came back, but I don't think I was supposed to. I think I broke a rule or something and now no one can die properly. They are stuck like I was."

She stared at him in fascinated horror, and he seemed so young now, a child who had accidentally smashed a family treasure – a vase or figurine, perhaps – while tossing a ball around the house, and was now waiting for his parents to get home. She patted his hand awkwardly while she thought of something to say. In the end she settled for simplicity.

"When?" she asked.

It was the right question and he seemed to take comfort from being able to answer it easily.

"Two weeks ago. Just over. I felt like I was trapped there ages and at least two years passed in this world, the world where people live. But then I came back and that sort of reset the timeline. I woke up in the moment I had died and everything was back the way it had been. Or that's what I thought at first. Now it looks like I sort of cheated, coming back to life and all, I mean. I didn't mean to," he said, his voice plaintive, desperate again. "Honest! I had been trying to help people. But now it looks like I made it worse. Now no one can move on after they die and it's my fault."

She shushed him gently, leaning into him and humming softly as if he were the baby she never had. The idea filled her with a tender sadness and a profound sense of lost things, things missed or never had, things irredeemable, and the silence of the empty church seemed to swallow them up and hold them in its dim and austere embrace.

* * *

Tracey took a deep breath and knocked on the door of the terraced sandstone cottage, one of what were known locally as Club Row up on Higher Road. They were small houses, originally built for handloom weavers and financed cooperatively in the late eighteenth century. Tracey had looked them up before coming to visit.

Her classmate, Jeanie Martin, opened the door, her customary look of surly resentment turning briefly to surprise when she saw who had knocked. She was wearing heavy, National Health specs which made her look more gawky and awkward than usual, but didn't soften her fighting edge.

"What do you want?" she sneered, one hand on the edge of the door as if poised to slam it.

"I came to talk to you about the written stone," said Tracey in a tone she hoped sounded direct but humble.

The girl's eyes narrowed and for a moment the conversation could have gone either way. Jeanie was quick with her fists when put out. Tracey braced herself, but without another word, Jeanie stepped back, admitting her into the little cottage.

Tracey wasn't especially tall but she ducked reflexively under the stone lintel as she entered. Everything in the house seemed very slightly undersized, as if it had been built for smaller people which, she reminded herself, it probably had. She followed Jeanie through to a stone flagged kitchen where a woman Tracey recognised as the girl's mother was rinsing a basket of newly laid eggs in the sink. Jeanie took a seat at the table, but neither she nor her mother spoke and Tracey just stood there, feeling penned in.

"I came about the written stone," she said at last.

Mother and daughter exchanged sidelong glances but their faces – both set and unsmiling – gave nothing away.

"Better late than never," said Mrs. Martin, putting the last egg down and wiping her hands on a mottled grey tea towel. She was thin, like her daughter, and with the same intense eyes and strong, masculine jaw, the same pugnacious attitude which made her chin jut upwards, as if daring someone to try and slap it. "Our Jeanie told you to move it back where it were. Y'aven't done that though, 'ave ya?"

"Not yet," said Tracey. "My mum and dad tried yesterday but it got stuck or something."

"Right," said Mrs. Martin noncommittally, giving her a hard and baleful stare so that Tracey shifted from foot to foot before deciding to sit – albeit uninvited – opposite Jeanie. The noise of the chair on the stone floor sounded unnaturally loud in the little room, but Tracey took her seat and returned Jeanie's glare with interest.

"It was moved once before," Tracey said. "That's what the librarian said."

The woman's eyes narrowed fractionally at this, but she nodded.

"Aye," she agreed, "and not without mischief."

"Broken bottles and the milk turning to blood," said Tracey.

"And worse," said Jeanie, her gaze still fixed on Tracey across the table.

"But putting the stone back was easier than it had been to

move it in the first place," Tracey pressed on. "Only took one horse when it had taken nine before."

"So they say," said Mrs. Martin. She was still standing at the sink doing absolutely nothing, looking at Tracey, her hands folded together at her waist.

"But we tried that and it won't shift," Tracey said. "So the legend must be wrong."

"Is that right?" Jeanie echoed, affronted. "Expert now, are you?"

"I just think the inscription and the stories about it are maybe not as big a deal as you think," said Tracey. It wasn't really true, but she felt cornered, flustered and didn't know what to do.

"You don't know the 'alf of it," said Mrs. Martin straightening slightly as if the conversation was beneath her dignity. "You come in 'ere, bold as brass, talking about what the *big deal* is when your family – your family! – has disobeyed the one command this village has followed for a century and a half! I oughtn't to give ya house room."

Her face didn't change, but her voice got slower and deeper in ways promising some fierce outburst, but Tracey was too busy processing the numbers to be cautious.

"A century and a half?" she said. "The stone was laid in 1655."

"And moved once since," said Jeanie, "by another stupid, greedy farmer who thought he knew more than the rest of the village."

"We didn't move it!" Tracey protested.

"Ken Shakeshaft, then," said the girl's mother, as if the difference was insignificant.

"No!" said Tracey, her indignation mounting. "The stone moved the night Agnes Tattershawl died. I don't know how. Ken and my dad moved it into the dairy to use, but it weren't us who shifted it in't first place."

Mother and daughter fell silent at this, and another suspicious glance flashed between them, but Tracey took advantage of their being briefly off balance.

"So the stone was moved 150 years ago?"

"July of 1859," said Mrs. Martin grudgingly. "The week of the railway crash."

Tracey frowned and shook her head questioningly.

"Runaway quarry load of stone almost hit a passenger train," said Jeanie, as if everyone knew something so obvious. "One railway worker killed on the quarry train, and a boy thrown from the passenger train."

"What has that to do with the written stone?" asked Tracey. She hadn't meant to sound annoyed, but she was tired of being made to feel ignorant.

"Told you, didn't I?" said Mrs. Martin taking a step toward her. "Same week, wasn't it?"

"So?"

"*So?*" Jeanie echoed. "So what made the train crash?"

"How should I know?" Tracey shot back. "Sounds like coincidence to me."

"The farmer who moved the stone didn't think so," said

Jeanie's mother with grim satisfaction. "Not after what happened. Went to his grave believing it was his fault."

"How could it be?" Tracey pressed, though the woman's black certainty was starting to worry her.

"When he moved the stone he released the boggart, didn't he?" she said. "And the boggart got stronger the longer it were out. 'ad to learn, didn't it? To remember. And it played its tricks while it grew, till the farmer . . ."

"Scared and greedy for what he was losing," her daughter inserted.

"Put the stone back," Mrs. Martin continued, "but he didn't battle the boggart. Didn't fight it, which is the only way to truly bind it in the earth. He moved the stone back, but that only contained part of it."

"Part?" said Tracey, quieter now.

"Aye, that's reet," said the woman, taking another step and leaning over Tracey's face, her eyes burning. "Split it, he reckoned. Some part of it were trapped under't stone, but another part was loosed to the air. I 'eard it from mi gran direct. She said the boggart divided, and part of it attached to sommat else."

"Like what?" said Tracey, not wanting to hear the answer.

"Like a ghost," said the woman, her face inches from Tracey's. "The ghost of a boy killed in a railway accident. A boy who became a monster."

"Who was the boy?" Tracey whispered.

"His name," said Jeanie, "was Thomas Ezekiel Leech."

The Leech, thought Tracey, her scalp starting to crawl.

"And now the boggart is whole again," said Mrs. Martin. "Because you moved the stone."

Tracey shook her head, not so much in contradiction as revulsion.

"No?" said Mrs. Martin fiercely, spittle flying from her lips, her eyes quite mad. "Ask Agnes Tattershawl and Jed Atkinson. Or give it another few days and see for yourself."

Tracey looked up.

"Why?" she asked, her voice meek and dazed.

"The boggart hates that land and them what lives on it," said Jeanie. "It'll take you all. Count on it."

"Take us?" said Tracey. "What do you mean?"

"When Ralph Radcliffe first laid the boggart under 't stone it cost him," said Mrs. Martin with grim finality. "You look in't Ribchester parish records. His whole family fell to the boggart before he bested it. Between February 1654 and the laying of the stone, Ralph Radcliffe's family was ravaged by the boggart. The son of his brother Robert, the daughter of Edward Radcliffe, John Radcliffe's wife, William and Ralph himself. Five deaths. You think on that."

CHAPTER
TWENTY FIVE

Tracey didn't doubt what she had heard from the Martins, but the news that Ralph Radcliffe himself had died during the events which had led to the laying of the stone puzzled her. How could he have laid the stone in 1655 if he was already dead? Perhaps surviving members of the family had acted on his dying wishes? Still, it felt strange, and she wondered if there was a detail of the story she still hadn't grasped. Instead of going home, she made for St. Wilfrid's in Ribchester.

She reached the medieval church with its squat tower and low slung body, and stood outside, listening for sounds of a service going on inside. Hearing nothing, she entered through the side porch and stepped into the nave, feeling the silent seriousness of the place. She wandered through the timber vaulted interior, feeling the light which slanted through the stone tracery of its arched windows warming the skin of her arms, unsure where to go or what to do.

"Can I help you?"

The speaker was a middle-aged man with close-cropped hair, balding on top. He was wearing wire-rimmed glasses and a maroon woollen cardigan with leather elbow patches. He was smiling and his voice was low, reverential of the place, perhaps, but amiable.

"I'm not sure, to be honest," she answered honestly. "I wanted to consult the parish records."

"Ah," he said, his smile expanding. "A little family tree research?"

"Something like that," she answered, matching his smile and hoping that would mask the half-truth. "The Radcliffe family. Mid seventeenth century."

"Well, the original records are in storage for safe keeping," said the man, "but I believe we have some transcriptions. They are a bit patchy in parts where the originals are damaged or illegible, but if that would be of service . . . ?"

"That would be great, thank you," said Tracey.

"I'm the vicar here," he said, extending a soft-skinned hand for her to shake. "Harold Jenkins."

Tracey was momentarily taken aback, only now registering the white dog collar under his cardigan.

"Tracey Blenkinsop," she said.

"Not Radcliffe," said the vicar.

There was no judgment in his tone, so Tracey nodded.

"We live on the same land the Radcliffes did," she said. "I'm interested in learning more about them."

"Most commendable," said the vicar. He didn't sound local, but maybe that was just the accent of his profession. "It is always good to learn where we came from. By *we* I mean all of us," he clarified. "The community. We seem to spend so much time thinking of ourselves and our immediate families, don't you think? *My life. My children.* We think so little of the whole, of the needs of others. It doesn't seem healthy. But then perhaps I am very old-fashioned."

He was, she thought, but that didn't mean he was wrong.

"Here we are," he said, guiding her through a narrow door into what she thought was called a vestry. There, from an unassuming wooden cabinet he produced a stack of still less assuming three-ring binders in which were a sheaf of mimeographed pages, the ink purplish and uneven. "Not ideal," he said, "but perhaps enough to get you started. Now, mid seventeenth century, you said, yes?"

"That's right. Thank you."

"My pleasure," he replied, flipping pages and indicating with a sweep of his finger. "Here we are. Christenings on this side, marriages here, burials here. As you can see, there are lots of gaps, and the marriage records cease at 1635 for some reason. There are large blanks in all records from there until 1653, but perhaps you will find something of interest. I'll leave you to it for a little while, if you don't mind. Have to get ready for the evening service, for which you are, of course, welcome to stay. I find it quite soothing after I've been hard at work."

He left her with another smile and she got to work.

The records were, as he had suggested, patchy and indistinct. They did not include the ages of those who died, and many of the first names seemed to be recycled – Ralph, John and Robert predominated, with a scattering of Williams and Henrys – so it was difficult to figure out who was who. Many burials – presumably of the young – were listed only by who was their father, and women often referenced solely as "wife of . . ." which Tracey, even here and with terrible things on her mind, couldn't help but find irritating.

Even so, a pattern began to emerge, and even with the absence from the records the Radcliffe family – assuming they were all related – had clearly suffered a great deal of loss in both the 1620s and after, averaging one per year from what must have been a very small community. She wondered if the gap from 1635 to 1653 was itself significant, but decided there was no point thinking about that. And besides, there were two things more compelling and odd which immediately seized her attention. She copied down the relevant entries, and her transcription of the burials ran thus:

Raphe Radcliffe in Dillworth
    26th February 1653 (fo 201)
Son of Robte Radcliffe in Dillworth
    4th March 1653

A chyld of Edward Radcliffe in Dillworth
   25th January 1654
Raphe Radcliffe in Dillworth
   26th February 1654 (fo 202)
Son of Robte Radcliffe
   4th March 1654
William Rauckcliffe
   26th May 1655
Wife of John Racliffe de Greenmer Laine
   30th May 1655

So between 1653 and 1655, the date on the written stone, there were seven burials of Radcliffe family members, which was a lot, and much higher than there had been in previous years. Dilworth was the tiny section of present day Longridge where Written Stone Farm was, where Tracey lived. But the sheer number of deaths wasn't the strange part. The first strange thing confirmed what the Martins had said; Ralph Radcliffe, whose name was carved into the stone and who was credited as laying it in place, died in 1654, the year *before* the stone was carved, a week before the death of another nameless Radcliffe child. She was considering the second and altogether more peculiar detail when the vicar returned.

"How are you getting on?" he asked cheerily. "You seem to have, as the Bard would put it, a brow of much distraction."

"This," she said, indicating the page. "See? Ralph Radcliffe died 26th February 1653 and a son of Robert Radcliffe died 4th

March 1653. But then come down a year. Completely separate entry. Ralph Radcliffe died 26th February *1654* and a son of Robert Radcliffe died 4th March *1654*. Two identical entries exactly one year apart."

The vicar leaned in, his open face creasing into lines of bafflement.

"That is remarkable," he said. "Must be a mistake. But a strange one for sure." He looked up suddenly and his face cleared. "But the calendar changed," he said. "The old calendar had the new year beginning at the end of March on Lady Day, so a date in January or February might appear as 1653 when it actually fell in what we would call 1654. That system didn't alter until . . ."

"1750," said Tracey quickly. "The Calendar Act, I know. But that adjustment wouldn't have been made in the original records, would it? These are sequential, with another death in between them, and there's nothing to suggest the second set of entries was somehow squeezed in as a correction after 1750. And see here, 'the wyfe of Robte Radcliffe in Dillworth 24th March 1632.' If these others were duplicated to adjust the dating to the modern calendar then that should too, but there's only one listing."

"It is, I confess, most extraordinary," said the vicar. "I suppose it can't just be a coincidence? Different people sharing the same name?"

"Two of them buried on the same day exactly one year after as their namesakes died?" said Tracey. "No chance."

"No," the curate agreed. "As you say. It must be a transcription error. That is most vexing. After all, a man cannot die twice, can he? No one comes back from the dead. Not outside scripture, of course."

Tracey said nothing, but her mind was racing.

* * *

Preston's mum went to visit his grandma alone on Sunday afternoon.

"If she's up to seeing visitors, I'll call," she said.

But she didn't call, and when she returned home two hours later she looked gray and exhausted. When Preston asked how grandma was doing she tried to smile, but her face buckled under the strain and she said,

"She's taken a bit of a turn for the worse."

"What does that mean?"

"Well, just keep her in your prayers."

Preston gaped at her. It couldn't be. It was too fast.

"But we don't have a diagnosis for sure, do we?" he said, knowing he sounded desperate.

"I don't think we need one, love," she said. "Or that it would make much difference. I'm sorry," she added, a single tear spilling from each eye and rolling unchecked down her cheeks, "but I think you need to prepare yourself. I know you were close."

"Are close," Preston corrected without thinking.

"*Are* close," she admitted. "But you have to be realistic, Preston."

"I don't understand," he said, meaning it on every possible level.

"No, love. I know."

"There must be something we can do."

"There's really not," she answered. She took a long shuddering breath and she wiped her eyes. "We'll keep watching over her, and the doctor is very good. Very attentive. And perhaps you can visit her while she sleeps. Just don't expect her to be, you know, alert or conscious."

Preston shook his head as if trying to clear it.

"I don't understand," he said again.

"I know. She's my mum," said his mother simply, and the tears ran down her face again.

He thought about that as if realising it for the first time, that grandma was to his mum what his mother was to him. Why this seemed like a new idea, he couldn't say, but it made him reach around her and squeeze her shoulders. He had been making his mother comfort him when the depth of her grief was surely as great or greater than his.

"I'm sorry," he said.

She nodded and for a moment he thought words were beyond her, but then she added with a wan smile,

"It won't be long now."

Preston stared at the old wooden antelope figure on the mantel piece. It was vaguely African and very sixties. He had no idea why they had it, but it had always been there. Sitting here now, in the middle of this unfathomable conversation about his grandma dying, it was like he was seeing it for the first time; it seemed so irrelevant and bizarre that he wanted to hurl it across the room.

It won't be long now.

And then what?

A horrible possibility occurred to him. The dead were trapped. Had been since he had returned from the nine twenty-two no-place. No one could move on.

Including his grandma.

She would be stuck forever, lost and alone in an increasingly shrinking, maddening, half-life version of the town as she knew it. He would watch her gradually go mad with loneliness and despair, and he would see a rage in her he had never seen in life. Because she would turn on him. She would blame him.

As she should.

She would die and then she would be stuck, her and countless others, all because her grandson had cheated death.

Preston went up to his room and sat on the edge of his bed, his head in his hands. Suddenly it was all too much. A gasping sob broke from him, rippling through him like poison or electric current. It was a long moment before he realised the bedroom door had been pushed quietly open and there was his dad, aghast, horrified by the scale of Preston's grief. He knelt down at his son's feet, reaching for him, his face confused and desperate.

"Preston?" he managed. "Son! What's wrong?"

Preston embraced him, clinging desperately to his father like a drowning man holding onto a raft, hugging him as he hadn't for years, and his words burst out like blood gushing from a wound.

"I am," he said.

CHAPTER
TWENTY SIX

It was getting dark by the time Tracey got back to Longridge and she turned onto Written Stone Lane with a sense of growing dread. She felt fragile, vulnerable, like a wounded bird which catches the reek of the fox on the air, but can't see it. How long had it skulked in the shadows of this place before being entombed beneath the great sandstone slab beside her house? Centuries? Millenia?

And now it's out, she thought. *And hungry*.

Agnes Tattershawl. Then Jed Atkinson. They were so unlike her in age and disposition that it was hard to see herself as the next logical target of the boggart's wrath, but she felt it in her bones nonetheless. She had thought it even when the spirit was plucking the clothes from her bed, even more so when it had appeared as the night-swallowing crow outside the dairy.

It wants you.

It had called her Radcliffe, which was wrong. She just lived on what had been his land. And why her rather than her parents or the Shakeshafts? They all lived on what had been the same fields where the Radcliffes had battled the boggart almost four centuries earlier. What made her special? It was true that strange things had happened here of late and that all the adults had seen them, but she didn't think they had been haunted as she had, pursued, victimised. Why was that? Because she was young? Agnes Tattershawl and Jed Atkinson weren't. But then they had been what the police sometimes called targets of opportunity. They had strayed into the boggart's range, and that was all the monster needed.

She was different. It had been stalking her for weeks, a little more with each encounter as if it wanted more each time.

Or was *capable* of more.

That too. It was growing in strength. The Martins had said it would, and odd though they undoubtedly were, she believed them. She still felt safer inside than out, but perhaps the cottage walls and doors would no longer be enough to keep it out.

And you have to get there first, she thought grimly, as she made her way up the lane, alert to every rustle in the nettles, every creak of the hawthorn hedge as the wind blew in the dark. She picked up the pace, the crunch of stones under her shoes unnaturally loud in the stillness of the evening.

She caught the scent before she heard him. The wind gusted, and with the aroma of the damp, chill night came something at once incongruous and distressingly familiar.

Hai Karate.

She looked up before the words had fully registered in her mind, and there he was, in his blue track suit and stoat-like smile, standing between her and home.

"Mr. Goggins," she said.

It wasn't him. It couldn't be. But it seemed so like him that the name came out.

He said nothing, just stood there, leering, smug and in control as he always was in class, like he knew secret things about all the girls. She felt suddenly small and powerless, as if there was something paralysing in the cloying aroma that breathed from him. He took a step toward her, an idle, would be casual step, but she saw how his weight was carefully balanced, like a footballer player timing his tackle. He sighed even as he smiled, as if there was something he had to do that he didn't want to, that she had *made* him do, but that was a lie. He relished what was about to happen.

That wasn't the only lie. The sharpness of the aftershave had increased when he breathed out, like it had come from inside him, billowing up out of his very lungs, as if whatever was wearing his form didn't really understand what the scent was.

"You're not him," said Tracey, clarity making her strong. "You fished around in my head, in my fears, perhaps, my nightmares, and you came up with him. You look like him. Smell like him. But you're not him."

The thing that looked like her PE teacher pretended to look confused, but he kept coming and Tracey was suddenly terrified.

She didn't know what to do. This was surely the boggart, and as such it was ancient and had killed many times before. She had no idea how to fight it.

So she didn't. She fought Mr. Goggins instead.

"You're a terrible teacher!" she said quickly. "You're a bully. And you stink! You think women like that stuff? It's revolting. *You* are revolting!"

That last comment, shot with the venom of real feeling, landed, and the Goggins thing seemed to flicker. Its eyes were momentarily red and burning, mouths rather than eyes, and for the merest blink of an eye the figure became hunched and covered with black, animal bristle. Then the PE teacher was back.

Tracey stepped forward and kneed him hard in the crotch.

The figure crumpled for a moment, as if forced to follow the logic of the disguise in which her thoughts had robed it, and then it was up again, up and animal and flickering between forms, now a monstrous horse, now a faceless Victorian woman in a coal scuttle bonnet, now the vast crow from the dairy, its wings spread.

But Tracey was already running, past it and up the lane toward the lights of Written Stone Farm. It took a few moments for the boggart to settle on its form and then it came swooping through the night after her. She sprinted blindly, almost losing her footing on the uneven ground, propelled by terror and determination. The boggart came after her in the form of the great crow, talons reaching for her hair, wings beating inches from the back of her neck, but the advantage she had claimed in its moment of indecision was just enough. For now. She reached

the cottage door, fingers scrabbling at the latch, and threw herself inside.

She heard the boggart-crow hurtling around the walls of the cottage, cawing its fury, rattling the tiled roof with the beat of its gigantic wings, and she knew she would not get that lucky again. The boggart had grown stronger and she had dodged as long as she could.

She was still leaning against the front door and breathing heavily when her mother burst out of the kitchen.

"Where have you been?" she exclaimed. "I've been worried sick! Doctor's been here all afternoon; no hide nor hair of you to be seen!"

"The doctor?" Tracey echoed. "Why? What for?"

"Doctor Farthingale! Your dad and both the Shakeshafts have come down with something nasty. Can't keep food down. Doctor says it's like poisoning, but not. Wanted to know if you were all right and I couldn't even tell him!"

Her mother's anger gave way to something else and her face cracked a little, her eyes gleaming. She took a step toward Tracey and threw her arms around her. For her part Tracey, who was used to her mum being still and calm throughout all manner of crises, caught her mother's panic like a contagion, and in her mind a single phrase floated up.

Like poisoning, but not.

* * *

"Preston!" his mother called. "Phone!"

Preston had been sitting motionless on the edge of his bed. Now he got up with a swelling sense of dread, sure that something he had sensed was coming had begun at last. He stepped out onto the landing and round the corner to the narrow stairs. His mother was at the bottom, holding the receiver against her pullover.

"*A girl,*" she mouthed.

Preston nodded wordlessly, took it from her and waited for her to go back into the lounge and close the door before speaking.

"Hello?" he said.

Tracey did not introduce herself but she didn't need to. He had known it would be her.

"The night we met out there on Ribbleton Avenue," she said, "when you were in your scout uniform, what happened to you?"

Preston couldn't speak. He turned to face the corner, head bowed, shoulders hunched, eyes tight shut and jaws clamped together biting back the sob he could feel tightening his throat like a noose. The silence dragged on between them and at last Tracey spoke again.

"The Leech is the written stone boggart," she said. "It used to be something else, I think, a kind of elemental spirit of the land, but it terrorised the area till it was bound under the stone by Ralph Radcliffe in 1655. I'm not sure how he did it but it cost him his family. Later a Victorian farmer moved the stone and released it again. The boggart wasn't out long enough to get really strong, and the land owner was able to confine it again just by replacing the stone, but a part of it escaped and bound to the spirit of a boy killed in a railway accident in 1859. His name was Thomas Leech."

The sob Preston had been holding back erupted from him then, coming out as a messy wet gasp, an ugly, miserable sound of despair, boundless and irrepressible. His mouth froze in an open rictus, teeth together, eyes still squeezed so tightly closed that the tears could not escape. Speech remained impossible, and for a moment he thought Tracey had gone, and then her voice was uncoiling from the telephone receiver as if it was coming in through a badly tuned radio.

"It knows your name, Preston," she said. "And I think you know why. The night we met something happened to you. I shook your hand and went home and I touched the stone before I went inside. Was that what woke the boggart? My touch? Or your touch, through me? Not that alone, surely. I think you met this ghost boy, this Thomas Leech. I think you tried to help him pass over, and maybe you did. Maybe the soul of the boy was freed and went through one of those doors like William Bell and Mabel did. But in doing so, I think the part that was the boggart returned, still live and free, to the thing that was imprisoned under the stone, the stone I touched. Somehow it got out and has been growing in strength ever since.

"It's a shape-shifter," she went on. "Picks through your fears and chooses its form."

She sounded revolted and angry, at the boggart and her own

impotence in the face of it. Preston listened but could think of nothing to say.

"There's something else, Preston," said Tracey. "When the stone was laid to bind the boggart in 1655 Ralph Radcliffe was already dead. He died and was buried the previous year but, I think, had instructed his family to set the stone in place and make sure no one moved it again. But here's the thing, Preston. Ralph Radcliffe *also* died in 1653. I think he came back. I don't know how, but I think he somehow cheated death and came back to life, him and the son of a family member. But it didn't work, and he had to die again, properly this time because that was how he trapped the boggart. The stone ensured it stayed put, but he couldn't go on living when he knew he was supposed to be dead."

Preston felt the truth of this like a knife in his lungs, and a tiny cry leaked out of him.

"The boggart is back, Preston," said Tracey. "It came back the night we met and it has killed twice since. It will kill again. It wants me, Preston, me and my parents. It thinks we are the Radcliffes that tricked and entombed it. My dad is sick. So are the neighbours. Came on sudden and the doctor can't figure it out. I think it's the boggart. It's coming for us and I don't know what to do."

The silence this time was longer still. Preston knew she could hear his heaving, desperate breathing but she said nothing, waiting. Twice he tried to speak but felt the words turning to sobs in his mouth, and had to swallow them down. Every muscle in his body ached with the strain of his rigid, unmoving stance. Finally he opened his eyes and took a breath as his tears flooded down his face. He managed four words.

"I'm on my way."

CHAPTER TWENTY SEVEN

Preston wrote a letter to his parents. It was short and unspecific, but carefully phrased. In truth he had suspected this moment may come for several days now and had been trying out the words in his head, rearranging them, holding them up to the light to see if they felt right. It was important that they didn't think it was their fault, that his leaving was like the girl in the Beatles song. He couldn't say much, but they needed to know that much. He doubted he would ever get the opportunity to properly explain, and they would never really understand.

He hesitated, looking around his bedroom, taking it all in, then breathing it all out. He left the letter to his parents square on his pillow where they would find it in the morning, slipped down the stairs and out the back door. He did not bother to take a key.

Preston didn't know the late bus schedule to Longridge and knew that if they were running at all at this time it would be infrequent. He considered riding his bike but the batteries in his lamps were dead and it was a long way to ride in the dark. Even so, the idea of going to the church and asking Nora MacIntyre for a ride came to him because it felt right, not because it made practical sense. In real terms he barely knew the woman.

But she understood. He was sure of that.

In the end he rode his bicycle to Blessed Sacrament and rang the bell of the presbytery with a pale and unsteady hand. If she told him to get lost, he'd cycle the rest of the way, lights or no lights. As the electric bell rang shrilly deep in the bowels of the house he worried that the priest himself might come to the door, but that didn't happen. Mrs. MacIntyre opened the door, her face steeled for whatever churches had to deal with at this time of night.

It changed as soon as she saw him. It didn't soften exactly, didn't become comforting as his grandma's would, or anxious and wary like his parents. It just changed, opened up like the door itself, ready to deal with whatever came next.

"I have to go to Longridge," he said. "There's something I need to do."

"Longridge?" she echoed, her high forehead furrowing.

"I know how to open the gate," he said. "For the dead."

Was it true? Not exactly, perhaps. He was guessing. But he had a pretty shrewd idea.

She stared at him for a second, then nodded once.

"Wait here," she said.

She was gone perhaps two minutes, emerging in a raincoat, her car keys in her hand. As she opened the door to the little Triumph Herald, she caught his eye across the car roof and hesitated.

"Why me?" she said.

There was a lot he could say to that, much of it about why he couldn't explain everything to his parents whose spirituality wasn't flexible enough to include ghosts and who would think he'd lost his mind or turned to drugs, but he settled on something simple.

"You helped me once before," he said. "You don't remember, but to me it was absolutely real."

She listened, processed, nodded once, and got into the car.

* * *

After speaking to Preston on the phone, Tracey had been overcome with a nervous energy that left her pacing her little room. She had visited her father but he looked oddly lifeless, barely conscious of her presence, and though she had sat beside him, his hand in hers, she had eventually found it too upsetting. As her mum had said, his dinner lay untasted on a tray. The bathroom smelled of disinfectant floating over the sourness of vomit. The speed with which this had happened, the strangeness of it all, was surreal.

"There's nothing for you to do, love," her mother had said. "Listen to your music and then try to get some sleep. I might need your help around the place tomorrow."

So Tracey had put the radio on for the look of the thing, but she had been barely aware of it, and sat with her face against the window, looking out into the night. It was after ten when she saw the headlights splashing the hedgerows of the narrow lane as a little car rocked its way toward the cottage. She was downstairs and outside before it came to a complete halt.

She had assumed it would be Preston and one or both of his parents but the woman in the driving seat seemed to be someone else entirely, plump and efficient looking with a hard, pale face. Her eyes found Tracey standing on the cottage doorstep and something strange and complicated flitted through her expression. She was surprised and confused, but also somehow resigned, accepting. Tracey found herself wondering if they had met before, but when she went to meet Preston, the woman held her hand out formally and said,

"Nora MacIntyre. I work at Preston's church. You must be Tracey."

There was that feeling again, as if they had crossed paths before, long ago, or in a dream. Tracey was immediately wary of the woman, but Preston caught her expression and said,

"You can trust Nora with your life."

The church lady seemed surprised by this, but nodded, as if making a decision then and there.

Still, Tracey thought. *Some wannabe nun comes to say prayers*

in our house? Dad will go spare.

She caught herself. Remembering that he was in no state to do any such thing, and looked at Preston.

"You have a plan?" she asked.

That sounded immediately absurd, but no one laughed, though she would have almost been glad if they had. It would have meant that she was overreacting, that this was all a set of coincidences, paranoia and superstition: nothing, in other words, that couldn't be cured by daylight and a good night's rest.

But she knew that wasn't true.

"The woman who died out here," said Preston. "The heart attack?"

"Agnes Tattershawl. What about her?"

"That was the night we met, right?"

"Yes," said Tracey.

"Big woman?" said Preston. "Dressed like Nora Batty?"

Tracey almost laughed. That was exactly how Agnes had dressed.

"Yes!" she said. "How did you know?"

"The next day when I came out here," said Preston. "On our first . . . When we went for a walk. I saw her in the graveyard by the church."

"Saint Lawrence's," said Tracey. "Is that important?"

"I should have realised earlier," said Preston. "*She* was the Leech's first victim after I separated it from the boy. I thought it was the caretaker at my school but I was wrong. Agnes was the first victim. If I'd spoken to her then, we'd have known."

He looked troubled, angry at himself.

"That doesn't matter now," said Tracey. "We need to decide what we are going to do." She flashed an uncertain glance at Nora, still – even now – embarrassed by what she was about to say, then added, "It will be here any minute."

"Where is your mother, Tracey?" said the church lady.

Tracey felt a spike of irritation. The sound of voices would surely bring her mum out soon enough, but if this woman thought the adults were going to take charge, she had another thing coming.

"She's inside looking after my dad," she replied. "But she doesn't know about all this. She won't believe it. And they are safer inside."

"Does it make a difference?" asked Preston.

"Yes," Tracey said. "The boggart is focused on the house and on us because it's close to the stone, but it's not the original Radcliffe farm building, and I think that helps. Or maybe it's just that the house is a more domesticated space, a human place. Either way the boggart's not as powerful indoors."

"Then shouldn't we face it there?" said the church lady, rolling with everything as if it was all quite normal.

"No," said Tracey, certain, though she could not say why. "We have to beat it here where it was beaten before and bind it in the same place."

"Where's the stone?" asked Preston. He had brought a little torch and now flashed it around the ominous rectangular pit in the browning grass and nettles where it had lain.

Tracey sighed, a long collapsing breath that leaked some of the fight out of her.

"It's in the dairy," she said. "The grown-ups put it there," she said, shooting the church lady a warning look as if she was guilty by association, "and now it won't move. The last time the stone was moved . . ."

"1859," said Preston bleakly.

Tracey caught his eye but kept going.

"It was hard to shift the stone from where Radcliffe had put it, but easy to move it back. This time it's the other way round. I think that means that the stone has some power of itself, that it was designed to keep the boggart pinned down, and it *wants* to do that. But this time the boggart is stronger, more whole, and it's fighting whatever power is in the stone."

"So what do we do?" asked Preston.

"One of us distracts the boggart, engages it, while the others try to move the stone back."

Tracey spoke briskly, but she couldn't quite hold Preston's eyes. He knew immediately what she meant.

"Me," he said. "I have to face the boggart. The Leech. It's my job because . . ." He seemed to search for the words, the decision, but then he drew himself up and completed the sentence with conviction. "It's my job because I'm the one who released it. I'm the one who's not supposed to be here."

The church lady gave him a quick look and opened her mouth to protest, but he stared her down.

"It wants you," said Preston, turning to Tracey again. "But it blames me. Hates me. I'll be the distraction."

"Or maybe," said a voice. "It wants all of you and will take all of you."

There was a woman coming up the lane, old and heavy, wearing a familiar coat. She had curlers in her hair and was eating from a bag of chips wrapped in newspaper. For a moment they seemed to smell sharply of vinegar, but then Tracey realised that the pungent scent was actually, predictably, Hai Karate aftershave.

Tracey froze.

"Go," said Preston.

Tracey just stared at him, momentarily incapable of thought, and in that moment the cottage door opened and her mother appeared in the doorway.

"What's going on here?" she demanded. "Trace? Who are these people?"

* * *

Vivien Blenkinsop had heard a car and then the muttered sounds of conversation from upstairs but it had been too dark to see outside. Stepping out of the cottage she had been amazed to see her daughter – long past her bedtime – talking to the Oldcorn boy she had been courting with an old woman she didn't recognise, apparently the owner of the little blue Triumph Herald. She was about to launch into an outraged tirade about sneaking around at this time of night when she saw another figure hurrying up the lane. A middle-aged man in a three piece suit, the waist coat bulging around his middle and shocks of windswept grey hair at his temples.

Doctor Farthingale.

Everything else went out of her mind.

"You're back," she said. "Thank you. I was getting so worried. Jim seems to be getting worse. Have you figured out what might be causing it? Is it a poison?"

The doctor seemed to hesitate as if considering how to proceed then looked up and said,

"I'm afraid it's not good news."

Vivien felt her knees give and she had to prop herself against the doorjamb. Her eyes closed for a moment and her mind flooded with a single word.

No. No. No.

It can't be.

"But he just took ill today!" she managed.

"Mum?" said Tracey moving toward her. "Mum! What are you talking about? Mum! Look at me."

She was shouting now. At her own mother. Viv and Jim had never so much as raised their voices to her, let alone a hand, a point of principle they had stuck to like religion, but now here she was, screaming at her, the little madam, while her father lay at death's door only yards away. It wasn't right. She ought to show more respect. She needed to be taught a lesson.

Vivien lunged for her daughter, one hand raised, and Tracey shrunk away in horror and confusion.

What are you doing?

The voice came as if from far away, but it was her own voice, her real voice, and it stopped her before the blow could land. What *was* she doing? Her eyes met Tracey, and her daughter looked like a frightened dog, cringing away from her, her eyes full of tears. Vivien shook her head to clear it, and then she was babbling and weeping.

"I'm sorry, love. I don't know what I was thinking. I'm really sorry . . ."

"It's all right," said Tracey, wiping a tear away. "It's not your fault. It's . . . her. She gets into your head."

Her?

Vivien's eyes fell on the unfamiliar woman, but Tracey grabbed her arm.

"Not her. *Her!*"

She pointed squarely at Doctor Farthingale. Except that he wasn't the doctor now. He was . . .

"Agnes?" Vivien gasped.

Agnes Tattershawl, who had dropped dead of a heart attack out there on the road. Again she felt her knees give, deeper this time. This was impossible. It was madness. And suddenly it was clear. Whatever had struck her husband down, left him barely conscious upstairs, whatever had done the same to the Shakeshafts, had got her. She was sick, delirious, seeing things that were not there . . .

"Mum!" screamed Tracey. "Whatever you are seeing, it's not real. It's the boggart. The thing from under the written stone."

More madness. More impossible nonsense.

But as soon as she thought that, she saw Agnes Tattershawl – who had been buried at St. Lawrence's weeks ago – smile sympathetically, and something clicked into place in Mrs. Blenkinsop's head. Because Agnes had never been sympathetic to another human being in her life. Not once. She had always been a self-righteous busybody who delighted in the misfortunes of others. Agnes was dead now, and the person standing in front of them, the person with the sympathetic look on her face, could not be her.

Tracey was right. Her daughter made mistakes like everyone, especially girls her age, but when she decided something, when she really thought about it and then *decided* something, it was right. Always.

"Look at me, mum," said Tracey now. "It's not the doctor. It's not Agnes. It's what killed her, and it's what is trying to kill dad. We're not going to let it."

Vivien looked her daughter in the face and things seemed to clear in her head.

"No," she agreed. "We won't."

* * *

The Leech was in its element. The stone was well out of the way, and those that stood so pathetically against it were old women and children. It drew from their fear and confusion as it drew from the earth and the dark. Though it did not have the words or human association, it relished moments like this almost as much as the banquet to come when its long hunger would be sated.

It could smell their panic, the dread and the grief which trailed after it. All that feeling, the horror and anxiety, registered in what the boggart had in place of a brain as colour, vivid scarlet, deep, angsty purples and roiling, sickly greens. It pushed, using whatever petty human rubbish it found in their heads and made the colours bloom.

They did the work for it.

It opened its ravening jaws and the Oldcorn boy put the words in.

* * *

"You have to come with me," said Preston's grandma.

He should have been ready for this. As he had driven up from Ribbleton besides Roarer's sister, he had thought about what Tracey had said, about the boggart changing shapes, and he had tried to guess what it would look like to him. Pete Maddingly, he had thought, all leering and threatening to bash his face in, but that seemed stupid now. Childish. Perhaps if he had imagined this fresh horror, that it might take the form of his grandma, he would have been better prepared. But then again, maybe not. As it was he felt strangely powerless before it, even though he knew it was not real. He shook his head, but he could feel the tears welling up.

"You're not . . ." he began, but could not say it. "You're still alive."

"Not for much longer," said his grandma. Her voice. Her face.

Her bright eyes sad now, resigned.

Hope your double double vision vision's getting better . . .

"You'll get better," Preston insisted. "They can do wonders these days . . ."

But she was shaking her head and he knew she was right.

It won't be long now.

"But what will happen next?" said his grandma.

Preston shook his head from side to side over and over, not a denial but a shutting out. He didn't want to hear this. He couldn't think about it. It was too much.

Nine twenty-two.

Nine twenty-two.

Nine twenty-two. Always.

"I'll be stuck," said grandma. "Trapped in death like you were, with no way out. Like them."

And as she said it, he felt them, the dead. They were in the fields around them: the spectres of Agnes Tattershawl, Jed Atkinson, Mr. Simpson the caretaker, the communion lady, and a dozen more whose faces Preston didn't know. All dead since he came back. All entombed as surely as the boggart had been beneath the stone. All trudging dreamily closer, so that Preston was the centre of a tightening ghostly circle. Their faces were masked with torment and bitterness. At him. His coming back to life had trapped them. His escape had shut the door to the realm of the Sincerely Dead and they were lost.

"You know what you have to do," she said. "For me. For all of them."

"Yes," said Preston.

And that was true. Boggart or no boggart, she was right. It was time. However much he had tried to hide from it, Preston had known it was coming, He had dodged and clawed his way back to life, but that had been a cheat, and the moment of life he had recovered had now passed. It had only been a couple of weeks, but the time he had won back, glorious though it had been, was over. Like Ralph Radcliffe before him, Preston had to die again.

This time, forever.

CHAPTER
TWENTY EIGHT

To Nora, it was Roarer, which is what she had expected. It lied and soothed and got him wrong, but it was still hard to see him – not as a wisp of mist or flicker of light, a half presence she felt rather than saw – but as a solid, real boy, almost a man, just as he had been when he had died so very long ago.

And now that she was here she found she did not know what to do or why she had come.

To help, she thought vaguely. To do for others as she always had, unseen and largely unregarded, scowled at by the congregation for living so close to the priest they venerated. She knew the way they saw her: hard, officious, managing the father's schedule, his life, as a way of keeping him to herself.

What good was that? What good was she?

The priest was the star. She was some minor wardrobe assistant, a perennial intern, doing the bits she could, unobtrusive and unappreciated, resented for her rules and timetables, always underfoot as she cleaned and tidied. She was a footnote to other people's lives. Not a real person.

There was nothing for her to do here. Her realm was the trivial window dressing of religion: flowers and vestments and brass polish. Not the real stuff of faith and virtue. She wasn't even sure how much of those things she had left. She should get in her ridiculous little car and go home.

Nora, reached into her handbag for her keys.

*   *   *

She'll leave, Tracey thought, watching the church lady. She'll get her keys and go, abandoning them to the thing which stank of aftershave as the fields filled with an ever-tightening circle of lost and vengeful spectres.

The possibility opened up like a door in her head, and she ran for the house, one word burning in her head.

Keys.

*   *   *

Tracey's mother stepped aside as her daughter pushed roughly passed her and into the cottage. For a moment she gaped after her, staring into the unnatural brightness of the little hallway of the house she had wanted to leave, mystified and caught between relief and disappointment. Tracey was running away. She had said they would stand and fight to save her father, but now she was running. Vivian Blenkinsop couldn't blame her, and in truth, Tracey's retreat made Vivian's own feel less cowardly, more reasonable.

Reason.

There was so little to any of this. Demons and spirits, curses and magic out of old legends.

It's nonsense. I won't countenance it.

Her husband's phrase appeared in her head and stopped her cold. Nightmares and spooky feelings were one thing, but she had seen the blood in the milk churns, watched it spill down the lane, leeching into the earth like poison.

That had been real. As was Jim's mystifying illness and the doctor who wasn't really a doctor any more than he was the walking corpse of Agnes Tattershawl. And now there were ghosts coming up the lane, shimmering half-people, their eyes desperate and angry fingers pointing at the Oldcorn boy as they got ever closer.

Reason, she decided, was no use to her here. There was evil at work, evil directed at her family, and *that* Vivien Blenkinsop would not countenance.

Tracey may have fled, but her mother would not. She turned to face the thing which looked like Agnes, and all her confused anxiety burned off in her rage.

"How dare you!" she roared, "coming to *my* house . . ."

But Agnes was not there.

Where she had stood was a thing like a huge man but with long limbs and hands ending in claws, a thing of darkness covered over in black animal bristle, its eyes burning red. It looked wet and filthy, as if it had just crawled up from the bottom of a pond, and it was bent over, so that man-like though it was it rested its weight on its hands. It skulked like a fox, jaws lolling, and she caught the reek of it – damp earth and the decay of long dead things. It made a sudden movement, loping on all fours toward her, and all her righteous fury evaporated in the horror of the thing.

She fell back and it came on, snarling, not a person now, or even a spirit: it was a beast, full of rage and hunger, and before it Vivien Blenkinsop felt her strength fail.

* * *

Preston threw himself at the thing as it flickered between forms.

Grandma, to Pete Maddingly, to William Bell, the enraged knife man from the Wellington, and then to the bloated Leech monster he had fought on the train as it rattled through Grimsargh, its body studded with the vague faces of those it had consumed. He wrapped his arms around it and they fell together, rolling and tearing at each other. In the darkness the Leech felt sinewy and covered in course hair, like the body of an immense spider but roughly shaped like a man. It was extraordinarily strong and batted aside his feeble stabbing punches as if his muscles were no more than wads of damp paper.

The Leech shrugged him off and slashed at his belly with a long claw. Preston felt the fabric of his jacket and jumper open as if carved by a razor but thought he had otherwise escaped. It was not until he stopped rolling in the damp weeds where he had fallen that he felt the bright pain of the cut. He clutched at his stomach and his hands came away slick.

Still he rolled to his feet, wincing. The monster was watching Tracey's mother like a great cat, coiled and ready to spring, standing beside the dark gash in the earth where the ancient stone had lain.

It was time.

"Enough," Preston said, getting to his feet. "You want me. You can have me."

He spoke quietly, but the Leech heard nonetheless. He saw it in its sudden stillness. It turned on its long, spindly insect legs, head lolling in a grin, and its voice appeared in Preston's mind as if he were speaking the words himself.

"Your life for theirs?"

And that was how it had to be. Preston had known it for a while now, had felt the ache of that bitter truth swallowing up his future, all the possibilities of a life he would not get to live. It ripped him in two as if he was made of old parchment, a slow ragged tear which opened him up and emptied him of hope. All the possibility of the future, good and bad, of a life lived to its limits, collapsed, shrinking like the last flare of a one of the church candles. The wax gone the light shrunk to a pinprick, a speck, and then was gone leaving only a column of smoke to show it had ever been there. In seconds that too would vanish, and the candle's light, its life, would be no more than a memory, and an insignificant one at that. He had assumed life would go on forever, or for so long that it felt like forever, but it was as if he had come to the end of a path and there was no room to turn around. For a second it was like being back in the Miley tunnel, a tight, brick tube which led nowhere, a place he had blundered around until time had run out, leaving him staring at a wall with death bearing down on him like a runaway train and nowhere to go. The future he had always taken for granted was gone, and this moment, here in the dark and cold of a weedy Lancashire lane, was all that was left to him. And only for a moment.

He thought of his parents, his friends, and Tracey above all, wishing he could see them all one more time, to say the things he had never got around to, though even as he wished for it, he knew he wouldn't find the words. He never had before. He looked to see if he could see Tracey, one last time, but she had gone inside.

Probably as well.

Seeing her would make it that much harder to go. He needed to stay strong, for her, for all of them. He tried to speak, but couldn't make a sound. His eyes were stinging. He didn't understand how he could feel so very old and so very young at the same time. He swallowed, then tried again to speak.

"My life for theirs," he managed to repeat. "Yes. On condition that you leave them alone forever, and that the doors to the realm of the Sincerely Dead are open again."

The Leech batted the idea away lazily with a twitch of one hand.

"That was your doing, not mine," it said. "Preston Oldcorn owes a death. When that is fulfilled with no evasion, with none of the old Radcliffe trickery, these ghosts will pass on."

"And the rest?" said Preston, panting from breathlessness and wincing at the pain in his belly. "Tracey and her family? You'll leave them be."

Silence descended on Written Stone Lane, a long, brooding silence loaded with dreadful possibility.

"You have my word," said the boggart.

* * *

It was a lie. Of course it was.

The boggart smiled in its dank and stagnant heart and it made the words the boy wanted to hear, but they were lies. Or at best, a half-truth. The ghosts *would* pass on. That was not the boggart's doing. The boy's clawing his way back to life after their last bruising encounter had jammed the gates shut, but a death in his name would open them again.

But as for these others, the living who dwelled on old Radcliffe's land, those who usurped the boggart's natural haunt and had thrived on its long bondage? Those whose boy champion was to die for them like some deluded saviour putting all his faith in self-sacrifice, leaving them defenceless and cowering before the boggart's dubious mercy?

They would pay as bloodily as ever Radcliffe did.

Nora MacIntyre watched the boy hesitate, then nod.

That was all it was, but the monster turned upon him – visible for the abomination it was – and pounced.

Preston Oldcorn did not resist. Nora felt his grief more than his pain, his sense of loss – his parents, his friends, and the possibilities tied up in the girl, Tracey, who was nowhere to be seen. She felt his pain, the depth of his sadness, as keenly as she had when he had sat beside her in the choir gallery at church, gazing out over the dark expanse where the crucifix hung. She remembered that moment perfectly, the building bedecked with the flowers arranged by her arthritic fingers, the smell of the mop she used to apply the floor polish till her knees ached for her to stop, the vestments scrubbed by her scalded, calloused hands.

Her work. Her contribution to the world. Flowers and polish, timetables and laundry and the petty rules she maintained to keep things in their place and her world ticking over . . .

There had to be something more for her to do, some last act of value, of faith.

Running was beyond her, but she managed a trundling jog which accelerated as it went, opening her arms to embrace the monster as she hit it side on, gasping as she did so,

"Take me for him."

* * *

The boggart felt only the warm flesh of his victim, and in its delirium, it did not register the squirming confusion of the struggle until it bit down into the boy's flesh and tasted . . .

Age.

It tore its bloody muzzle from the corpse and roared its fury.

Another cheat. A substitution. A sacrifice.

No!

The cooling body in its claws was not the Oldcorn boy but the old church woman. It spun around, raging at the deception, spitting curses and the promise of death and torment. It saw the shadows of the dead which were looming in the lane hesitate, and then quite suddenly there were doors and gates everywhere in the night. Some were plain and rustic, others ornate, some were wood, others were wrought iron, some painted, others raw, rusted or unfinished. They opened as one and the spectres moved through them into blankness.

The boy was still alive, but the ghosts were gone.

The boggart roared loud enough to set the cottage windows bursting and the tiles to jumping from its sagging roof. The cheat changed nothing. It cared not for the dead. It wanted the terror and lifeblood of the living and it would take them all.

It turned on the boy, prone in the nettles where he had fallen, and the boggart reached through the earth and brought the stinging plants tight around him, holding him in place. Preston Oldcorn cried out, but it was the last sound he would make.

The last sound.

The boggart's focus, which had been singular, like looking

through a telescope, wavered. There was something pushing against its consciousness. The night, which had been utterly still was filling with noise, a swelling roar, uneven but relentless.

An engine, iron made mobile by human ingenuity, was coming toward it, and behind it trailed something else, something which smouldered like the hatred of an old adversary . . .

The boggart Leech hesitated, turning slowly, and there were lights coming from the old farm yard, great eyes that blasted the darkness aside and filled the world with brilliance and colour.

The boggart's power buckled as the darkness – its element, its friend, and the root of all its strength – shrank down to nothing but the shadow of its own body as the tractor rumbled toward it.

On top, staring down defiant, was the girl.

* * *

Tracey turned the steering wheel a fraction to keep the monster dead ahead, and gunned the tractor's engine. It struck the boggart as it tried to shift into some other form and the iron plough on the front seemed to cut right through it, as if the metal had some dreadful power over the monster. The tractor rolled on, driving it back and into the very pit where it had lain for centuries, and as it did so, the chains behind the tractor dragged the written stone as if it weighed nothing at all. The sandstone slab slid into place as if sucked there, like water vanishing down a drain.

A terrible wailing shriek split the night as the boggart was pinned in place, the great stone sliding slick and feather light into its old, familiar spot as if it had never moved, leaving only a whiff of dirt and aftershave which blew away into the night and was gone.

The air, the very darkness itself seemed shocked into silence.

Tracey turned the engine off and slid down from the high seat, rushing first to Preston who was getting groggily to his feet. She folded him in her arms and, before he really knew what was happening, kissed him firmly on the mouth.

He was warm.

* * *

Preston wept for Nora MacIntyre. The creature had set upon her like a tiger but her body was somehow unmarked now and would go down as another heart attack, an accident brought on by stress. Preston knew otherwise, saw her sacrifice for what it was, and vowed never to forget it. She had given herself for him, so that the possibilities he had dreamed of might yet come into being. The selfless generosity of the act left him speechless and humble. He sat quite still, drinking in the night and with it, air, oxygen.

Life.

Real life, not the half-life he had been living. Because he could feel it now, the sense of being himself again, blood pumping, heart pounding. He had thought he was alive before, but now it was like getting water out of his ears and hearing the roar of the world for real at last.

Tracey's kiss had been the last act to revive him, stirring him from slumber like the princess in a fairytale, though she did not stay with him long, hurrying to check on her stunned mother. She was rushing to the cottage door when her father appeared asking what was going on and whether there was anything in the house to eat.

It was over.

The future which had seemed closed to him, the tight and narrowing tunnel he had felt trapped inside when he had agreed to the Leech's demand, had opened up again, and there was sky and possibility ahead. He would go home and his parents would be there, unaware of how close he had come to being lost forever, and life would go on.

After he had breathed a bit, and washed, after he had supervised the ambulance men who came for Nora's body, ensuring they showed the respect she deserved, he sat upon the long stone beside Tracey, listening to the night.

"Will it stay, do you think?" he wondered aloud.

"The boggart?" said Tracey. "So long as the stone stays, yes."

"We should find a way to make sure it does," said Preston. "I can't go through this again."

"No," she agreed. "Do you think you'll still see ghosts?"

He considered that for a moment, then shook his head. Mr. Simpson and the rest had vanished when Nora had given her life in his name and opened the gates to death, but it was more than that. He felt different, grounded in the world and in the moment in ways he had not been before. Tracey felt it too. He could tell. He had seen her face after their kiss on the bus. She had known he was not right. That had changed.

He took her hand. Like his it was warm with life, with the promise of things to come.

"So now what?" she asked, the hint of a smile crinkling the corners of her mouth.

Preston shrugged, thinking about all they had gone through, the ghosts, the boggart, the stacked history of the town where people had built their lives for centuries uncounted.

"The present," he said. "And then, the future."

THE END

AFTERWORD & ACKNOWLEDGEMENTS

Though I was born in Preston and come back from time to time, I am mostly writing from my home in the USA, which can be tricky. Frequently I don't know what I need to research about a place until I'm actually telling the story for the first time, and hopping across the Atlantic every time I realise that I don't really remember the layout of a key building is hardly practical. This is doubly true in the case of historical details not covered by the books I have with me, or when I run into information online which seems shaky or incomplete. In such moments I turn to friends, family and experts in the Preston area who have been kind enough to help me get things as right as I can, lending their time, knowledge and insight to help me hang my scribblings on something resembling fact. Where I've made mistakes, I take full responsibility. But where I get things right, I'm often in the debt of others.

I'd particularly like to thank local historian Keith Johnson who helped me make sense of the various changes to the town centre, and to Sheila Vivien Berresford and Andrew Peter Forster, past and present landlords of the Wellington Inn. Thanks to UCLan staff and to Edwin H Booth himself for helping me map the structure of the Booths store and café building (now the Waterstones where I briefly worked shortly after it opened). Father Edward Gannon helped with some matters of liturgical history and my long suffering mother, Annette Hartley (now back in the Longridge of her birth) fielded a thousand questions, and tracked down various details including some concerned with the history of the Radcliffe family. Others have chipped in when I have fielded questions on the Preston Past and Present Facebook group and its Longridge counterpart. Thanks to all of you. A book like this could not have been written without such supportive friends. A special thanks to those who have also nudged my memories or given me feedback on early drafts of the book, notably my old school pals Stephen Melling, Alf Biggins, Ruth Yeulett, and Chris Bruney.

While Mabel the Booths waitress is my own invention, I remember tales of a ghost on the top floor from my Waterstones days. The story of William Bell and the fight which began at the Wellington but ended fatally on Pleasant Street is a matter of historical record, and the details of Bell's subsequent deportation are exactly as I had Preston report them in the novel. I should say that while I have stayed as close to fact as I could manage in matters of buildings, geography and local history, the people who inhabit the present of the narrative – those teachers, pupils, priests and the like who surround Preston's daily life – are all made up, and any resemblance between them and actual people, living or dead, is best put down to coincidence.

Stories surrounding the Written Stone were already very old when they were documented in Tom Smith's 1888 *History of Longridge*, and they already included the tale of what happened when a farmer attempted to move the stone (which in my narrative I have placed in 1859 to coincide with the Longridge railway accident). A boggart is the local form of the hob goblin or malicious spirit generally bound to a specific area, variant forms of which occur throughout Britain. Its name is etymologically related to bugbear – a supernatural thing of horror or disgust (and therefore to the later use of 'bug' to mean insect) and bogeyman. The Lancashire form, as exemplified in tales of the Grizelhurst boggart as well as the Longridge boggart, emphasise the spirit's shape-shifting ability, the aspect of the creature used by J.K. Rowling to define her boggarts in the *Harry Potter* books.

In November of 1983, some five years after the fictional events of my narrative, the Written Stone of Longridge was officially classified as a Grade II Listed Building (source ID 1147440, English Heritage ID 183016). I do not know the circumstances in which this protective status came about, but I like to think that somebody set out to ensure that disturbing the stone should be prevented by more than tradition or, if you prefer, superstition. If so, they were successful, since moving the stone – in accord with Ralph Radcliffe's inscription – is now prohibited by law. The parish records concerning the Radcliffe family, incomplete and confusing though they are, are exactly as I have presented them, including the curious duplication of Ralph's death in both 1653 and 1654. An error of some kind, perhaps . . . But then again, perhaps not.

I was a great lover of music, TV and film as a kid. Still am. But in those days it wasn't as easy to track down and enjoy what you liked as it is now: no DVDs, CDs, digital downloads or YouTube. In 1978 we didn't even have VCRs. That meant that your only way to keep up with what you liked was to listen to the radio, to go to the pictures and to watch whatever BBC and ITV had to offer, because if you missed it, you might not get a second chance. For many of us, keeping track of such things became something of an obsession, and popular culture therefore stamped and shaped my adolescence. To this day, a snatch of a familiar song can take me back to a precise moment in my past, all the sights and scents, the mood of the moment, flooding back. I wanted to make sure that the cultural soundtrack of this book was correct, so I've been careful to get the TV offerings, singles charts, North End scores and the like accurate to the weeks the story represents. It's important to me that I get such things right, and if it gets a little overly documentary in the telling, I apologise.

A final special thanks to Debbie Williams and the UCLan publishing staff and students who have made a greater success of these books than I could ever have imagined. I'd also like to thank readers in general and those of the Preston area in particular, especially those who have reached out to me over the last year or so to say how much they appreciated seeing their streets, shops, schools, churches and so on in print. I'm a great believer in the power of representation, in people seeing something of their own particular experiences captured in books, so that the art feels like it belongs to them. Too much fiction (and I include film and TV) is in love with a version of the world whose glamour has nothing to do with ordinary life as experienced by ordinary people, and I fear that we are made to feel smaller, less important as a result. That said, it's a strange thing to write about your home town and the world in which you grew up when you have been gone for so long, and I was concerned that the book would be sneered at or ignored by those I most wanted to like it. Instead the town and its people have been enthusiastically supportive, welcoming and helpful in ways I didn't dare hope for. Thank you.

It's like coming home.

Best wishes and thanks for reading
Andrew – AJ – Hartley

HAVE YOU READ . . .

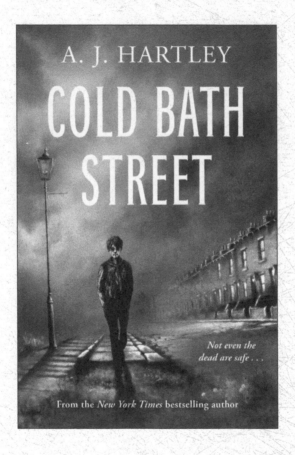

A. J. HARTLEY

COLD BATH STREET

Not even the dead are safe . . .

From the *New York Times* bestselling author

The spine-tingling prequel to Written Stone Lane.

OUT NOW!

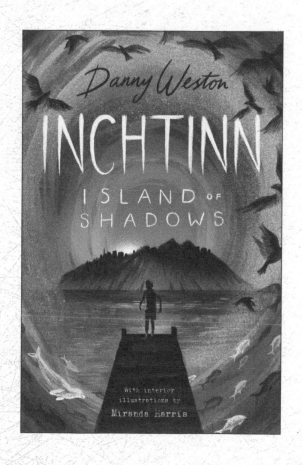

If you loved Written Stone Lane, you'll love this!

www.uclanpublishing.com